I0663921

Violent Crossfire

Evil Darkness Strikes America

Stephen L. Thompson

Violent Crossfire

Books by Stephen L. Thompson

The Crossfire Series

Colorado Crossfire
Believer's Crossfire
International Crossfire
Israeli Crossfire
Spirit Crossfire
Faith Crossfire
Chinese Crossfire
Texas Crossfire
Dark Crossfire
Island Crossfire
Jagged Crossfire
Violent Crossfire
Russian Crossfire
Nuclear Crossfire
End Times Crossfire
Revelation Crossfire
Gates of Hell Crossfire
Assassins Crossfire
Albatross Crossfire
Global Crossfire
Far East Crossfire

The SFO Series

Station Force One – Onset

Violent Crossfire

The Crossfire team continues in its battles with the enemy of all mankind and their human tools of the Omicron Cartel. A new member of the team appears and new dangers erupt as the United States is threatened by a nuclear attack concealed by demonic forces.

-   Stephen L. Thompson

Violent Crossfire

Published by
Stephen L. Thompson
Facebook.com/CrossfireNovelSeries

ISBN- 978-1-943879-11-3

Published in the United States of America

Foreword

To my Christian readers –

The Crossfire series of action/adventure stories include depictions of violence which are unusual in Christian literature. It would be nice if there were no conflict or violence in our world. But we live in a time when evil is increasing instead of diminishing, when some men seem to be controlled by selfishness, madness, or evil forces. When the enemies of decent mankind are bent on subjugation of other men and women, righteous men and women must stand against evil. Please remember that the yoke of oppression is not lifted by prayer alone. God is our shepherd and we are his sheep. As long as there are wolves about, God will use some of us as sheep dogs to defend the rest of us. These stories are about people like that and the forces they fight against. The stories describe violence because it occurs in the real world and it is active in the lives of all people whether they recognize it or not.

To my non-Christian readers –

The Crossfire series include depictions of spiritual warfare and spiritual activity with which the non-Christian may not be familiar. These stories describe the realms and activities of both God and Satan because they are real and active in the lives of all people whether they recognize it or not.

Steve Thompson

CHAPTER ONE

Only the fingers of her right hand supported Alexis as she hung from the projecting rock. Demons of fear gibbered in her ears and failure loomed like a black specter in her mind's eye. In the darkness of night she could not see the abyss below her but she clearly sensed the hundreds of feet yawning underneath her. She knew if she fell her body would slam into sharp granite rocks at over one hundred and twenty-five miles per hour.

The rush of the wind reminded her that the subzero temperature was amplified by the blowing wind that drove the cold through her like needles. The thought flashed through her mind that she could freeze right where she was.

It wasn't the fear of death that chilled her insides but the fear of failure. This was the first time she had been in a situation that she wasn't sure she would survive. Her four fingers were supporting all of her weight and the strain on her arm and hand was quickly becoming intolerable. Adding to that the cold was quickly numbing her bare hand clenching the frozen rock.

Glancing down she could still see the copilot floating serenely down from the mountain tops in his parachute. Of course he didn't care because he was dead, but it still irritated her that he had the chute and she didn't. Another cold blast of frigid air tugged at her tenuous hold on the rock. The grim thought that she might end up as an icicle didn't improve her mood at all.

Using reserves of strength she didn't know she had she pulled herself up and swung her left hand up and onto the rock above her. As in her three previous tries her fingers slid on the ice and she couldn't get a grip. She prayed a very earnest prayer. "Father Yahveh, in Yahshua's name, I need your help because I'm not able to save myself this time."

Just as her left hand was starting to slide off of the icy rock above her she got a grip on a small crevice. She carefully put more weight on it to see if it would hold and it did. As she shifted the weight to her left hand it was as if her right arm screamed in relief from the pain of holding her up by itself. Alexis realized she really was the one screaming in relief.

She also noticed that the fear had receded from her mind and wondered if that was because Yahveh's presence had caused the fear to lessen or if the new hope was responsible for the relief. In the bitter cold of the night air she smiled to herself. She could feel the presence of Yahveh's Holy Spirit in her dire situation and knew she had never been alone on the mountain.

She drew on all her strength and training and pulled her body upward in one quick lunge. Leveraging her torso over her hands she managed to get her chest and stomach onto the top of the rock. She rested for several seconds to relieve the strain that had gripped her arms. A little training clock in her head told her that the sub-zero temperature wasn't going to stop robbing her of body heat and energy so she carefully thought through her next moves concerning the slick, rock-hard ice cap above the rocky edge.

Letting go of the rock with her right hand, she found the fingers didn't want to bend any farther than they had while gripping the rock. She forced them to grab the hilt of the small dagger she had stuck into her belt. Her hand was getting so numb she wasn't sure she actually had the little knife until she brought it up and saw it in her hand, the blade glinting starlight from a hole in the clouds racing by above her.

She raised the knife up and brought it down at arm's length and it sank into the frozen ice above her. She stabbed it into the ice several times and then stuck it into the ice above her head. Letting go of the knife she jammed her fingers into the hole she had chopped and tested the hold.

Transferring her weight carefully to her right hand again, she repeated the operation with her left hand. The icy wind whistled as it tugged at her body. The wind sang of defeat and loss to her burning ears.

Alexis pulled her legs up onto the shelf and continued to repeat the ice chopping, right and left, three more times. She was very grateful for the tough blouse and pants she was wearing as she slowly regained level ground away from the edge of the precipice.

Now that the adrenaline surge which accompanied the imminent danger of falling was waning, so was her strength. She had trained in her U.S. Army Ranger Team in conditions a lot like this and knew the danger in the lure of taking a blissful rest or a short nap. She would never wake up again. At least she would not wake up in this world.

Not trusting the soles of her shoes she continued to belly crawl across the ice using the little knife as a piton to keep her from slipping backward. In minutes she had reached a rocky stretch that didn't have snow and ice on it. Careful not to cut her hands on the sharp rocks she slowly pulled her aching body upright and staggered into the lee area of several large rocks.

The rocks cut the blast of the wind but didn't do anything to restore her energy or heat. Another prayer for salvation from the mountain and Alexis turned around and sat down to conserve her energy and heat for exactly four minutes. Every part of her body was rapidly cooling down and she knew her core would reach shutdown soon if she didn't get some heat energy soon.

As she tried to concentrate she noticed that her mental processes were sluggish from the cold and that wasn't good. Forcing herself upward she started to walk across the rocky ledge when she tripped on something soft. Catching herself clumsily to keep from smashing into the ground she felt around and found that the soft mass was a leather jacket. It was *her* leather jacket!

She'd lost it as she had slammed across the mountain with the dead copilot on their initial contact with the ground. What amazed her foggy mind was that even though it hadn't been zipped up, she had been wearing it and it still came off.

She struggled into the bomber jacket and felt the warmth of her body, as little as it was, contained around her and not just radiating into the night air at the ten or twelve thousand foot elevation. Shoving her hands into the pockets she pressed against the rock in the dark to stop the tendency she had to shiver uncontrollably.

There was no paper or lighter in the pockets to make a fire, not even gloves. But she wasn't going to let that defeat her. Yahveh God had restored her jacket to her and she said a prayer of thanks for his mercy.

The ledge had turned out to be a semicircle about two hundred feet long by sixty feet wide but it ran out and fell off into the darker depths at both ends. The black cliff above her was insurmountable without climbing gear as was the cliff below her.

Defeat beat at her again but she beat it back with love for Yahveh God and His Son. She prayed for His will, even if that meant she didn't make it. She thought of just running off the edge and falling forever but the ornery streak in her wouldn't let her waste whatever was left of her life in a useless gesture like that.

She continued to pray and felt her prayers were answered as she was bathed in a soft white light. Looking up, she saw a bright light approaching her from above. Her addled senses thought it might be Rose, the angel she had seen once before.

Then the roar of machinery overrode the noise of the wind and another light joined the first. Alexis was amazed as the first light came down to the ledge and became recognizable as a military jet helicopter. She absentmindedly noticed it was a Huey troop carrier and the pilot was hovering half-on and half-off of the ledge so that the rotors didn't hit the mountain side. The additional wind the rotors created slapped at her but the hope inside her was like a roaring fire. As the craft hovered in front of her she staggered toward it and she watched as the door on her side opened. Two people in arctic parkas jumped out of the door onto the ledge and ran to her. They threw a third parka over her shoulders and hustled her into the chopper.

As the door was slammed shut, cutting off the icy air, the heat inside the helicopter felt like flame against her skin everywhere. It felt like it was burning her but she knew the sensation would end quickly. In the dim light she saw David Zahavy pull his hood back from his head and as she leaned toward him she fell into a large darkness. David caught her and held her tightly. The only thing Alexis knew as she passed out was that it was a warm, welcome darkness and she could rest for a while.

The Team pilot, Su Li, expertly lifted the chopper off of the rocky shelf in the gusting and fickle winds by sliding away from the mountain side. She had learned to fly her first helicopter in an early version of the Huey and she was well accustomed to its abilities and its weaknesses.

As Su Li gained height she started tipping the chopper toward their destination outside of Denver, Colorado. She checked her radar and watched as the Apache gunship formed up with her and protected them.

Su Li looked in the small mirror and in the red-lit interior of the chopper she could see Sarah adding a blanket to Alexis' coverings. She also could see David hanging onto Alexis with a look that dared anyone to interfere. Su Li smiled and attended to the conversation with the ATC controller as they left the mountains and turned south toward the Crossfire Fortress.

CHAPTER TWO

Alexis slowly awoke in feathery warmth with soft light around her. She opened her eyes to see Laura Malone standing beside her bed smiling at her.

Alexis returned the smile and then remembered the icy ledge. She tried to sit up quickly and dizziness washed over her along with weakness. Laura grabbed her shoulders and pushed her back down to the pillows softly. "Easy Tiger lady, you've gone through a lot and you need to come back slowly." Laura touched the communicator on her belt and spoke into the blue tooth microphone at her cheek. "She's awake."

Alexis rested quietly while the dizziness faded away by doing an inventory of her body. Everything seemed to be all right. She could wiggle her toes and could feel the sheets with them. Her hands were bandaged, but all the digits moved properly and while they felt like she had been working out, there was no pain.

A strange man walked into the room and gently moved Laura out of the way. It quickly became obvious that he was one of the medical technicians from the base at the top of the mountain the Fortress was located in. The medtech proceeded to check her out from head to toe. He took her blood pressure and checked her temperature. He took the bandages off of her hands and examined the skin. Dry, flaking skin but no frostbite. Shaking his head at the impossibility of that he smiled and pronounced her well enough to move around. He packed up his instruments and left the room.

Alexis scanned the room and noticed David sitting quietly in an overstuffed chair to one side of the room watching everything. She smiled at him and he smiled back. Getting up, he stretched and walked over to the side of the bed and, ever so softly, took her hand. "Welcome back."

He started to leave and she hung onto his hand. Squeezing it tightly she spoke with gratitude from her heart. "Thank you for coming for me." This came out a bit raspy but understandable. Impetuously he bent down and kissed her on the cheek. The look in his eyes was more than camaraderie, "Wild horses couldn't have kept me away and I never, ever leave an agent out in the cold." It was obvious to both Laura and Alexis that she meant more to him than just the fact she was an agent. That fact made her feel flattered and protected. He brushed a tear away from her face, patted her hand, bent over, gently kissed her on the cheek again, and walked out of the room.

Laura looked after him as he left. When he was gone she turned back to Alexis. "He's right you know. After we discovered you were gone he moved mountains to locate you and then to rescue you. He was not to be denied. He told Charlie to devote all his resources into locating you and would not take no for an answer. He's been by your side ever since he found you on that mountain."

That really made Alexis' feel warm and loved. Then another part of her anatomy demanded her attention and she had Laura help her out of the bed and to the bathroom. After a shower and a lot of damage control to her hands, face, and hair, she slowly got dressed and then sank to her knees next to the bedside and prayed her thanks and love to Yahshua and Father Yahveh. She felt the closeness of divinity and the love she felt made her so happy she wept. She then got up and repaired her makeup, again, and finally went down to the kitchen area of the Fortress.

As the other Crossfire Team members saw her they came over and gave her a gentle hug and told her they were elated that she was back and in one piece. It was obvious to Alexis that they really meant it. Alexis had never felt so loved and at home since she had left her parents home to join the Army.

After being fed a light breakfast by Sarah Connelly, Alexis wandered into the War Room and sat in her command chair at the console. Noticing the silence, she looked up and saw everybody staring at her with expectation. She grinned lopsidedly, "What?"

Jack Malone grinned at her and then sat up and asked her to tell everyone what had happened to her since their confrontation with the members of the Omicron Cartel outside the Cherry Creek Mall two days ago. Alexis realized that she needed to be debriefed and the routine of it felt good. She let her memories flow back to the beginning of her dilemma.

-----------------------*********-----------------------

She had been assigned to accompany Laura, Sarah, and Mark to a covert meeting with what was supposed to be an OC member that wanted to switch sides in the conflict between OC and the Crossfire Team. Mark thought it would be a trap and prepared everyone for that eventuality.

Even though they were in civilian clothes, Alexis knew that there were more weapons scattered throughout the group than most police tactical teams. They were going to be ready for trouble if it came their way.

-----------------------*********-----------------------

As her memories ended she started her debrief, Alexis listed the weapons she had been carrying. Two Para Ordinance 10-45s and two extra clips, a miniature 45 caliber Derringer, over and under, a Cold Steel Tanto fighting knife and two back-up knives, one was a SWAT Spike Steel Tanto and the other was a special National Clandestine Service spike that hid in her sleeve lining on her left arm. She also had her GPS tracker in her hair disguised as a barrette.

As Mark made contact with the supposed turncoat, Alexis was watching for any sign of a trap. At that point she faltered in her narrative. "I really don't know what happened. I was looking for anything out of the ordinary and then I woke up captive on a small jet aircraft, a Sabreliner, I think."

Looking at Jack she hypothesized possibilities. I could have been Tazered, stunned, or gassed, I don't know which. I don't have any signs of a Tazer or a stun gun but then I didn't feel any residual effects of having been gassed either."

"Regardless, as I said, I woke up suddenly. I knew my hands were bound by metal, probably handcuffs. At NCS we were trained to wake up without giving evidence that we were awake. Unless they were monitoring my vital signs they would not be aware I had awakened."

Alexis stopped to take a drink of water. "I listened carefully to a low conversation going on in the seats before me. Primarily, it was about how they were going to "pry" information out of me when we got to California. There was a mention of a Doctor Ramos who was a specialist in memory retrieval but the process was fairly destructive to the person giving up the memories."

Looking around at the others she realized they knew exactly what she was describing. "I carefully opened my eyes and saw two men sitting in the row in front of me to my left. One was apparently the copilot and the other was a guard for me. I carefully worked a lockpick out of the seam of my right sleeve and went to work on the handcuff lock. Twice I had to feign sleep when the guard guy turned around to look at me."

"I got the locks undone but didn't remove the cuffs. The copilot said he had to go to the can and got up and went to the back of the aircraft to the little potty they had back there. I waited until the other man yawned and was off guard. I slid out of my seat and kicked him in the side of the head at the temple by kicking over the seat backs. In a dying reaction he triggered off all the rounds in an Uzi he apparently had been holding in his hands and that I hadn't seen. All thirty-two of the rounds went into the cockpit through the wall. The plane shuddered and started to fall into a dive. Probably from the weight of the dead pilot on the steering yoke."

"I realized that regaining control of the aircraft in the cockpit was probably not feasible due to the damage caused to the flight controls by the rounds fired by the dead guard. I headed toward the rear and the door to the aircraft. As I was making my way uphill against the increasing nose-down attitude of the plane, the copilot emerged from the toilet hanging on for dear life. He also realized the futility of trying to save the aircraft and grabbed the single emergency parachute from a rack and quickly put it on. He then managed to open the rear side door by an explosive charge."

"I knew my only chance of survival was that parachute and ran at the copilot as he prepared to jump out the door.

I hit him like a linebacker attacking a running back, knocking us both out the door into the slipstream of the falling aircraft. The wind and shock of the sub-zero temperature almost broke my hold on him but we rotated to the left and he blocked the direct blast of the wind on me."

"At this point the copilot tried to knock me off of his back. When he couldn't dislodge me he drew an automatic pistol with his right hand and tried to angle it back at me. I grabbed his arm and twisted it up behind his back. As I cranked on the arm he fired the pistol thinking he would hit me somewhere. Instead the bullet struck the back of his head near his neck with the hydraulic pressure neatly removing the top of his head. He died immediately and became rigid. Wiping his blood off of my face on his jacket I was then able to move myself around to the front of his body and deploy his parachute."

Alexis looked at Sarah and saw sympathy and understanding. She had obviously had a similar crisis in her life as a Mossad spy.

Alexis continued with her debriefing. "Understand that I did not know where we were or the altitude of the aircraft when we left it. It was dark enough that the ground was simply a darker black than the sky, which was partially overcast with limited star or moon light. I survived the shock of the chute opening and prepared to guide the chute when I saw the ground coming up really fast, immediately below us. Apparently we had been flying over the Rocky Mountains on the way west and had lost a great deal of altitude before we ejected from the aircraft. I managed to use the copilot's body as a buffer as we hit the first mountain wall. The chute partially deflated and we fell about fifty feet onto a ledge. The impact of striking the ledge ripped my hold off of the copilot. I was able to do a reasonable tuck and roll but somehow the contact with the mountain removed my leather jacket and sent me sliding down a dome of ice toward the edge of the ledge."

She shook her head, "The wind re-inflated the parachute and lifted the copilot back off the ledge above me. At this point I was attempting to stop my slide and couldn't afford to try and regain my hold on the parachute or the copilot's body. I slid over the edge of the ledge and was able to grab onto a rock with my right hand to stop my fall. After that I was able to regain the surface of the ledge with the help of my NCO spike. After reaching the safety of the cliff face, I found my jacket and discovered I had no avenue of escape from the ledge. My body temperature was cooling rapidly and I was going into hypothermia when David and the others found me."

She leaned back in her chair and looked at her rough hands. "All in all, not a situation I would like to be in at any time in the future."

Sighing, she smiled, "But the Savior helped me every step of the way or I wouldn't be here talking to you now. I can pinpoint at least ten times between waking up on the aircraft and getting into the helicopter that required His help to have even had a small chance of victory". Everyone in the War Room could agree with her statement because they saw the Father's hand operating every time they were in conflict with the enemy.

CHAPTER THREE

After Alexis had finished describing her ordeal on the mountain, the rest of the group brainstormed the events surrounding the abduction.

Jack summed up the initial event. "I believe you were gassed Alexis. I have had the same thing done to me and it doesn't leave a lot of signs that it happened. Regardless, as they took you down and spirited you away while they tried to capture Mark and Sarah. Not succeeding in that effort they tried to disengage. We ended up with one attacker dead, one injured, two captured, including the injured guy, and three that got away. After the battle, the FBI took control of the two surviving mercenaries for interrogation."

Jack took a sip of water and continued his recitation of the events. "As Mark suspected, it was an OC trap, pure and simple. They thought that they had at least achieved a partial victory by bagging you. Obviously, they made a mistake in that judgment and you made them pay for it." He looked at Alexis and waved his hand to indicate the others in the room. "We have discussed the entire event of your capture and now we know about your escape. I dare say we are all proud of your abilities and very grateful to Yahveh and Yahshua for your survival."

Several hundred miles to the southwest of the Fortress there was another discussion going on about the same events. Howard Tollison was the latest director of the Eastern Directorate of the Omicron Cartel. He was proud of the fact that the glare of his eyes kept men worried and women afraid of him.

Tollison knew that he owed his elevation to this lofty position entirely to the Crossfire Team for removing the previous men that held this position. He was glad to be in the command seat but felt nothing but intense hatred for his promoters. To prevent a repeat of their successes, Tollison had his mind set on destruction of the team at any cost. One of OC's agents in Washington had reported that it truly was the Crossfire Team that had eliminated Voltron, their command and control center in Egypt.

Tollison was very aware that losing Voltron eliminated the day-to-day orders that had run OC. The Crossfire Team had located the Voltron complex in Egypt and shut it down. Worse yet, the Crossfire Team also scored a major victory against OC by finding the Arab Strike Force executives who had been running that operation. Those individuals were now probably residing in Guantanamo Base in Cuba under the interrogation of the U.S. Military, Tollison knew of no way of getting them out of there.

The Voltron plan to use a united Arab military force to attack Israel was gone, although Tollison could not figure how the Crossfire Team had stopped the attack after it had already started. Tollison was very aware that he and his western U.S. counterpart, Carl Sammos, were now in control like they had never been before. The long term strategy and world overview had been eliminated with the loss of Voltron. That left the United States efforts of the resurgent OC controlled by the ambitions of Carl and himself. After meeting, they had aligned their considerable assets on a single goal; total destruction of the Crossfire Team. Tollison knew that most rational people would avoid attacking an enemy that had defeated them so many times, already. But he and Carl were sure they would succeed where the earlier efforts had failed.

Tollison shook his head as he thought about another major setback to OC. That was the loss of his personally-selected director of operations, Raisia Ivanova. In an unauthorized but bold move, Raisia and five men had decided to capture Jack Malone by themselves. Their effort not only failed but Raisia was apparently killed by Malone, and the rest of her OC team captured by the FBI.

While this infuriated both of the new directors, the most galling thing was the subsequent "trade" they had arranged to not bomb several schools to get Raisia back. The Crossfire Team did return Raisia but she was dead. Then showing OC how ineffective they were, the team and the government found and disabled the bombs set in the schools. At that point Carl Sammos said, "Now we are not only seen as fools but stupid fools, too. This cannot be tolerated!"

Seething with anger and a great desire for revenge they decided to demonstrate to the Crossfire Team and the rest of the American government that OC wasn't to be trifled with in any way.

CHAPTER FOUR

The Saturday shopping was in full swing at the Mall of Georgia in Buford, a suburb to the north of Atlanta's huge metro area. It was a summer's shopping spree created by Fourth of July sales at the anchor stores and some of the larger chains within the mall.

Judy Colter herded her twin six-year old daughters toward the mall entrance and chaffed that she had to park so far out due to the crowds.

She looked ahead of her and knew that the hot, humid summer heat drew a lot of both shoppers and movie goers into the acres of air conditioned mall to enjoy their Saturday. It would be a hassle trying to keep up with the shopping and the kids. She envied her husband and his weekly golf game.

She checked her watch because the girls had an appointment at twelve-fifteen for a photo session here at the mall. It was right at twelve and they could make the appointment if they could wind their way across the vast parking lot and through the throngs of people.

Suddenly there was a monstrous, deafening blast of sound and a force that knocked all three of them to the ground and backwards. Both girls started screaming and Judy was trying to understand what happened and pull her mind back together. She looked up in a mixture of fear and wonder as two cars flew over them and crashed to the ground behind them, smashing other cars.

Fear for the girls overrode any other emotion as Judy looked around. She crawled over to the twins and pulled them to her. There were noises and screaming everywhere and the girl's big eyes told her to look back at the mall.

There was a huge fire that engulfed two of the smaller stores and a three hundred foot section of the mall arcade. Billowing black smoke roared up into the sky as screaming people raced away from the mall carrying small children.

In the aftermath of the explosion there was only more screaming and wailing to be heard from the dust and darkness that was the middle of the huge mall.

Judy checked her girls and herself for injuries and only found scratches and abrasions from their fall and tumbles on the ground. Absentmindedly, she noticed that their summer dresses were ruined. But then, the photography studio probably wasn't even there anymore. Judy realized that she was in shock herself.

In minutes there were dozens of fire trucks and rescue squads converging on the blast site. Judy watched as the paramedics and the firemen rushed into the mall to attend to the injured and the fire. Her heart almost broke when a second blast roared out of the rubble and destroyed the first responders. She just sat in the parking lot holding her girls and weeping. She knew she should do something, but not sure what.

She staggered to her feet and watched as the police isolated the blast site, evacuated the mall and surrounding buildings, and kept everyone away from the mall. They couldn't stop many exceptionally brave paramedics who would not be deterred from trying to help the injured and dying. As a paramedic reached her and started checking the girls, Judy realized that this was a horribly black day which was symbolized by the giant pillar of smoke rising into the hot air over Georgia.

Laura watched the TV news as it showed the horrific effects of the bombs at the shopping mall in Georgia. Her heart ached as she saw the littered bodies of innocent men, women, and children who never had a chance to live their lives or even a clue as to why they were being killed.

The newscast was interrupted by an announcement that a caller from the Omicron Cartel Group had claimed full responsibility for the terrorist attack by telephone to one of the news groups. Laura prayed about the evil and asked for peace for the survivors and mercy for the killed, Yahveh confirmed OC's involvement in her spirit.

OC's stated goal wasn't to change national policy or even to attack the United States for any foreign power. They were telling the government that they could inflict major death and damage whenever and wherever they wanted to. Laura knew this despicable act was in response to the recent death of their senior agent by the Crossfire Team.

Laura thought about the red-haired woman, Raisia Ivanova. She had been a highly trained Russian agent before she had sold her services to the OC. Less than two weeks ago she had attempted to kidnap Laura's husband, Jack. Laura shook her head. "That was easier said than done." This was a fact that Raisia and her team found out. The trap backfired and Raisia had been captured by the Crossfire Team and the FBI.

Laura remembered Jack's description of the fight. The battle had been in a side walkway in a mall. During the fight to kidnap Jack, Raisia's hand had been broken. Transported to a secret military site in the Rocky Mountains the military doctor had treated her injuries and sedated her. Unknown to any of them, in true Russian spy fashion, Raisia had a serum in her blood that when combined with a sedative agent it turned into a deadly poison. This was to keep a spy from being drugged and blabbing. That was what killed the young Russian woman.

Laura looked up as Jack, and Mark Connelly walked into the War Room of the Fortress. They stood there and watched the pictures with Laura. Jack put his hand on her shoulder in a gesture of comfort. Laura looked up with tears in her eyes and put her hand over his.

Mark shook his head, "That was not only incredibly cruel and horrible, it was monumentally stupid."

Laura looked at him with a questioning look.

Mark sat down next to her and took her left hand in his. "This action has taken the OC out of our hands and placed it at the top of the list of the Department of Homeland Security. I just heard from the President. This country will not allow anyone to commit this type of terrorism. We're to stand down as far as investigating, looking for, or attacking the OC because the alphabet agencies are going to be hunting anyone allied with this group. I think new OC directors overstepped their bounds this time. I'm sure that Voltron would never have allowed OC to do anything as dumb as this. The President and the Congress will not be satisfied until the OC is nothing but a bad memory.

Jack shook his head. "Does that mean we can't take them on if they try to attack us?"

Mark smiled faintly, "No, not at all. It just means we need to take their bodies to the FBI if that happens. Remember that Satan is a promoter of this group and even Homeland Security will defer to us if there is any significant demonic involvement."

Laura continued to monitor the newscasts of the bombing. The death toll continued to climb until all the people involved at the mall were accounted for and rechecked. All in all, two hundred and nineteen people had lost their lives and six more died as their wounds overcame their ability to live. Over one hundred of the dead were innocent children.

Damage was in the millions of dollars and the hew and cry for justice was almost as loud as it had been during the poisoning of Israel and the United States two years before.

All known, or suspected, directors and associates of OC were being arrested as well as their mercenary troops. There would be justice and no judge was going to allow any of these people to make bail.

Six days later the computer guru of the Fortress, Charlie Wu, charged into the War Room waving a handful of papers. A well-muscled Oriental man with a handsome face, Charlie had a recent background as a top Chinese internal security agent. Both he and his wife, Linda had been functioning as exceptionally loyal agents for China until they had found Yahshua and became Christians.

Jack stood up to intercept Charlie and ask what the problem was, this time.

Charlie was slightly out of breath in his hurry to get the news to the team. "Crayton and I have discovered an OC operation that the other agencies aren't aware of, yet. There is a definite spiritual component to this one which is preventing the knowledge of this raid from being understood by anybody."

Laura asked, "Then how did you discover it?"

Charlie waved his free hand in the air. "Okay, I wrote a program for Crayton that allows him to extrapolate intentions and operations based on the previous occurrences and new data as it unfolds. Especially if there are energy whirls involved."

Mark smiled, "Maybe we should call you the computer prophet rather than the guru."

Charlie looked irritated for a second. Then he took a deep breath and calmed himself. "Guys, this is real and it's going to go down in less than twelve hours in Phoenix, Arizona."

Jack felt a dreadful certainty in his spirit. "Charlie's right. Let's gear up and move."

CHAPTER FIVE

The warm summer breezes blew gently across the serene landscape and brought the sweet smell of a recent rainstorm to the citizens of Phoenix, Arizona as they drove south on Interstate 17 toward the downtown area through the late Friday afternoon traffic.

In a nondescript, single-level commercial building located next to the west side of the Interstate, just south of West Rose Garden Lane, the environment was anything but gentle, serene, or sweet.

Carol Moffet had grown up living a protected childhood and being home schooled K-12 by loving and considerate parents in Yuma, Arizona. She secretly felt she had occasional wild times, which would have been considered as boring by most public school graduates, and she felt she was a bit of a rebel. After finishing the high school grades she found that she excelled at computers and physics and had gone to a private school for her college work. She was rated as one of the best software engineers in the world of geophysical research by the time she graduated with honors.

She had taken a premier position with the new "GTherm Corporation" and quickly established herself as a very young but brilliant theoretical physicist in the new world of Geothermal Power. She easily assumed the position of leadership in her design group and was respected by everyone despite her young age of twenty-two.

Everyone respected her it seemed, except for these thugs that had just invaded her world. The emergency alarm had gone off and everyone rushed quickly to the vault-like door to the lower level as they had been trained. She had checked to make sure everyone else had cleared out and then headed for the door herself.

An explosion had blown the front doors to the facility into the building and the blast had knocked her to the floor of the lab. This actually was a blessing in disguise as one of the door panels ripped a jagged hole in the air, right through the space she had been standing in a second before.

As her hearing tried to return she saw a bunch of military types with rifles rush into the lobby and head for the control room of the lab where she was struggling to get to her feet. She watched in horror as the janitor, Joey Garland, was gunned down where he stood in shock at the invasion.

She realized she was about to die and it just made her mad. She saw one of the armed men swing his rifle in her direction and she defiantly glared at him. She wasn't going to show him any fear. It was too late for that.

Suddenly she was tackled by another person with military gear and found herself on the floor as bullets flew above her. The person that tackled her rolled over and fired an extremely loud rifle at the incoming troops. The man that was trying to kill her was knocked off his feet by the rounds and the other raiders sought protection behind desks or consoles.

She was grabbed unceremoniously by an arm and dragged behind a two-million dollar analyzer console, which suddenly sounded like a jackhammer was hitting the front of it. The overwhelming noise and zing of bullets flying past her fell off as other weapons around her started firing back at the invaders.

She looked at the person who had just risked their life to save her and was stunned to realize it was a woman. Not just a woman but a very pretty black-haired woman, holding a smoking rifle, who grinned at her in the midst of the violence and chaos. Carol noticed that the woman was carrying as many guns and knives and bullets as anyone she had seen in pictures of Viet Nam or Iraq. The dark-haired woman tipped her head to the right and led Carol away from the front lines to the slightly safer area behind the Blend Console.

Carol was amazed to find two more women also dressed in combat gear that were firing their rifles at the invaders. Both of these were blonde-haired and would be beautiful if they weren't in the middle of combat and had battlefield cosmetics to hide their faces in the dark.

The black-haired woman that had saved her, duck-walked over to the blonde women and said, "See! I told

21

you I could get her out of the line of fire." Then she added her rifle to the firepower against the attackers.

Carol sat there amazed at the three warriors. She never knew women that could do what they were doing and still present an aura of femininity. The fact that these three had just saved her life didn't hurt her admiration of them.

The firing fell off and she heard the black haired woman say, "Oh boy. This isn't good." Carol risked a peek over the console and was even more shocked than she had been at the raid. Striding forth from the area where the attackers were huddled behind anything metal was a creature that wasn't of this world. The evil it radiated was horrible and penetrating; it sickened Carol's stomach and made her scared more than anything had ever scared her before.

This one was probably male but sleek and almost contemporary-looking in its appearance. The outlandish features were its jet-black skin and almond-shaped eyes. It had slicked back hair and pronounced eye-brows in a dull reddish hue. It was wearing a long black cape and had a black body covering which couldn't hide its misshapen form. The being came forward with a determined stride, ignoring the bullets fired its way.

The dark haired woman fired two rounds directly into the creature but they had no affect on it.

Shaking her head, one of the blonde women put down her rifle and stood up. She started praying out loud as she eased around the console and walked out to meet the creature in the middle of the lab area. Carol's heart sank as she saw the woman approach the six-foot tall demon.

As they neared each other the creature disregarded the woman's lack of fear and suddenly raised two unnaturally long arms to display razor-sharp claws instead of fingertips. Carol let out a strangled plea to God to protect the woman from the beast.

As if in answer to Carol's plea, suddenly, golden armor and a golden shield explosively appeared covering and shielding the smaller woman. More impressive than the armor was a metal sword, gleaming like the purest chrome with some form of power flowing off of its surface. The creature slashed with both its clawed hands at the golden image in front of it. The claws slid off the armor without leaving a mark. The blonde woman feinted to the right and when the creature moved the other direction the blonde woman reversed her direction and plunged the sword through the chest of the demon and yanked upward on it. The sword split the upper half of the demon into two like it was paper. The demon disappeared into an oily black smoke with a horrible, hissing scream.

Two of the mercenaries, enraged by the defeat of their creature fired their M-16s at the blonde. She casually deflected the rounds with the sword in her hands. She advanced on the mercenaries and they scrambled to get as far away from her as possible.

In the meantime, two men dressed in combat armor like the women, had moved to the sides of the attackers as they watched the battle between the woman and the demon. The two men opened fire on the enemy soldiers and took down several of them. The remaining troops retreated backward, toward the front door, firing as they went.

Another voice was heard yelling, "Fire in the hole!" The black haired woman turned and fell on Carol, covering her with her own body armor as everyone sought shelter. A new blast tore into the retreating mercenaries and decimated them. The blast was sufficient to shake the entire building, knock out the lights in the lobby, and the lab, and to blow out any remaining glass in the first-floor windows. Debris fell on the woman covering Carol and slammed down around them.

Carol felt the weight on her lift up and off of her. The woman shook the dust and debris off of her. In the darkness and dust, six incredibly bright beams flashed on. Each of the team was using what Carol found out later was a Streamlight NF-2 LED NightFighter flashlight to search for any remaining threats. Carol had Googled the flashlight later and learned that the NightFighter is one of the brightest, most versatile compact combat flashlights on the market. It uses a Luxeono™, super-high flux LED that is 10 times brighter than a high-intensity LED.

As the emergency lighting struggled to come on, the flashlights were switched off and Carol, who had timidly ventured out from behind the console in the darkness noticed a sixth person with the group. A very trim, middle-aged man with a distinguished face and an infectious smile. The black haired woman referred to him as David. He was the one that had thrown the last explosive.

There were sounds of sirens approaching the building from several directions. The solidly-built, good looking black haired man handed his rifle and sidearm to the black haired woman and went out the blasted entrance, apparently to speak to the officers.

Carol stood there with her arms folded over her chest and watched the efficiency of all of the team members as they quickly confirmed the fatal status of the mercenaries and checked the bodies for Intel.

The dark haired woman saw her standing there and walked over to her. "Hi! My name's Sarah, what's yours?"

Carol was still attempting to process everything that had happened in the last little bit and had to think to come up with her name. "Carol Moffet, I'm the chief programmer here." She stuck out her hand to Sarah. "I want to thank you for saving me back there, several times."

Sarah shook her hand in a surprisingly solid grip and waved her other hand around. "Sorry about the mess. We didn't have time to stop them before they got here. In fact, we were barely able to get into a defensive position before they attacked the building."

Carol looked over at the blonde haired woman who had fought the demon and asked Sarah, "Does she do that golden thing very often?"

Sarah grinned, "Occasionally, as the circumstances demand. How come you were out in the open when all the brave men were safely below?"

Carol grimaced, "I was too slow checking to see that everyone else was safe."

Sarah stepped up and hugged the smaller woman. "Thank Yahshua that you are safe."

Carol looked honestly into Sarah's eyes and saw that honesty returned. "I will, and I will ask Him to bless you all for your part in our safety."

The dark haired man came back into the building and called quietly, "Okay guys, we're out of here."

As Sarah turned to leave, Carol caught her arm. "Who are you people?" She noticed that the woman rotated her arm which broke the hold Carol had without effort.

Sarah smiled again, "We're just servants of the Most High. We're called the Crossfire Team." And then she was gone.

Carol looked around at the debris and bodies leaking blood everywhere and thought that Joey would have a hard time making it right. That was until she saw Joey laying there on the floor in a big pool of blood as part of the death and destruction. That made her mad and sad at the same time.

The shock was wearing off and the emotions were asserting themselves and she felt hot tears run down her cheeks for Joey. She realized she didn't give a whoop about the dead attackers. They had asked for it and boy, did they get it. Seeing other people, she scrubbed her eyes and cheeks to clear away the tears.

The rest of the employees were timidly coming back up from the safety of the floor below and one of them asked her, "Good God Carol!, were you up here during the fighting?"

Carol coolly looked at the man and answered. "Yes Bob, I was. After all, who would possibly want to miss all this?" She waved her left arm indicating all the bodies and destruction. Bob's eyes widened as he considered her statement.

Carol looked out the gaping hole that had been the front door to "GTherm" and prayed that she would have a chance to see more of the Crossfire Team.

CHAPTER SIX

The command vehicle they had acquired from the FBI carried the six-member Crossfire Team back to Sky Harbor International Airport in Phoenix. Sarah's mind wandered as they drove.

--------------------------*****--------------------------

Sarah studied her husband Mark, as he talked on his cell phone. She knew he was linking up with Charlie Wu at the Fortress in Denver. She also knew he had sources that were not available to most people, although she now knew quite a few of those people herself.

Mark's quiet manner belied his strength and power. She loved his casual friendly attitude but she had been with him in quite a few actions. She coolly appraised his solid good looks and rugged features. She realized that she loved him more than any other person in the world and would not be very pleasant with any woman that tried to split them up or made a play for Mark. Considering Sarah's background in the military and as a field agent and assassin for the Israeli Mossad, her unpleasantness could be a truly frightening proposition.

Sarah used to have feelings for her old boss, David Zahavy, which she always kept to herself since he was married and had kids. After meeting and marrying Mark she realized that she had let go of her earlier feelings. Watching David and Alexis talking quietly in the back of the van she realized that Alexis had become the object of David's affections since his divorce. Sarah checked her feelings and was glad to find only happiness for them both, now that David was divorced from his wife and estranged from his children by religious differences, let alone by time and distance. David needed a relationship that she herself could no longer offer and Alexis was a good match for him. She quietly sent a prayer winging its way to Heaven for their relationship. Sarah then looked back at her new husband with pride.

Mark stood about six foot, two inches tall and weighted in around 200 pounds. Dark brown-black hair framed a face that had 'honor' written all over it. His time in the United States Navy Seals had set his mold toward being a protector of the innocent. He thrived on complicated situations and was definitely a strategist of the highest order. The integrity he had in everything he did was like a giant rock foundation. He was a man you could count on to keep his word even if he had to die for it. Oh, he had his faults, but then who didn't? He was a very detailed planner, but then if the situation went into the unknown he was just as quick to throw the plans out the window and go on instinct and training.

Mark's physique was what the average American thought of when they pictured the perfect Marine. An honor scout personality in a body like that of Arnold Schwarzenegger. Oh yeah, throw in the mind of an engineer. He was bulked out somewhat but when he worked out it was more for greater endurance than physical bulk. Whatever! It made him a man who could turn a girl's head just by walking by. That still bothered her somehow. Hmmm.

Jack Malone was driving the van and his wife, Laura, sat next to him in the front seat. These two people were very humble yet dynamically affected everyone around them. Their faith was the rock on which the team's faith began and the basis for all of the actions of the Crossfire Team. Jack's combat capabilities had become awesome and his military competence was rapidly approaching that of a tactical officer. Jack had become a warrior because he had been called to do so by Yahveh.

He was a good-looking man with blonde hair and gray-green eyes. He normally dominated any scene he was involved in. He stood about six foot four inches and was, in his own way, just as muscularly solid as Mark was. His muscle mass was more fluid and compact and he didn't show the 'buffed' shape that Mark did. But he was anything but soft. He was a good fighter and didn't ask any quarter in a conflict. Sarah should know. He had beaten her at unarmed combat and that was something nobody else had done since her early Mossad training days.

Laura was a beautiful and refined young woman with a full head of blonde hair and light green eyes. No longer an amateur at combat, she had a sharp mind and a grit and determination that sustained and complimented Jack's leadership capabilities. Their faith had sustained them all in the beginning and built up the belief of everyone on the team. Laura's endowment by God with the physical armor and sword of God to combat the incursions of demons into man's world had been a miracle and had saved them countless times. Both of the Malones had become more humble as they advanced in their capabilities because they realized that they were only servants, tools if you will, of the Most High Creator of the Universe. Every time they saw God in action it made them realize their place in God's world.

Sarah considered herself introspectively. Her mandatory military training had led to her recruitment by the premier Intelligence Service of her country, the Mossad. Her training and operational background had hardened her attitude but, so far, not her looks. She knew she was a darker-haired version of Laura with a decidedly darker background. She knew she weighed about 130 pounds and stood right at five foot ten inches tall. Her conversion to Christianity from Judaism had been dramatic and complete during the team's exploits in Tel Aviv two years before.

-----------------------*****-----------------------

A bump in the road caused the van to bounce and that action snapped Sarah's mind back to the present. The van settled down but Sarah was now in the present and aware of everything going on around them. The Arizona nighttime sky was full of stars and there didn't seem to be any hostile actions near them that she could detect. She stayed alert as the van pulled into the airport.

CHAPTER SEVEN

The van pulled up to the military part of the airfield. They proceeded to the USAF Reserve Officer Guest Quarters and the team disembarked. Removing their armor, they cleaned their weapons and reloaded them. They also refitted their combat equipment and stowed it expertly. Each person was a trained and intelligent warrior and knew the importance of properly maintained equipment and weapons.

Using the Guest Quarter's facilities they rotated through the showers and cleaned the smell of cordite, blood, and battle off of their beings. Redressing and rearming in a more concealed way they checked to see if they'd left the place clean before heading out in the night air to the jet. Each person loaded their gear into the luggage compartment before boarding the CitationX for the trip back to Denver. The Crossfire Team pilot, Su Li, checked each one as they came on board for injuries or problems. Not finding anything more serious than scratches and some bruises she asked them to sit down and belt up for takeoff.

The plane had been pre-flight checked, and as Su Li taxied out of the hanger onto the taxiway she ran the engines up. Su Li taxied the jet down the taxiway leading to the runway careful not to get in the way of the commercial heavy jets using the same facilities. Getting clearance from the tower she smoothly accelerated down the runway and lifted off way before the normal point for most aircraft. The fact was that this particular private jet had been refitted with military engines gave her twice the normal engine power. This much improved the power-to-weight ratio and had everything to do with the quick takeoff.

As the plane leveled off at the 35,000 foot operating altitude, Mark used his cell phone to link up with Charlie at the Fortress again and asked, "Did you get good video coverage of the action at GTherm?"

Charlie confirmed that they had several different views of the action from the combat cameras included in each warrior's gear. "I do have a good record of that demon and that bothers me somewhat. Normally, spiritual beings don't register on recording devices."

Mark passed the question up to Laura who considered it for a few seconds. Some of the Heavenly training she had received a few weeks ago opened up a memory. She smiled faintly and told Mark, "Demons that violate Yahveh's laws, including the act of coming physically into the human dimension illegally, meaning without Yahveh's permission, no longer have the spiritual protection they used to when they were acting legally. That is why they can be seen by all humans, shot and killed, and why they can be recorded, sometimes."

Sarah tipped her head to one side. "But, I shot it two times and the bullets didn't affect it. I thought that demons in our dimension had to be here legally for bullets not to harm them don't they?"

Laura thought about that for a few seconds. "We'll have to ask somebody with more knowledge than me about that. It's a good question."

Mark relayed her comments to Charlie who understood the synergy and what he felt was the correctness to the explanation. He thought quickly and asked Mark, "Do the demons realize their vulnerability when they cross into our dimension without permission? And why didn't Alexis' rounds harm this demon if he transgressed his spiritual protection?"

Mark gave up relaying messages and got up and handed the phone to Laura. She grinned at his pique and took the phone graciously. "Charlie? Okay, here is how this works. The lower level demons don't get a chance to consider whether an action is dangerous to their existence. They get their marching orders from superior demons and that's what they do. They are nothing like us and don't have the luxury of independent thought about everything and how it would affect them."

Charlie thought about that and commented. "Thanks Laura, that gives me some new parameters to consider in our planning, but what about Alexis' bullets she fired at this demon? They didn't affect him and if our theory about them transgressing and losing their protection is correct this doesn't fit the facts.

Laura thought for a minute. "I'm still not sure why he wasn't affected by the bullets. I need to pray about that."

Jack listened to the ongoing conversations while he thought about his team's future operations. OC was now in the crosshairs of every law and justice organization in the world. He felt that the Crossfire Team's role in the disassembling of the Omicron Cartel would be minimal. That would leave them free to pursue...What?" Then he realized his mistake. HE was trying to plan out the future of team's actions when they were dedicated to doing Yahveh's will. He looked up and caught Laura's eye as she was finishing up with Charlie. Jack tipped his head to the left and she nodded. Laura got up and gave Mark back his phone and walked over to where Jack was sitting. Sitting down beside her husband she thought she knew what was coming. Smiling at him she asked, "Time to pray?"

Jack laughed; she was right on top of things as usual. He nodded. They held hands and started praying to Yahveh, the Creator of the Universe. One by one the other members of the team felt the communion and fell into the prayer. As they continued to pray, Jack felt the closeness as the Holy Spirit of Yahveh settled down onto them. The communion was divine and personal yet it encompassed them all. Jack's concern about the future of the team's effort was answered in a flash and Jack knew that they had an even worse enemy to confront than OC.

This was like being in the river of life, so refreshing to the spirit and so thoroughly the Spirit of Yahveh that the mind and body relaxed and became spectators to harmony and peace of the proximity of the Elohim as his children.

After a while the Spirit lifted and everyone felt so refreshed and in harmony with the Heavenly Kingdom and the will of Yahveh it was amazing.

Su Li came out of the cockpit and stared at all of them with a frown.

Jack asked her, "Are we on autopilot? What's the matter?"

Su Li blew out a breath. "Yes, of course we are on autopilot. Do you think I would walk away from the controls otherwise? Thank Yahveh that we have this good of an autopilot. The prayers you were generating brought the Spirit of Yahveh all right. Did you stop to think that it also fell on me? I barely had time to engage the autopilot before I lost sight of the controls. Do you know that we were basically unpiloted for the last twenty minutes?" She seemed upset with them for praying which left her out of control of the aircraft.

Laura laughed. "Su Li, how can you possibly think that Yahveh would allow you to commune with Him if there was even the smallest possibility that your skills as a pilot would be needed? Not on all of our lives. The Father had everything in His hands."

Su Li relaxed and realized she had just committed the sin of pride. Thinking that she was as so important as a pilot when Yahveh was directly involved with them. She silently prayed her confession and repentance to the Lord of the Universe and asked Him to bless Laura for reminding her of the real order of things. She smiled, "Thank you Laura, I was a little puffed up on myself, wasn't I?"

Jack thought back to his recent decision that resulted in the prayer in the first place. He got up and put his hands on Su Li's shoulders "Don't feel alone in suffering with the old habits, we all do it. She looked up at him from her shorter stature and nodded, "Thank you."

Su Li went back to the cockpit and Mark decided to join her and continue his training as a backup pilot.

Sarah thought back over her life since she had met Mark and the Malones.

CHAPTER EIGHT

Sarah's memories flew back to the first time she had encountered the Malones.

-----------------------✱✱✱✱✱✱-----------------------

She had been one of the top Mossad field agents which wasn't saying too much because of the attrition rate in her business. The normal life span of an Israeli field agent seldom spanned more than a handful of years.

She had been on assignment in Houston, Texas in the United States to investigate a privately owned operation of one Max Lister who was suspected of evil intent against the Israeli homeland. Lister had aligned himself with the desert madman of Libya and was fermenting a crisis in America. It turned out that the crisis was to be a major internal distraction for the Americans so that they would not be able to aid their Jewish ally until it was too late.

She had investigated Lister's "Children's Ranch" operation, looking for information concerning Lister's plans for Israel. She remembered the partly cloudy, hot, humid day when she had run into the Malones who were also investigating the ranch for entirely different reasons.

Their first meeting was confrontational and she had to admit that they had bested her. Jack with his fourth-degree black belt martial arts and Laura with her Christian faith. She had teamed up with them at first to see what they could do to help her on her assignment. She was intrigued by their associate, Mark Connelly, an ex-U.S. Navy Seal turned counter-terrorist in civilian life.

In the firestorm of events that followed that day they had gone on the warpath against Lister with the help of the President and the power of the United States. She had been amazed at the effective relationship between Yahveh and the team. She had personally witnessed spiritual things that contradicted her Jewish upbringing and faith. Lister had fled, like the coward he was, to Libya, seeking protection for himself from his new infamy as an

International terrorist and child molester. He died at the remote Libyan airbase in the desert when a Libyan nuclear weapon was detonated by the Libyan military at the base, apparently by mistake.

Seeing the effectiveness of the team, she set a plan in motion to get the three Americans to accompany her to Israel to assist in a troubling case with the Arab Strike Force. The ASF had concocted a new poison and were bringing it against Israel and also against the U.S. Before the conclusion of that saga, she had chosen Christianity after she watched her good friend and mentor brought back to life by Yahshua. While she prayed for David's resurrection and healing, she herself was healed. Seeing the truth, she gave her life to the Savior and became a Messianic Jew herself. She fell in love with Mark Connelly and married him. But, not before the Father in Heaven used her to lead an International prayer meeting that saved millions around the world from the poison.

There had been other missions with the team including Satanists, island-grabbing thugs, a billionaire, a challenge between Yahveh and the false idol god of the Zarthanians, meteors, and so much more it was like ten movies going by at once.

-------------------------******-------------------------

Sarah smiled as she realized she was doing the right thing in serving the Father and the Son as part of the Crossfire Team. It dawned on her right then that it had all the earmarks of being a God thing and then everything else fell into place and became understandable. Her life had become worthwhile. She looked over at Laura and found her looking back. Laura got out of her seat next to Jack and climbed over to the seat between Sarah and Mark. Sitting there she took Sarah's left hand in her right and said, "You smile like you're happy and that makes me glad. You have really grown since you gave your life to Yahshua. Did you know you were very cynical and professionally stern almost to bitterness when we first met?"

Sarah squeezed Laura's hand as the memory burned in her mind of being mortally wounded by a Russian military round through her neck. She knew it was real even though it no longer had happened, maybe. But she did remember that one of her dying thoughts was how glad she had been to have known Jack and Laura. Looking at her best friend in this world, she grinned and told her, "I wouldn't have missed this adventure for all the gold in the world."

Laura said a silent prayer and told her. "That's good, because it's only going to get harder from here on out. I know I haven't told you this, but I am so glad you are with us. You give my spirit courage to face the combat and still laugh. Like you did for that young woman back at "GTherm", when you grabbed her out of the killing field.

That comment made Sarah think of the innocence and naivety of Carol Moffet. "You know. I really liked her grit when she knew she was about to die and wasn't afraid. I'd like to know her better."

Getting a leading from Heaven, Laura said, "You'll probably get that chance. I have a feeling we're going to meet her again, and soon."

CHAPTER NINE

Laura gently shook Jack's shoulder. He came to full awareness in their suite at the Fortress without any confusion or surprise as he always did when he was rested. He rolled onto his back and smiled at his wife. "Good morning to you too, Sweetie. What's up?"

In their present lifestyle, anyone who got a chance to sleep was allowed to sleep until they woke up. When sleep was interrupted then something needed attention that couldn't wait.

Laura smiled back at her tousle-haired husband and leaned down and gave him a kiss on the cheek. Standing up she said, "Bart Cooper from the NSA is asking to speak to you."

Jack's memory of his interaction with the government man was clear. Jack had bailed him out of a sticky situation when OC was attempting to destroy the agency. Jack had counteracted their influence with his own money and contacts, which included the Chairman of the Joint Chiefs of Staff, General Miles. Jack had been aware of the OC attempt to discredit the agent and a word from Jack to General Miles got to the administration which cleared Bart Cooper and led to the discovery of the person doing the lying. Bart heard from General Miles himself as to why he was still employed and not in jail. Apparently, he hadn't forgotten.

Laura handed Jack the cell phone and left him to deal with the agent. She had six other things going on at the moment as they searched for the next enemy they had been warned was looming on the Crossfire Team's horizon.

Bart Cooper had a tone that reminded Jack of the late actor Gary Cooper. He used the same inflections and had the same laconic assurance that the actor used to portray in the movies. Jack liked the older movies because they were less filled with sex and needless horror than the present ones. The agent greeted Jack with, "General Malone? My name is Bart Cooper and I work for the National Security Administration. I'd like to tell you that I really appreciate what you did for me two months ago. I'd also like to give you a heads up that we have uncovered." Bart's reference to Jack as "General Malone" was in reference to his being placed in that rank by the President during a world crisis where each of the team had to lead troops to prevent the detonation of multiple nuclear weapons at the top of the world.

Jack's interest was piqued. "The appreciation is welcome and I'm glad that I could help you. What has the NSA found that the other alphabet organizations aren't interested in keeping to themselves?"

Bart chuckled in a low voice. "Obviously you've worked with the CIA and the FBI before. This one was provided to the other groups but my superiors felt it would be more up your alley since it has some supernatural vectors to it."

Jack's curiosity was aroused at that statement. "What is the problem?"

Bart took a deep breath. "It seems that some Intel from one of our U.S. military crypto-analysis efforts concerning the Omicron Cartel indicates a demonic influence on the communications between Howard Tollison, who we believe to be one of the two directors of the remaining OC operations for the U.S., and one of his henchmen in the Hawaiian Islands. The transfer of information is being directly hidden by supernatural power rather than by a human-generated cryptography. It has taken three of our top analysis two days to come to this conclusion but it is based on similar efforts detected during one of your team's earlier operations in Colorado, as recorded by the FBI."

Jack remembered the attempted missile attack on Denver and the demonic covering of the action in that matter. "Yes, I remember that mission. Go on."

The NSA agent relaxed when he heard understanding in Mr. Malone's voice rather than skepticism. "It appears that the OC is interested in a geothermal operation in the Hawaiian Islands but beyond that we haven't been able to decipher the conversation. I will tell you that this is very disconcerting to our management and to the present administration. My contact with you was directly requested by the President's office.

Jack could understand the interest the President would have in the matter. "Bart, if there is evidence of demonic tampering with those communications, it is a major indicator that the operation is very important from Satan's viewpoint and therefore to OC. I believe we can assist your organization in this matter." Jack then told the agent to send the information to them as an encrypted package and gave him Charlie's phone number to set up the connection; he thanked the agent for calling them.

Jack considered the information Bart had given him and then prayed for guidance. He got a leading that definitely meant that the team needed to attend to this immediately. It was a strong leading and didn't leave any wiggle room or delayed scheduling.

Jack used his computer screen to locate Mark, Sarah, Laura, and Charlie. Happily he saw that they were all in the War Room. Jack called Laura and told her to ask everyone to remain there until he could talk to them. Jack smiled when he remembered that trying to collar all of these characters at one time was like trying to herd cats.

Racing though a quick shower he decided to put off shaving until after the meeting. Throwing on a matching set of slacks and dress shirt in blue, he pulled on his socks and shoes. Grabbing his keys and billfold he subconsciously felt for the NovaStar pendent. It was in place. Jack ran through the apartment and down the hall to the general utility room in the center of the suites. Bounding down the curving stairs he trotted across to the door to the War Room and entered.

The group had been in multiple conversations when he entered. These conversations all broke up and everyone gave him their full attention.

Jack waved everyone to their work stations and sat down at his own console. Speaking through the communications system he knew that everything that was said was recorded in full stereo and video.

"I just heard from the NSA that the devil is at work again with OC and it concerns the geothermal power plant in Hawaii. Do any of us have any detailed knowledge of geothermal power or an idea why the enemy wants to get at it? This will probably be similar to the one in Phoenix.

Mark commented that they still didn't have any real idea why OC attacked that plant, so they would be hard put to identify a reason for the new interest in the Hawaii facility, unless they were attempting to discredit geothermal power generation for unknown reasons, with the attacks creating enough concern to shut the plant down.

Laura spoke up. "I would like to recommend that we get an expert on geothermal power to enlighten us as to the applications and dangers of such a facility. I also would recommend that we see if Phoenix "GTherm" would lend us Carol Moffet since she was the one we had the best contact with on that mission."

Jack looked at Mark who nodded acceptance. "Okay, Laura, see if you can make contact with "GTherm" and if they would let us borrow their chief programmer for a few days. If so, see if she would be willing to join us here, say, tomorrow."

Laura agreed and asked Sarah to make the arrangements. She winked at Sarah to remind her of the earlier prediction.

CHAPTER TEN

Answering her boss' page, Carol Moffet was surprised to see him smile and hand her the telephone handset. Her surprise was because her boss seldom smiled and almost never let anyone touch anything in his office. A bit of a perfectionist, but a good supervisor, anyway.

Taking the phone she said, "Carol Moffet."

Her eyes widened in even greater surprise when she heard Sarah Connelly's voice on the phone. "Hi" Carol said, "It's good to hear from you again so soon. What can I do for you?"

This surprise was sufficient for her to have to sit down in one of the boss' desk chairs without asking permission. A quick glance showed him still smiling. "You want me to come to your "Fortress" in Colorado to discuss geothermal energy?"

Sarah laughed a hearty laugh. "No, Carol, we want you come here and teach us about it because it looks like we will have to be involved with it again and soon. Can you give us a sufficient overview that will allow us to determine why the people that attacked your facility are interested in geothermal power generation? We really don't have any insight into the industry or any potential uses a terrorist group might derive from controlling one of the plants. Do, please come on up. I would like to see you again and show you our "facility".

Carol asked Sarah to wait a minute. Looking at her boss she was about to explain the request when he said, "its okay, Carol. They explained it to me and I think your operation is running smooth enough you can take a few days off." He glanced around the office as if he could spot a spy. Then he whispered, "They're directly connected to the Oval Office so let's do what we can to help them."

Carol again wondered about the mental stability of upper management but accepted his approval without a comment other than a nod.

She said to Sarah. "It seems I have approval for the trip. When do I have to get tickets for and where will I go when I get there?"

Sarah laughed again. "Not to worry. Your tickets will be waiting for you at the airport tomorrow morning at 7:00 a.m. and I will meet you at DIA when your 9:00 a.m. flight out of Phoenix arrives here. See you tomorrow."

Carol said, "Okay, see you tomorrow" and handed the telephone handset back to her boss. Thanking him for the time off, she got up and headed back to her desk. Looking at her watch she realized she only had two hours before quitting time and she had to shop for something to wear.

"What do you wear to a counterterrorist meeting?" she asked herself. "Probably something with a bullet-proof lining."

She sketched out a quick list of what to do and who to assign to what during her absence. She decided to give her acting authority to Bob Kirkland, the supervisor that reported to her for the programming operation. He was sharp and capable of handling the duties. She had started training him last month to stand in or to replace her if she got promoted.

After settling matters for her absence she sat at her desk and pondered whether or not to call her parents and tell them what she was doing. Her eyes widened when she realized this could be covered under Homeland Security's umbrella of classified information. She decided to call her mom and tell her that she was going to Denver for several days on a training trip. That should keep them from worrying.

After a partially successful night of sleep at her apartment, Carol was an hour early at the United Airline ticket counter to pick up her tickets. After showing her identification she loaded her suitcase onto the weight table and was glad to see she was under the 50 pound maximum. She got her tickets and processed through security and waited at the gate until they called for boarding. She presented her ticket to the agent at the gate and he frowned. "Miss, you were supposed to board with the other first class passengers. Please proceed past the line directly to the plane."

Carol was taken aback because she hadn't even bothered to look at her ticket and didn't know she was in first class.

Seeing the somewhat stricken look on her face, the agent misinterpreted it as social unease at passing the lined-up coach passengers in the jetway. He motioned for a junior agent and told him. "Please take Miss Moffet directly to the aircraft and see that she gets priority service for seating in first class."

Carol followed the young man past all the other passengers on the jetway and was quickly allowed to enter the plane and shown to her seat. After being seated she quickly turned on the individual television screen that came out of the arm of her chair and stared at the news being shown there. That way she didn't have to look each one of the boarding passengers in the eye. She was quite grateful when the door was closed and the routine for takeoff was being followed. She had done quite a few flights but never before as a first-class passenger.

She liked the perks that came with the first-class seat and was also glad that they got to disembark before the other passengers.

As she entered the main terminal from the flight area she spotted Sarah right away. The tall, athletic, raven-haired woman was dressed conservatively in a beige skirt and matching jacket over a white shirt trimmed with lace. Her shoes were short heeled black pumps and the smile on her face was infectious.

Carol went over to shake hands with Sarah only to be hugged instead. That was good. Carol's family had always hugged everyone as part of their Christianity and acceptance of others. Sarah held her hands out at arms length and nodded at Carol's outfit.

Not knowing what to wear she had decided to go with business casual and had on black slacks with low heels in matching black. Her blouse was deep red trimmed in black and matched her handbag. Carol had brought her calf-skin leather jacket trimmed in white synthetic fur in the event it got cold at night in Denver.

Sarah asked about luggage and they went to get it. After grabbing her bag off the turnstile they headed out toward the parking lot shuttle. Carol was pleased with the

Denver skyline and atmosphere. It was similar to her home in Yuma, Arizona. She'd seen the City of Denver on the way in and liked its layout.

CHAPTER ELEVEN

Sarah easily loaded Carol's bag in the back of the Escalade which told Carol that the lithe woman had unseen strengths. She noticed a definite accent as well as the darker color to her skin tones that spoke of the middle-east, probably Israel as her home.

As Sarah drove through Denver toward the west she explained the area to Carol who had never been there before. Before long they entered into the foothills and drew close to the mountains.

Just before Silver Plume she left the highway at exit 228. Driving down a newly paved, concrete road she came to a circle in the road with an island planted with trees and plants. Halfway around the circle was another road with a sign on either side. The signs were in green and white like the state signs in Colorado. Both signs said, "Private Property Do not enter". The signs and the convenient circle back to the road out were obvious indications that illegal trespass was discouraged.

Beyond the signs the road climbed a slight grade and disappeared over the top of the hill. There were rising rock walls on each side of the road that also discouraged trespassing.

Over the rise there was a new sign in stark black and white that spoke volumes about disobedience. "UNITED STATES MILITARY RESERVATION. UNAUTHORIZED VEHICLES AND PERSONNEL WILL BE DEALT WITH SEVERELY!" In smaller print there was a warning about tire damage, vehicle impounding, and possible death.

Towering vertical walls rose on either side of the road and there was nowhere to go except back or forward. This was a single lane road with ditches on each side and carbon-arc lighting for the nighttime.

After crossing the three sets of tire-shredding grills, the road turned to the right and then arched back around a curve to the left. At this point, signs were no longer needed as the road ended in a twenty foot gap that Carol estimated to be thirty feet deep. Across the gap was a granite cliff with a massive gate set flush into the cliff. Several TV cameras were visible as well as a variety of ominous, closed ports.

Sarah operated a remote control. They waited several seconds until the gate had swung outward and up from the bottom and the top went inward and down. The entire assembly moved outward and descended into the gap to form a bridge across the open span. The bars of the gate were twenty-four inch square beams with six-inch thick walls. This would allow the heaviest truck or tank to cross it but would also resist all but major military ordinance attempting to breach it.

As Sarah drove across the bridge/gate, a series of lights came on in the tunnel behind the gate. The marble walls rose twenty-five feet to the arched ceiling in the thirty-foot wide tunnel. The tunnel was thousands of feet long and made a gradual turn to the left and then another turn to the right before resuming a straight path for six hundred more feet. Deep inside the mountain at the other end of the tunnel there was another bridge/gate combination that was already in the lowered position.

Sarah drove past the second gate and turned left into a large enclosed parking area. It was obvious that the tunnel and parking area were built deep inside a granite mountain. But upon exiting the SUV Carol found the air was fresh, flowing, and smelling of mountain greenery such as spruce and pine trees. As Sarah unloaded Carol's suitcase from the Escalade Carol looked around and asked her, "Don't I have to check into a hotel?"

Sarah shook her head. "We have plenty of room for you here. Plus, you're a lot safer here than in any hotel." Carol wondered what she needed to be safe from.

A well-lit entrance stood at the end of the parking area. As they approached it a NovaStar sign lit up requesting identification. Sarah identified herself and had Carol step up and say her name. After this, the sign went out and a satin-chrome finished set of elevator doors opened. They got on the elevator and the doors closed silently.

The elevator first went sideways, then down, then forward. When it stopped and the doors opened Carol was amazed at the room she saw, it was beyond visually impressive.

The elevator opened directly onto the living room. The living room was a circular-shaped open area of over two thousand feet of floor space. The entire far side of the circle from the elevator was floor-to-ceiling windows. The ceiling was twenty feet above the carpeted floor. The ceiling was almost all polished stone in a light brownish-white color which complemented the spectacular view of the valley below and the mountains on the other side of the valley. Again the air smelled fresh and mountain clean.

Comfortable furniture and dramatic art was placed strategically around the room. The lighting was subtle with recessed lamps providing back lighting and tasteful use of light panels throughout the room that didn't leave any place in dimness or gloom. A large rock fireplace and chimney graced the right wall and a large display television screen was prominent on the left. The colors and scents and accents were done with class.

Sarah led Carol through an automatic doorway into the War Room next to the living room. Equally tasteful, this large room had a massive, circular conference room table dominating the space. Jack looked up from his console and stood up to greet Carol. Carol was pleased to see him again, this time without all the weapons. Looking at the circular table with the multiple positions set into it she asked him to explain the setup if he would.

Jack smiled at the young woman. Pointing at his position he told her, "The microphones and speakers at each position are designed to be completely secure and isolated to each station. What you say will only go where you indicate you want it to go. To another member or group here at the table, or to anyone with a phone or a wireless connection anywhere in the world. The keyboard will connect you to anywhere."

Carol was awed with the precision and beauty that was designed into the efficient electronics as well as the decor.

After leaving Jack to his work, Sarah showed Carol to one the bedrooms a level above the living quarters. The upper floor was reached by multiple stairwells, two escalators, and two elevators. It was an interesting arrangement because there was a large gathering room at the top of the stairs with more comfortable furniture and a TV/DVD/Stereo and a small kitchen. Radiating off of this room were twelve short hallways that each led to a master bedroom, bath, and study. It was obvious that each of the bedroom suites were hallowed out of their own part of the granite which gave privacy to the occupants of each room. Pulling Carol's wheeled suitcase, Sarah walked down the eighth hallway and opened the door to the suite. Easily lifting Carol's luggage she placed it on the settee at the end of the king-size bed. Looking at Carol she said, "This will by your place while you're here, is it okay?"

Carol realized that her mouth was hanging open and snapped it shut. Looking around the room she could tell that it had been professionally decorated. Artistic paint mixed with silk wall coverings. Automatic light systems in the living/seating room, bathroom, closets, and of course, the main bedroom. She smelled the slight touch of a beautiful scent of ozone to the air like a rainstorm had just passed through. The furniture seemed to be a part of the wall and or the floor and mirrors expanded the already large room. But the most amazing thing of all was the floor to ceiling windows on one wall that showed the mountains with snow blowing off of the peaks. She could also see the Rocky Mountain Aspen trees twirling their green leaves.

Carol looked at Sarah in wonder. "How do you get this window on the mountains in the middle of a granite mountain?"

Sarah smiled a beautiful smile. "That is the one feature I never get used to myself. Actually, Jack Malone and his father invented this and they call it the "Viewport". There is more than a mile of solid granite between that wall and the view it shows. I don't understand the physics of it, but I sure love the view it provides."

Sarah got a twinkle in her eyes. "You want to see something else that will stun you?" Carol nodded her head. Sarah told her to lean back on the pillows and close her eyes.

Carol laid back and closed her eyes. Sarah pushed two controls and then told Carol to look. When she opened her eyes she let out a shout of wonder. The room was gone except for the bed, the bedroom furniture, and the two of them. The mountains were in full splendor in every direction. It was as if they were in a field with no structures anywhere near. Carol could actually feel the breeze as it blew the grasses and mountain shrubs she could see around her. It wasn't unpleasant at all. She could hear sounds of the distance in all directions. It was the most incredible thing she had ever experienced. She looked at Sarah with wonder in her eyes. "How do you do that?"

Sarah moved the controls again and the view disappeared except for the window in the wall. The restful room was back. Sarah showed her how to change the settings on the remote control. "Just wait until you do that at night. Mark and I were just lying in bed watching the stars and it is fantastic. We actually had a wolf come up to one of the lenses and it looked like he was going to walk into our bedroom, but of course he didn't. She headed toward the door to the suite and then stopped and opened the top to a jewelry box on the dresser by the door. She walked over and handed a NovaStar medallion to Carol. Sarah got serious and told her about the capabilities of the defense system and warned Carol to always keep the medallion on her while she was resident in the Fortress.

Sarah's mood lightened and she said, "Come on, let me show you the rest of the place."

The level below the living room housed the exercise gym, laundry, storage areas, a firing range, and additional rooms for food and supplies.

In a separate area on the living room level was the arsenal, the control room that defended the Fortress and a set of offices for Mark's security company.

Then Sarah took Carol down to the lower level and through another tunnel. They found themselves in a huge, sunlit green house, arboretum, and garden. There were several birds flying around in the area. Sarah then showed Carol another hall that led to an Olympic-sized swimming pool with changing rooms and a sunning area. Carol saw the large exercise and training room. Then they toured the mechanical equipment area that controlled all of the systems and then wound back up at the living room.

Sarah told her about the crews quarters on the fifth level where the SOG warriors and David's Israeli support people were housed.

Sarah showed Carol the two studies, library, and a room for private worship that were off of the living room. All of the rooms they had seen were well lit with large windows and gorgeous views of the surrounding mountains.

Sarah went into the kitchen and made a drink and a snack for the two of them Seated in the dining area Sarah continued to tell Carol about the Fortress. "First off, this dwelling sits directly in the middle of a five-mile square military reservation. That means that the government can restrict it in many ways from intrusion. The Civil Air Rules have been amended to prevent any over flights of this reservation under 10,000 feet altitude. It doesn't intrude on any of the existing air lanes around Denver and it was planned that way. Mounted in the top of this granite cliff are three batteries of surface-to-air missiles which are maintained by the United States Marines. They are federally approved for use against any hostile aircraft violating the zone."

She stopped and took a sip of her tea. "The room we are sitting in has a minimum barrier of six thousand feet of solid granite between it and the outside world at any point. Anything less than a full nuclear strike will not breach this defense and we're not sure that it would."

"Like I said before, I have to congratulate Jack on his "Viewport" vision systems. He owns a company called Technology Alternatives in Denver that is now working with all branches of the service to supply this technology as needed. Such clarity and detail in a non-electronic, direct vision system as used in the sun rooms and the tropical garden are going to change horticulture as we know it in the near future."

Sarah asked Carol if she remembered the huge hinged gates that they drove through when they entered the property. Carol nodded and Sarah continued. "The entry gates have been tested to 360 percent of load and still did not fail to prevent access. This was still true even when one gate was partially destroyed by tank fire. There are weapons systems at each gate that will destroy all but the most armored main battle tanks and have shown the capability to knock down all shoulder or vehicle-mounted missiles prior to impact and then redirect fire automatically on the launch position. There are many more defensive systems for this dwelling."

Waving her arm in a circle she smiled, "The upgraded NovaStar System2 used in this Fortress is extremely deadly, and I do mean that as in lethal. Never forget that, and always keep that ID tag on you as a backup if there is a penetration. If you have your ID tag then you can fight from room to room in full cooperation and safety from the NovaStar system." Carol had never "fought" with anybody or anything and couldn't see her role if an "attack" could ever get into this fortress. Carol looked down at the tag and smiled her thanks to Sarah for the trust it represented. She looked at the amazing woman next to her. "How is all this powered? I mean, I don't think that you'd be silly enough to depend on public power."

Sarah said, "The primary power for daily living is from horizontal wind turbines supplemented by a solar cell farm near the top of the mountain. Backing those sources up or in the event normal sources are compromised, there is a five-hundred megawatt nuclear reactor buried twelve hundred feet below and six hundred feet north of the bottom level. It is serviced by Navy technicians on a bi-monthly training rotation for nuclear submarines."

Carol asked how they could have a nuclear power plant and surface-to-air missiles without breaking dozens of existing laws.

Sarah shook her head. "The military designation for this property was assigned by the President through Executive Order. But for public consumption, and that includes anyone you might discuss this with, this is an advanced mountain training base for Force RECON, SEAL, Green Beret, and Navy nuclear units. They train all year around here but primarily utilize the mountain face and hills exclusively. They don't interact with the Fortress, unless they are needed."

Carol was thoroughly impressed by the technology and security of the Fortress. Sarah didn't bother to tell her about the Computer Center or the Helicopter base at the top of the mountain as it was obvious the young woman was nearing overload with information about the Fortress.

Sarah picked up their dishes and put the plates and silverware in the dish washer. "Why don't we go meet the rest of the team that's here right now? Some of them are on individual assignments so we will video tape your presentation if that is all right with you."

Carol nodded, "Thank you Sarah for showing me this magnificent place. I will probably wish I lived here long after I leave."

CHAPTER TWELVE

Carol went upstairs and got her notes from her room. She was still amazed that she was allowed to use this fabulous room. She took the escalator down to the main living room floor and met each of the individuals she had seen at the GTherm facility during the battle as well as new ones. She was introduced to Laura, David, Alexis, Mark, Charlie and Linda Wu as they arrived in the living room. They all assembled by a series of chairs that Laura had set up in front of the 56-inch HD-DLP television screen.

Charlie and Linda Wu were delightful and it was only later that she learned that they were recently converted Christians and had actually been two of China's best Internal Security agents before their defection to the U.S.

Before she got started with her lecture, another beautiful Oriental woman joined the group and got hugs from everybody. Carol was introduced to Su Li, the team's pilot. Carol began to wonder if there were any "normal" people on the team. Still, she was amazed by the camaraderie displayed by these people. They were like the people at her church with their smiles, hugs, and obvious respect and love for each other. It was hard to imagine that these people were hardened warriors that stood against the enemy and killed them with ease and professionalism. But, she had seen them in action and could tell from the assurance each of them exhibited that they were very competent. She just hoped she didn't come across as naive as she really was in comparison.

Everyone settled down and Carol began her description of geothermal power.

"The word *geothermal* comes from the Greek words *geo* (earth) and *therme* (heat), and means the heat of the earth. Earth's interior heat originated from its fiery consolidation from dust and gas over 4 billion years ago and is continually regenerated from the decay of radioactive elements that occur in all rocks."

"It is almost 6,500 kilometers or 4,000 miles, from the surface to the center of the Earth, and the deeper you go, the hotter it gets. The outer layer, the crust, is three to 35 miles thick and insulates us from the hot interior."

"From the surface down through the crust the normal temperature gradient, the increase of temperature with the increase of depth, in the Earth's crust is 17C - 30C per kilometer of depth. Below the crust is the mantle, made of highly viscous, partially molten rock with temperatures between 650C and 1,250C. At Earth's core, which consists of a liquid outer core and a solid inner core, temperatures may reach 4,000C - 7,000C. "

"Since heat always moves from hotter regions to colder regions, the Earth's heat flows from its interior toward the surface. This outward flow of heat from Earth's interior drives convective motion in the mantle rock which in turn drives plate tectonics - the "drift" of Earth's crustal plates that occurs at 1 to 5 cm per year which is about the rate our fingernails grow. Where plates move apart, magma rises up into the rift, forming new crust. Where plates collide, one plate is generally forced or subducted, beneath the other. As a subducted plate slides slowly downward into regions of ever-increasing heat, it can reach conditions of pressure, temperature and water content that cause melting, forming magma. Plumes of magma ascend by buoyancy and force themselves up into or intrude, the crust, bringing up vast quantities of heat. "

Carol showed pictures of various volcanoes. "Where magma reaches the surface it can build volcanoes. But most magma stays well below ground, creating huge subterranean regions of hot rock sometimes underlying areas as large as an entire mountain range. Cooling can take from 5,000 to more than 1 million years. These shallow regions of relatively elevated crustal heat have high temperature gradients."

"Perhaps the best known of these volcanic regions are in the countries that border the Pacific Ocean -- the geologically active area known as the "Ring of Fire" where the oceanic plates are being subducted under the continental plates. Other volcanic chains form along mid-ocean or continental rift zones which is where plates move apart, -- in places such as Iceland and Kenya, or over hot spots which have magma plumes continuously ascending from deep in the mantle. Such as the Hawaiian Islands and Yellowstone National Park."

Carol changed the pictures being shown on the television screen. Then she continued with her lecture. "In some regions with high temperature gradients, there are deep subterranean faults and cracks that allow rainwater and snowmelt to seep underground -- sometimes for miles. There the water is heated by the hot rock and circulates back up to the surface, to appear as hot springs, mud pots, geysers, or fumaroles. "

"If the ascending hot water meets an impermeable rock layer, however, the water is trapped underground where it fills the pores and cracks comprising 2 to 5% of the volume of the surrounding rock, forming a geothermal reservoir. Much hotter than surface hot springs, geothermal reservoirs can reach temperatures of more than 350C, and are powerful sources of energy. "

"If geothermal reservoirs are close enough to the surface, we can reach them by drilling wells, sometimes over two miles deep. Scientists and engineers use geological, electrical, magnetic, geochemical and seismic surveys to help locate the reservoirs. Then, after an exploration well confirms a reservoir discovery, production wells are drilled. Hot water and steam shoot up the wells naturally, or are sometimes pumped to the surface where -- at temperatures between around 120 - 370C -- they are used to generate electricity in geothermal power plants. Shallower reservoirs of lower temperature, 21C - 149C, are used directly in health spas, greenhouses, fish farms, and industry and in space heating systems for homes, schools and offices."

"In geothermal power plants, we use the natural hot water and steam from the earth to turn turbine Generators to produce electricity. Unlike fossil fuel power plants, no fuel is burned. Geothermal power plants give off water vapor, but have no smoky emissions. "

"Most geothermal power plants operating today are "flashed steam" power plants. Hot water from production wells is passed through one or two separators where, released from the pressure of the deep reservoir, part of it flashes or explosively boils, to steam. The force of the steam is used to spin the turbine Generator. To conserve the water and maintain reservoir pressure, the geothermal water and condensed steam are directed down an injection well back into the periphery of the reservoir, to be reheated and recycled."

"A few geothermal reservoirs produce mostly steam and very little water. Here, the steam shoots directly through a rock-catcher and into the turbine. The first geothermal power plant was a dry steam plant, built at Larderello in Tuscany, Italy in 1904. The power plants at the Larderello dry steam field were destroyed during World War II, but have since been rebuilt and expanded. That field is still producing electricity today. The Geysers dry steam reservoir in northern California has been producing electricity since 1960. It is the largest known dry steam field in the world and, after 40 years, still produces enough electricity to supply a city the size of San Francisco."

"In a binary power plant, the geothermal water is passed through one side of a *heat exchanger*, where its heat is transferred to a second, hence, "binary" liquid, called a working fluid, in an adjacent separate pipe loop. The working fluid boils to vapor which, like steam, powers the turbine Generator. It is then condensed back to a liquid and used over and over again. The geothermal water passes only through the heat exchanger and is immediately recycled back into the reservoir. It never touches the turbine."

"Although binary power plants are generally more expensive to build than steam-driven plants, they have several advantages. First, The working fluid, usually isobutene or isopentane boils and flashes to a vapor at a lower temperature than does water, so we can generate electricity from reservoirs with lower temperatures. This increases the number of geothermal reservoirs in the world with electricity-generating potential. Second, the binary system uses the reservoir water more efficiently. Since the hot water travels through an entirely closed system it results in less heat loss and almost no water loss. And, third, binary power plants have virtually no emissions. Also, moderate-temperature water is by far the more common geothermal resource, and most geothermal power plants in the future will be binary-cycle plants."

Carol put a picture of a geothermal power plant up on the screen. "Sarah mentioned the Hawaii facility. The Hawaii geothermal area includes the Puna Geothermal Venture, which is located about 21 miles south of Hilo on the Big Island of Hawaii. The facility is situated along the Lower East Rift Zone of the Kilauea Volcano. At the Puna Geothermal Venture, geothermal fluid is brought to the surface through production wells, which tap into the resource at a depth of almost a mile. The steam, along with its non-condensable gases, is routed to the power plant and used to produce electricity for the Big Island of Hawaii."

Carol put her notes down. "I have given the question of terrorist utilization of a geothermal power source a lot of thought, and frankly I don't get it. The most dangerous possibility would be for a surface rupture of superheated steam or possibly lava. The PGV in Hawaii is protected by several automatic shut down systems and doesn't provide enough energy to be any more devastating at its location than a very small vent in a volcano if it were to go to the worst case. I'm afraid that I won't be much use to you in determining why they would want control or to destroy the site."

Jack thanked Carol for her fascinating presentation. The meeting broke up and Carol walked over to Sarah. "Sarah, I'm not sure I understand why you scheduled me for four days when we seem to have already completed the presentation for you."

Sarah looked at Laura, "Carol, this was an introductory briefing to get us all onto the same page as far as geothermal energy is known. Our definitive need for your expertise is just getting started. Based on what you told us there doesn't seem to be any reason why OC is going to such an expense to interdict geothermal power sources. We are fairly certain they are going to strike at the Hawaii site but, "when" is the question. These things you can help us with as we brainstorm possibilities. You can deep six really unsupportable theories and your understanding of the system of generation could spot something any of us could miss. As they say in the Navy, this meeting was just the tip of the iceberg."

Carol suddenly understood the weight of her participation with the team. It went far beyond her original desire just to socialize with these people. They were about preventing terrorists and their evil acts like the one at her work and the Georgia Mall. In her typical method she analyzed the possible implications to her life, she might become marked as an enemy by this Omicron Cartel and that could affect her family as well as her own security.

She then prayed and asked Yahveh for direction. She definitely felt she was supposed to do all she could do to save Yahveh's children who couldn't defend themselves. She made the decision and forgot about the possible consequences because God wouldn't tell her to do it if he wasn't going to provide the best protection for her and her family.

The angels watched and knew that Carol Moffet would be very surprised at the consequences to her life by her association with the Crossfire Team.

CHAPTER THIRTEEN

Carol went down to the exercise hall and went through her daily workout. She admired the top-of-the-line equipment and computerized machines the team had to work with as they toned themselves.

While she was running on one of the eight treadmills she was joined by Su Li who started running on the machine next to Carol's. As the two women jogged along they both ran in silence while working on their breathing. Carol could see that the young Chinese woman was as serious about her training as Carol was hers.

Carol finished her run and toweled off the sweat as she watched Su Li run. Su Li selected a much faster pace and began running quite hard. After six minutes she slowed to an easier pace to let her heart adjust. Carol had never seen guys, let alone a woman, run that hard for that long.

When Su Li finished her run she grabbed a towel and smiled at Carol. "Do you run every day?" Su Li asked in a pleasant alto range voice.

Carol smiled back and shrugged, "Yes, if I can. Sometimes the job gets in the way but I will run if I can."

Su Li asked about her normal life and why she was doing what she was at GTherm. Carol explained her education and decision to enter the geothermal field. They continued to chat for a while and Su Li told Carol about her past and how she met the team.

Carol was wide-eyed with wonder. "You were there when Yahveh defeated the Zultarians in Zyngola?"

Su Li nodded. "I wasn't directly involved but I was on the periphery and saw the destruction of the idol-worshipers by the hand of Yahveh. It was more than impressive.

Carol was impressed by the stories she heard from this young woman. She was about to ask if Su Li had been involved in any battles herself when Jack and Laura walked into the exercise hall.

Laura came over and asked Carol how she was doing. Carol grinned, "I like your facility. I could get used to this."

Jack smiled at her and then addressed Su Li. "Laura and I were discussing defenses against multiple attackers. Would you mind helping in the demonstration?"

Su Li grinned, "No, I wouldn't mind at all."

Laura excused herself and walked out on the mat surface with Jack and Su Li. Jack and Laura went through a stretching exercise while Su Li did her own version of preventing microtears in their muscles.

Jack looked at the two women and explained. "Unlike the battles you see on television or in the movies, the bad guys don't stand around and take turns attacking the good guy. That is done only to showcase the star and their martial arts abilities in slow motion so that the viewer isn't overwhelmed by all the activity at one time. In a real street brawl as many attackers that can get near the target attack at once."

He put Laura in between himself and Su Li. "I am going to come at you from your left and Su Li will attack from your right at the same time. Ready?"

Laura went into a defensive stance and Jack and Su Li came in at her. Laura blocked Jack's right hand punch with a left hand inward block while she rotated toward him and executed a rear mule kick at Su Li. Su Li's approach was neutralized and Jack's punch rendered ineffective.

Jack and Su Li stepped back. Jack said, "That was good but how did it feel to you?"

Laura thought for a few seconds. "It felt wrong. I think you could have counterpunched with your left hand and Su Li could have gone for my legs."

Jack concurred, "We could have done that but, you correctly interpreted the types of attacks we both were attempting and you compensated for two independent attacks. As we practice you'll become more proficient in analyzing and compensating against multiple attackers.

Jack stepped into the middle and told them both to attack him. He had done this for years as a fourth degree black belt instructor. Su Li got Laura's attention and tipped her head slightly to her right. Laura gave a brief nod.

Jack took a defensive position and as the two women attacked, he suddenly stepped back out from between them to bring them both to the front where he could deal with them both at once.

Su Li's movement had her go to her right at the same time Laura went to her right. This should have placed them off of Jack's main axis and therefore make it easier to attack him. His movement caused Su Li to suddenly be too far away to attack and brought Laura right into Jack's left arm palm-heel strike to her chest causing her to fall backwards. Jack rotated to his right and then it was one-on-one with Su Li as Laura continued to fall to the mat.

Su Li was a highly accomplished martial artist in her own right and she quickly used her extra space to accomplish a short run, leap, and flying kick to Jack's head. Only Jack wasn't there. He had interpreted Su Li's move and anticipated it. By the time she was airborne, Jack had side-stepped to his right again and he used a right arm lift to throw Su Li's legs up over her head as she flew past.

Su Li compensated and landed like a cat doing a forward roll and coming to her feet. She moved into a back heel kick in the chance that Jack was following up on his move and closing on her. He wasn't. He'd just stepped back again and waited for the rest of the action.

Laura held her hand up for a break and tipped her head to the left. "Jack, did you know we were going to circle you?"

Jack shook his head, "No, I didn't. I just reacted to the situation as it developed. I stepped back to bring both of my attackers in front of me."

Jack had Su Li attack him with front punches and kicks and told Laura as he deflected the attack. "This is how they like to do it. One will attack you and if you focus strictly on him, the other one sneaks in from behind. Once you identify the number of attackers you must always keep track of all of them."

Carol was excited to see the martial arts performance by the three warriors. It reminded her of the efficiency of a highly-trained boxer she'd seen once. As jack started to explain more about how to sort out the various attackers and their styles his cell phone beeped.

Jack took the call. His face grew grim and he nodded as he hung up. "Okay kids we've got a situation with a demon in our world near 6th Avenue and I-25. The police can't do anything and the creature has killed two men already. This is probably one of Satan's traps but we are the only ones that can deal with this type of attack. Let's go!"

Su Li wrinkled her forehead and shook her head, "What are we? The new Ghostbusters?" Laura corrected her, "No, the Demon busters."

The three ran out of the exercise facility with Carol right behind them. As they reached the first floor, Sarah came from the War Room with Mark and the others. They had been galvanized after Jack had contacted them. There was room in the elevator for everyone and it went up at a tremendous rate. Carol wondered if she was the only one that felt like she was being crushed to the floor by the acceleration.

As the others ran out of the elevator to the personnel arms lockers on the helicopter hanger level, Sarah grabbed Carol's arm. She looked intently into the younger girl's eyes. "Are you sure you want to go with us? It could get messy." Carol could only nod that she wanted to go. Sarah felt the leading of the Father to let her come with them.

Sarah smiled at her and handed her a bulletproof vest and a helmet. "You can go but I don't want you to leave the helicopter unless I tell you to do so. Is that understood?" There was no arguing with this version of Sarah. Carol said "okay". As the large helicopter's rotors spun up to speed with Su Li at the controls, Carol wondered if she had made the right decision to make the trip. She watched and each of the team strapped on handguns, grenades, and loaded M-8 assault rifles. The mood was all business and no jokes.

As the helicopter was lifted free of the cavern that made up the hanger, Su Li pulled Gs as she threw the craft into the air and simultaneously rolled it to the left to line them up for the area just southwest of downtown Denver.

Mark was monitoring the police band and held up his left hand. Carol saw that everyone was wearing headphones and she grabbed a pair from a hook on the cabin wall. She heard Jack's voice as she put them on. ". . . seems that the demon is attempting to get at a family in a car but the car is an armored limo and they are still safe. The demon has killed a third policeman and blockaded the limo so it can't drive away. The police sergeant on site says that bullets don't affect the demon."

Laura started praying for guidance if she needed to confront the demon on a one-on-one. Jack was praying for guidance also. He directed Su Li to put them down within two hundred feet of the battle going on 6th Avenue and Sherman Street under an overpass created by the northbound lanes of I-25.

The Crossfire team jumped from the troop chopper as soon as Su Li touched the skids to the pavement. Jack spoke into his combat microphone to Charlie Wu back at the computer center of the Fortress. "Charlie, are you getting anything about this? It is out of character for the dark forces to be so blatant in their appearances. Do you see anything that looks like a trap to you?"

Charlie had six views of the battle on his screens. Since satellite observation was blocked by the overpass he had tapped into the traffic cameras and a feed from a news truck video recording the attack "Jack, I got nothing here. I don't see any other energy indications showing more demons or dimensional rifts."

Jack had directed Su Li to watch Carol and to be their big gun backup if they needed it. Su Li spoke to Charlie and in seconds she had the same feeds that he was watching. Carol worked her way forward and sat in the left hand seat in the cockpit to watch the screens.

David and Alexis went to the left of the battle centered on the limo while Mark and Sarah took the right. Jack and Laura went in up the center, directly for the demon. Laura's prayers hadn't given her a direction to take so she went with the last thing Yahveh had told her. "Save my children".

CHAPTER FOURTEEN

As Jack and Laura neared the limo from the rear the demon seemed to be so intent on getting at the people inside the limo he wasn't aware of their approach. This particular form of demonic representation tended toward the grossly ugly. Probably seven foot tall and four feet wide it had stubby legs and arms which it was using to pummel the armored vehicle. It had a large head for the body with an equally large and ungainly mouth full of sharp teeth.

From his position Mark was watching the demon closely. He keyed his combat microphone, "Jack, Laura, something is not right here. That monster should have broken into that car long before we got here. He's just making motions hitting and kicking the doors and roof. It's like he's killing time until we get here. Why don't you guys fall back with us and we'll deal with it on a team basis?"

Jack agreed with his friend, "Ten-Four Mark, Laura let's move back."

About that time the goofy looking demon stopped attacking the limo and turned to the two warriors. In a cultured and educated voice it said, "It's about time you got here. I was about to fall asleep beating on this car." He took three quick steps that covered a great deal of territory in almost no time and brought him close to Jack and Laura.

Laura was praying but her armor didn't appear. Jack leveled his M-8 at the demon.

The demon laughed a bass guttural laugh. "Try it! You can't hurt me you simple human. its past time we dealt with you two."

The demon spread his arms and both Jack and Laura were suddenly surrounded by flame-lit darkness. Pain struck both of them so harshly they immediately passed out.

Jack came to still in pain and found he could move. The memory of the last two days of beatings and lashings flashed through his mind. Instead of beating him down the torture had only increased his anger and resolve. Jack slowly turned his head to each side. His neck hurt and everything he saw was dim with only a faint light to relieve the red-lined darkness. There were noises coming from all over but no coherent speech.

Jack took an inventory of his body and condition. He had pain in his face, neck, arms, and especially his back. Even the bottoms of his feet hurt. He was naked and dirty. He was able to fight through the pain so that he could raise his head to look over at Laura. Due to the low light conditions he couldn't see anything very well. Suddenly, he sensed an evil presence that was supposed to frighten him. It just made him even angrier, not for what was happening to him but what they were doing to Laura

The demon walked forward out of the darkness. He had lost the play-doo version of his original form. His sleek face had almond-shaped black eyes that were full of malevolence and evil. As he approached he walked to Jack's right. His voice was still a deep rumble as he spoke. "Laura Malone, you killed my friend and I am going to enjoy killing both you and your husband." He spread his unusually long arms with long claws that were a picture of the demon at GTherm. I will flay the flesh off of your body one screamingly painful strip at a time!"

Even though it seemed her whole body was on fire and the pain was almost overwhelming, Laura locked eyes with the demon and said, "You may kill us and you may torture our bodies, but you can't get our souls. They belong to Yahshua. Very soon you will join your brother in chains in the pit. Then you both will get sent to the lake of fire for an eternity of torture that will make this seem like a picnic. Have a nice trip."

If she was looking for something to irritate their captor she found it. The pure hatred and evil on the demon's face intensified. He hissed, "Starting tomorrow you will pay for using that name in here a thousand times over and your screaming will be music to my ears." Then he turned and stalked off.

Jack knew that he and Laura were separated by bars and each of them was chained to the walls behind them. There did not seem to be any answer to prayer, the torment had been painful and looked to go on forever. No one knew where they were, or how to get to them.

It should of seemed hopeless but Jack's mind wasn't depressed or recognizing any hopelessness. He knew who they were as children of the Most High and he had studied Yahveh's promises to his followers. He knew that Yahveh had allowed this to happen to them for His reasons. All at once, one passage in the Bible stood out in his mind, Acts16:22. He called softly to Laura who had shared in the beatings and whippings which had left them both with bloody stripes on their backs. She wearily raised her head and tried to see her husband. She cried out in a hoarse voice, "Jack? Are you there? I hurt a lot, please help me." Her voice faded out. Jack strengthened his will and said bravely to his lovely, naked wife. "Honey, remember what Paul and Silas did in prison?"

Laura pushed through the fog in her mind caused by the constant pain and concentrated on her remembrance of God's Word. "Yeah", she croaked. Jack began to sing praises to Yahveh and Laura slowly joined in, weakly at first but stronger as she went along. The little song gained power and timber because the pain faded as they drew closer to Yahveh. They were both aware that Yahveh inhabits the praises of his people and the submission in such praise even though they were in such a grave situation gave Heaven the spiritual right to act on their behalf. The other prisoners were listening to them and started singing with them. Suddenly there was such a violent earthquake that the foundations of the prison they were in were shaken. At once the doors to the cells flew open and everyone's chains came loose. Jack noticed that the other prisoners were disappearing from their cells.

Suddenly a painfully bright light struck Jack's eyes as the overpass and the limo were back and the rest of the team members were running up to Jack and Laura as they crumpled to the pavement. Jack could hear screams and wailing from somewhere. Mark pulled out an emergency blanket from his back pack and carefully wrapped Jack while Alexis pulled out a large medicated pad and pressed it to Laura's bleeding back. Sarah quickly wrapped Laura in another emergency blanket.

Mark helped Jack to his feet and held him up as he shuffled toward the helicopter. David picked up Laura and carried her gently. The team quickly withdrew to the idling helicopter.

Never having seen such physical damage before, Carol watched as the two leaders of the team were loaded into the helicopter. She was appalled by the number of festering cuts and injuries to both Jack and Laura. She couldn't understand how they could have crusted blood and slime on their bodies when they hadn't been gone for more than a minute. Unable to do anything for them she started to cry out to God for her new friends and that led her to pray a heartfelt prayer for them. Carol's eyes widened as she prayed.

Su Li lifted the armed helicopter off of the street and headed for the Medical Center hospital in Aurora. Laura waved her hand and called Mark to her where she was lying down on her stomach. She spoke to him and he nodded. He keyed his microphone and spoke to Su Li who nodded her head. The helicopter tipped to the left as Su Li headed at full throttle speed for the Fortress. A news helicopter tried to follow the speeding chopper but quickly fell back into the distance as the far more powerful military engines of the team's helicopter quickly outpaced the commercial machine.

As soon as the helicopter was drawn down into the hanger on its hydraulic platform, Charlie was there with two wheeled litters from the medical room on floor five. They went directly to the medical facility where they cleaned the many small wounds and attended to the bloody stripes covering both of the Malone's bodies. Linda Wu expertly bandaged them. The Medtech was shaking his head and quietly told Mark that there were deep and very strange infections that hadn't responded to medicine in the wounds of both people.

Dressed again in loose fitting clothes Jack and Laura were helped down to the living room accompanied by the entire team that was resident in the Fortress at that time. Once they were gathered around, Jack and Laura told everyone about what happened to them and how they were rescued by the Father. After that Jack posed several questions for everyone's consideration.

He looked around through swollen and blood-shot eyes at the people who had become like family to him and asked, "Why didn't bullets hurt the demon that had come into our dimension? We know he was in our dimension because he was battering the car and had physically killed three policemen. How come Laura's armor and sword didn't manifest? How could a demon capture us in front of everyone and we couldn't do anything about it? How can we combat this type of one-sided battle in the future?"

Mark added a question. "Why didn't we go to the hospital but instead we came here? Some of those wounds on your chests and backs are infected with something pretty nasty."

Laura fought through the pain to look up at Mark. When she spoke her voice was still rough and scratchy and tended to fade out. "You answered your own question. These wounds are not natural and will not respond to human medicine. We need to pray to have the damage done by the demon healed by the power of God."

Carol was empowered by the word she had received from Yahveh and bravely stepped forward in front of this formidable group. Looking at Laura she said, "We must seek the Father as you said Laura. Yahveh told me on the helicopter that only He can heal your wounds. Seek Him and he will bless you and answer all your questions."

The entire group knelt on the carpet around Jack and Laura and touched one or both of them as they begin to pray for Yahveh's intercession and healing. Besides Mark and Sarah there was the spiritual leadership of David and Alexis. The battle hardened men and women of the SOG combined years of praying for the wounded and dying in the field of combat and seeing God's healings. The spiritual training of each person had risen and reached the level of direct intercession without doubt. Their direct experience and knowledge that Yahveh was not only real, that he heard their prayers and that He was willing to heal the Malones. In this group there was no doubt or wondering as to the roles of Yahveh and themselves. They had each seen Him in action many times and were confident in their faith while they prayed prayers that were very powerful in Heaven calling on the Father to act swiftly.

CHAPTER FIFTEEN

As the team and Carol prayed with all their hearts for the healing of Jack and Laura the heaviness of Yahveh's spirit settled on each of them. Carol was surprised by the weight and conversely the lightness she felt. No, that wasn't right, not lightness, elation! She reveled in the feeling of Yahveh's spirit surrounding her and flowing through her. But she knew enough not to be distracted from the purpose for her prayer. She strongly petitioned Heaven for a complete and total healing from everything that had been done to them by the enemy. She felt the nearness of God's Holy Spirit and she gave her whole being over to it in complete submission in her desire for Jack and Laura's healing.

No one remembered how long they knelt there in prayer but as the spirit lifted Carol looked up to see a smile on Laura's face. Gone were the bruises and cuts and bedraggled hair. The joy Carol felt went way beyond any emotion she had ever had before. Her tears ran freely down her face and she wasn't alone.

Mark stood to his feet and extended his hand to Jack. Jack strongly grabbed Mark's hand and rose to his feet. He knew he had been touched mightily by God. Not only was he healed but he was cleansed also. He hadn't felt this light and happy since he first met Yahshua in Colorado. He looked over at Laura and his heart sang with joy at the comfortable, peaceful look on her face. He helped her up and tenderly kissed her lips with a kiss that conveyed his total love for her. Laura melted into his embrace.

Everyone got to their feet smiling and crying for joy. Jack told them all to form a circle. They encircled Jack and Laura and put their arms around each other. Jack then prayed his gratitude to a loving Father who could heal with His touch. Jack gave all the glory and honor to Yahveh in love through His Son Yahshua.

The ten people in the circle were suddenly washed with light forming within their ring. Laura smiled at the gold and white swirls coalescing into a beautiful angel. She said, "Hello Rose, Mighty angel."

The angel smiled back at her and said a word in a language not heard on Earth. Each of the people in the circle felt a strengthening that felt like a crystallization or a coming together of pure power within them.

Rose closed her eyes and Yahveh transported all of them to a different realm. There were operations and movements that would have baffled the smartest person on the planet but were easily understood by everyone there. All things worked together and with perfect reason. The complete saga of the demon and the torture and the salvation and healing was a simple matter that had meaning in eight or possibly eleven dimensions and the whys were answered easily and made complete sense.

Many things were comprehended by the little group and then Rose said another word and Yahveh brought them back to four dimensions and the living room of the Fortress.

Jack slowly nodded his head, "I see why the Father allowed us to go through that torture. He had to allow it so that we could reach this level and be able to understand this new revelation."

Rose studied Jack intently. "Yes, you did see and understood. Yours shall be a mighty calling in the near future." She rotated around inside the circle. "I see that each of you has the understanding of the true and full universe. Hold onto that memory because it will serve you greatly as you battle Satan and his minions. You were allowed to see all because the Lord wants you to understand rather than just to accept. Each of you has proven that you have the faith to rely on the Most High on your faith alone." She returned to looking at Jack and Laura. "What you told Dibethalon was prophetic Laura. He is now with his friend in chains in the pit with the lake of fire before him. He is not at all happy with the turn of events. But all of his curses will remain on him in the pit and on into his distant future in the lake of fire."

Rose grew in richness of color as the gold became more prevalent than the fierce whiteness of the power of her being. God's power flowed out of her and everyone there was washed with a fantastic mixture of power and love and total acceptance that went beyond faith and hope.

Rose smiled, "As I said before, the Lord knows each of your hearts and that is why He allowed you to comprehend the complete need for the demon and his torture of you without having to try to explain it in only the four dimensions you live in daily. As you all can now understand the explanation here would have been a weak and incomplete presentation that would have relied simply on your belief rather than knowledge. The enemy is coming against this team in eight dimensions and to combat those attacks you needed to understand the "big" picture."

Rose smiled at them, "Each of you now know that there are a myriad of things that influence an event, not one or two. Knowledge of that caliber in all the dimensions is what you all will have when you live with Yahveh."

Rose swung around and focused on Carol Moffet. At this particular time Carol thought that there was nothing that could of have amazed her more than she was already amazed.

Rose smiled at the young woman. *"Carol, for a time such as this, you have been called by the Most High. Your submission is and has always been complete and now your reward is mighty. You are now anointed by the Most High to keep the full vision that everyone here had for a few seconds in the service of God. This will be for throughout your life on Earth as long as you listen and obey Yahveh. Your service will be to serve as the Crossfire Team's Knowledge Bearer or watcher on the wall in their conflict with Satan and his followers."*

Rose moved close-up to Carol and enfolded her in an embrace. When the angel moved back there was a small diamond-shaped white light on Carol's forehead and a second one at her throat. As the light pulsated everyone there recognized the light streaming from the diamonds as the same power that flowed from Laura's sword during battle with demonic forces, the all powerful Glory of Yahveh.

Rose continued, "These power symbols will be a sign to others when you are in prayer against the enemy just as is the armor and sword that Laura has been given. The Lord will also empower you in full knowledge as He feels you need the knowledge. Guard it carefully!"

The swirling power of Rose's being flowed over and through Carol and the young woman suddenly saw the way before her open up in a fantastic display of detail and expectation. Rose came close again and rested her hands on Carol's shoulders. "You have a sweet spirit and great drive but now you must exercise great spiritual judgment because what you learn can cause many things to happen on Earth and in Heaven, both good and bad. Always seek Yahveh's direction before you speak out of your new knowledge. Never forget that! It will be a daunting duty full of heavy responsibility. But with it you will counterbalance the enemy's new lack of respect for Yahveh's commands and provide insight for many people as they do the Lord's work, especially the team members."

Rose looked around the circle as the diamonds faded away on Carol's forehead and throat. "You have grown in numbers and in strength of spirit. I commend all of you to listen carefully to Yahveh's spirit as it guides you in His service."

Rose's colors swirled and she faded from view. In the somewhat dimmer room the ten people looked at each other with new respect and love. Spontaneously, the entire group gathered around Carol and touched her as they prayed for her new assignment and anointing with power and blessings.

Laura hugged Carol and then said, "I don't know about the rest of you guys, but I'm famished." Seeing the looks she continued. "Hey, it's been two tough days without food, okay?"

The entire group laughed and all but one headed for the kitchen.

Carol remained there by herself praying her thanks to the Father. As she finished she felt a touch on her arm and looked up to see Sarah standing there. Impulsively Carol reached out and fiercely hugged the Israeli woman. Sarah returned the hug and asked her if she was all right.

Carol's eyes sparkled and she nodded her head. "I have just had the biggest paradigm shift anyone has ever had. But I understand it and like all of the Lord's plans, it is perfect. Oh Sarah, I am so blessed and I owe it all to you for inviting me here."

Sarah looked at the young woman with new respect and some concern. "Carol, this isn't what I had planned for you when I asked you to come to see us."

Carol quietly said, "No, I'm sure it wasn't. But, it was Yahveh's plan and you were obedient even when you don't know it is Him leading you."

Sarah had to think that one over. "Okay, I guess. Are you hungry?"

Carol smiled a knowing and sincere smile that everyone on the Crossfire Team would learn to watch for in times of stress. "Yeah, I think I am very hungry."

CHAPTER SIXTEEN

After everyone had eaten their fill and had cleaned up the kitchen dishes they regrouped in the living room.

Jack was still elated from the absolute peace and contentment he had during his healing but he knew as a group that they needed to resolve the outstanding issues. "Okay people, we saw how the original questions and their answers were understandable in eight dimensions but how do we relate that understanding in our limited four-dimensional world? The questions were: "Why didn't bullets hurt the demon that had come into our dimension? How come Laura's armor and sword didn't manifest? How could a demon capture us and we couldn't do anything about it? How can we combat this type of one-sided battle in the future?"

Laura held her hand up. "I'll take number two since I was given the armor and sword. Converting what I saw while we were in our "eight dimensional state" I believe that Yahveh had to give Satan the right to interrogate us to provide him an adequate or equal opportunity to acquire the crucifixion nail. Since the nail became a nexus of potential spiritual power the Father's desire to have his saints keep it out of the enemy's hands is what created the imbalance. If my armor and sword had functioned it would have contravened Yahveh's permission to capture us. He is a just Elohim and therefore has to follow the same rules he made for the other spiritual beings or He wouldn't be Elohim."

Jack nodded his agreement with that assessment. "Then it required us to petition Yahveh to release us from the interrogation, which we did when we prayed to him through our psalm of praise?"

Laura considered that thought. "I believe it was also a test of our commitment in faith to Yahveh. If we had merely asked for release because we were in pain and suffering rather than accepting our lot as His will and praising Him despite the torture, we would not have been set free."

Mark spoke up. "The same answer works for question number one. The demon was allowed to enter our world and was invulnerable to bullets because he had Yahveh's permission to do so and as such was not "illegally" here. Hence, his immunity from gunfire. This would also apply to question three. He could capture you two because he had permission and Yahveh needed you to be vulnerable at that time. I think that you were supposed to be interrogated by the demon to find the location of the crucifixion nail and how to get it. But I think this particular demon's thirst for revenge overcame his orders and he was enjoying the pain you were suffering. He wasn't supposed to do that which gave Yahveh the express right to release you two. I'll bet it was Satan that gave the demon over to Yahveh to have him sent to the pit."

Carol listened to these warriors of God as they discussed the battles between good and evil, torture, submission and obedience. She thought to herself, "How can I be a part of these things? This feels like a dream. This morning I was a newly promoted, twenty-three year old senior programmer for a power company in Phoenix. Now Yahveh has put me in a position to help these people and their lives will depend in some measure upon what I do. I don't know that I capable of doing this!" She followed her natural habit, she humbled herself and prayed. "Father! Please give me the words and the confidence to do Your will in this matter. My human frailty causes me to doubt. I certainly don't feel worthy or capable of the task even though I heard your messenger say I would do it. Please, please, tell me what to do!"

Clearly she heard Yahveh tell her, *"My child, as I was with Moses, so I will be with you; I will never leave you nor forsake you. Be strong and courageous because you will help lead these people in their battle against the enemy. Be strong and very courageous and be careful to do and remember all my commandments. Have I not commanded you to be strong and courageous? Do not be terrified; do not doubt or be discouraged because I will be with you wherever you go."*

Carol recognized the encouragement was similar to the one God gave to Joshua in Joshua 1 in the Bible and she was thrilled and filled with encouragement. She took a big breath and stepped forth in front of these awesome people and said, "And the answer to number four seems to be me. According to the angel Rose, I am their antithesis whenever they "legally" attack you in the future. I'm not completely sure how that works but I believe my "gift" will become functional when Yahveh gives the enemy a legal right to attack the Crossfire Team in this dimension. I have faith that my part will help you because it is the Father's plan and His plans always work. And, He just told me that was my job under His guidance."

Seeing the intent faces of these warriors who had such a shared history among themselves she would normally feel like a babe in the woods and unworthy of this involvement. But, she felt Yahveh's full confidence and support. "Look, I realize I am brand new at this and until today you didn't even know me. I didn't plan to intrude by becoming a part of your team, even in my wildest dreams. Well, maybe in my dreams. But, the Father has ordained this and all I will do is ask each of you to pray and seek His will on my participation in the team."

Laura had been doing just that and spoke up. "Carol, this team is not proprietary to any one or any group of us. We were all called by Yahveh to do His will and your addition to the team, as sudden as it seems to you, is par for the course. You humble yourself to His will as do the rest of us. It is His team and He anointed you to be a part of it. I believe I can speak for each and every one of us in welcoming you to the fight. We are older and because of our daily involvement in the battle we are aware of how much of yourself you will be required to give to do this. It won't be easy and there will be pain and most likely, suffering to go along with the good times. We will all stand with you as you serve Him, but, regardless, it is His will." The rueful smiles on everyone's faces told Carol she was welcome.

David smiled a big smile and shook his head. "I have never had such clarity and understanding as I did when all the dimensions were opened to us. I felt positively dull and constrained afterward. I realize that brief time was a special gift from Yahveh but I long for that type of knowledge and vision. So, of course, I prayed about it and the Father reassured me that is the way it must be while I

am on this planet. I will do the best with what I have got."
He looked at Carol with a grin. "We are going to talk. I
assure you, missy, you are going to be busy when we have
cross-dimensional demon problems. Is that all right with
you?"

Carol realized she had the answer before the question
had been asked which was a little scary by itself. She had
the complete answer in time to respond to David's query.
"Of course it is all right Mr. Zahavy. I have been so blessed
by Yahveh with this capability which is for the team and I
expect everyone here to use my gifting as He directs us."

The Israeli smiled at the young woman. "Good! To
start with you can call me David as everyone else here
does, okay?" Carol nodded with a grin at the acceptance
she felt from all of them.

At that point it occurred to everyone that it was very
late and they agreed to retire. Carol walked down hall
number eight and realized that her life had been radically
and completely changed by the events of this one day. The
mature confidence and assurance she had from the Father
echoed throughout both her life and spirit. The closeness
and approval of the Father so filled her she almost could
not contain it. She realized that she was definitely done
with attempting to make something out of her life by using
her education and social skills to advance in the world. As
the angel Rose had said, *"For a time such as this."*

All of her previous life plans no longer mattered now
because it had become so minor compared to the
"anointing" she had been granted by Yahveh. As she
prayed her thanks to a loving creator she had a brief
glimpse of her new knowledge. She instantly saw that this
had always been her destiny as designed in Heaven. She
felt she now knew how to explain her new occupation to
her parents and her old boss. She suddenly noticed the
glow of the white diamonds fading out on the walls around
her. Her inherent sense of humor caused her to smile as
she recalled the saying that, "Diamonds were a girl's best
friend."

Letting herself into the beautiful suite of rooms she got
ready for bed and laid down on the bed and stared at the
ceiling for a minute. Then she remembered Sarah's
demonstration and found the remote control unit. Pushing

the correct sequence she was suddenly on the mountain top with nothing above her but the night sky so full of stars it was almost like daylight. Smiling to herself, she thought, "There can't be a better meditation place than this!" She lay back on the comfortable bed and began to pray her thanks and ask for direction in this new life she had been given. In the dark the diamonds began to glow.

In their suite Jack looked in the full length mirror and couldn't see anything of the two days of whippings and beatings he had taken. He smiled at Laura because she looked so happy. When she came up and hugged him he gathered her into his arms and decided that he would never let her go again. Laura felt so loved at that moment.

Mark and Sarah had crawled into bed and were discussing the day's events and Carol's dramatic inclusion into the team. Mark asked, "Sarah, I know it is Yahveh's plan to add Carol to the team and I'm good with that. But, I have a concern. What about the life she had? It is essentially gone to her and she is equally gone to those who knew her from before. It's like she joined the military service without time to put her previous life in order and say goodbye to the ones she loved."

Because of her pivotal role in bringing Carol to the Fortress Sarah had taken time to pray about the same concerns earlier and was able to answer Mark immediately. "Honey, I asked Yahveh that very question. Carol told me that she was so focused on her education and employment she never had time for social events such as dating. She's a young, single female, unattached except for her mom and dad and they will be happy for her. She will be able to make their lives much easier with her new income and she was already so in tune with the Father it was a small step for her to move completely into His service. Did you notice how much more mature and bold she was after her anointing by the Father?"

Mark thought about that and said, "Yeah, she did take a big step today. Did you have any inkling of what was going to happen?" Sarah shook her head and snuggled close to Mark and kissed him tenderly.

The Fortress fell quiet as the various members of the team went to sleep. With the exception of the computer center and security team which were on alert and active

24/7 to keep watch over the Fortress and the other members of the team not in residence.

CHAPTER SEVENTEEN

The next day started with Carol in the kitchen making breakfast for the rest of the team. It hadn't been planned that way. Laura smelled the breakfast before she got downstairs and walked in to see Carol attending to the stove and the oven. "Well, well" Laura said with a smile. "Couldn't sleep?"

Carol grinned, "Not a wink. I have this huge high and sleep isn't very important at the moment." Carol checked the progress of the pancakes and turned to Laura. "I have a favor to ask. I have to explain this sudden change of lifestyle to my mom and dad and I was wondering if you and Jack could go with me? I prayed about this last night and I think it would give them closure if they knew I was with godly people who agree with what I am doing."

Laura didn't say anything immediately as she started setting the table. She asked Yahveh if that was what He wanted and got a favorable leading. "Sure, we'd be glad to do that for them."

Carol noticed that Laura hadn't said, do that for you. The acceptance in that little shift was uplifting to Carol and she impulsively went over and hugged Laura.

Laura held the younger woman for a few minutes and then asked her, "when do you want to speak to your folks?'

Carol thought about that. "In the next couple of days if possible. They know I came up for four days of training so they won't start to wonder until the weekend." Carol stopped and thought for a second. "Oh, yes, we still have to finish the geothermal work. That seems like a lifetime ago already."

Laura laughed at that thought. In the next twenty minutes the rest of the resident team and part of the security team going off duty showed up hungry and there wasn't time for talk.

Jack, Laura, and Carol finished cleaning up the kitchen after breakfast was done and everyone attended to their own affairs until the first War Room session was to start at nine a.m. Laura hung up a dish towel and surveyed the result of their efforts. She had noticed that Carol was very efficient in the kitchen and had cleaned everything including the backsplash panels over the range and the sink. That was encouraging. She turned to the young woman. "Thank you very much for all your efforts and don't think you have to do this all the time. Everyone here is scheduled to do their fair share of cooking and clean up. You have just earned the right to join that schedule."

Carol grinned and shook her head. These people were so accepting and nice! Then Carol remembered their handling of the attackers at GTherm. That brought another thought. "They are violently efficient too."

Jack took Carol into the large office set off to one side of the living room. He had her sign all the required federal and state employment documents. Then he asked her if she had any qualms changing employers.

Carol laughed a hearty laugh. "This is hardly my choice, right? I will be glad to work for the Crossfire Team. I was making $65,000 a year a GTherm will my pay match that?"

Jack smiled at all the things this young lady was going to learn. "Your basic pay will be $100,000 dollars per year. But, since you will get all your housing, food, clothing, transportation, and equipment from us at no cost to you it is actually a lot more."

Jack then pointed out that she would also share in all bonuses that the Team received. Last year they distributed over nineteen million dollars to the nine members of the team. This distribution was an equal share for everyone involved in the team's activities. Each person had received a little over two million dollars. There were more members this year but the bonuses would be even larger due to the recent activities they had participated in lately. The bonuses were from private groups, corporations, and governments that the team had assisted or in some cases, saved from destruction. "I expect that you will get a partial share this year because of the time you're joining us but it will still be more than a million dollars.

Jack went on, "There is also the life insurance, medical insurance, dental and vision insurance where we cover everything."

Jack thought for a few seconds and then stared at Carol intently. "I want you to pray and see what the Father has in mind for you as far as training in the combat end of things. I am sure you could learn what is needed but I don't want to endanger you if that is not His plan. Let me know what permissions you get, okay? Laura, Mark, Sarah, and I will also pray about this aspect of your involvement. Right now, since you have little or no skills in this area I would expect you will be working with Charlie Wu and his wife Linda in coordination with our command and control activities. But, then again, I don't know what Yahveh wants you to do at this point."

Carol's first thought was, "Me, a warrior?" This would take a lot of prayer.

Laura walked into the office and sat down. She explained Carol's request regarding her parents and Jack agreed it would be a good thing for them to do. Checking his pocket computer with his schedule he said, "It looks like tomorrow afternoon will be free if Yahveh is willing and warfare doesn't arise."

Laura laughed at that. Carol didn't get the humor as yet.

The three of them went to the War Room and assigned Carol a console position. Jack showed her how to operate the equipment and the thought crossed Carol's mind of just how recently she had been admiring these work positions without a clue she would actually have one of her own.

Laura had set up the big screen with a series of pictures of the members of the team and described them to Carol. "Jack, myself, Mark, Sarah, David, Alexis, and Su Li you've already met. The next two pictures are that of Stan and Debbie Hargrove." Stan was a thirty-something Caucasian male who looked like a friendly uncle. Debbie was a petite brown-haired Caucasian woman with a cute face and a nice smile. "Stan used to be a police captain with the Salt Lake Police and Debbie is an undercover sniper for the government. They both work for Mark's security company when they aren't being called to help the team. We are having an all-member team meeting in three weeks and you'll be introduced to everyone then."

Laura moved her pointer to the next picture. "This is Carol Nolan an agent for the Colorado Bureau of

81

Investigation." The woman was a pretty black-haired Caucasian woman in her late twenties. "Carol is sort of a part-timer as far as the team goes. She is an asset whenever she's needed. The next picture is Victor Chamberlain." The picture was a full-figure photo of an African-American man with a trim body and a nice smile. The smile was intriguing to Carol. She realized she knew who he was. "Isn't he the food billionaire that provides food and money for relief efforts all over the world?"

Laura nodded, "Yeah, that's him alright. We were able to help rescue him and he is a backer of the team now. He became a Christian during his rescue and now does the Father's work."

"Then we have Sensei Jim Grady." Jim was a large Caucasian man shown in a black martial arts Gi and a defensive posture. He was balding with a friar's halo of gray hair from sideburn to sideburn. "Jim was Jack and Mark's Sensei, or teacher, in martial arts and has been a good member of the team, and warrior, since it began.

The next two pictures were of older Caucasian men in their sixties or so, in good health and resembling each other. "The first picture is of Steve Malone, Jack's father and the source of several of the inventions that Jack has produced at Technology Alternatives, his Colorado-based company. Steve, and his older brother, Larry Malone are supporters and backers of the team and occasionally involved in operations."

Laura pointed to the next picture. "This is Tim Carson; he is a Pastor of a Christian Church in the Denver area. He serves as the Pastor for our little flock and occasionally he gets in the trenches and fights along side of us. A good man to know."

Laura looked at Carol. There are more members both here and away that are considered a part of the team but I don't want to overwhelm you at this point. Two young Israeli men who are working for David Zahavy and a couple of dozen military types that are rock-solid Christians who live on the fifth floor and provide the muscle in any major military situations. You will get to meet them at the get together too. Right now they're mostly on leave or doing some part time operations for the military."

The team turned to trying to determine why OC had been attacking geothermal power generation plants.

The brainstorming session went for six hours with every conceivable scenario proposed and countered or eliminated as unfeasible. Carol's contribution was concise and frank. Bad ideas were discarded before they took up valuable time.

As the majority of the team met in the War Room, Charlie and Linda Wu and Stan and Debbie Hargrove were in the ComSec center seeking any and all information, no matter how insignificant, on the movements of any known OC troops either vectored toward or already in Hawaii. They had some leads but nothing substantial that indicated a definite push for the power station there.

At eight o'clock that evening the session broke up and Jack and Mark coordinated with Charlie. The decision was to get in touch any of their alphabet department contacts next morning and see if they could stir up anything there. Jack and Laura made plans to fly to Yuma to meet with Carol's parents and reassure them that Carol wasn't running off on some dang fool adventure.

CHAPTER EIGHTEEN

Su Li brought the team CitationX into the Yuma International Airport and received permission to park the aircraft at the Marine Airbase for protection. Jack rented a luxury car and took Laura and Carol the four miles into town.

Carol had called ahead to tell them that she was bringing home some people she wanted them to meet. She pointed the way to her folk's house and her mom and dad were out front when they pulled into the driveway to the modest colonial dwelling off of West Primrose Street. It was medium income area and the yard was well laid out and obviously had careful tending. Carol had explained that her dad had retired from his executive job with a local office of an international sales group. He tended to work outside on the yard while her mom preferred to work on internet sales which brought in additional income to supplement her dad's retirement.

After Carol had hugged both of her parents she introduced them to Jack and Laura. Jack shook the dad's hand and got a hug from her mom. Her dad told them to call him Carl and his wife was Shirley, not Mr. and Mrs. Moffet. Jack liked the older man's direct assessment of them and his offer of a cool drink on the shaded patio. Yuma is one of the hottest cities in the country and the average heat right then was over 100 degrees F and rising. Thankfully it was a desert dry heat and not humid like you found in coastal cities and places like Texas.

After they had been seated and given lemonade, Carl Moffet came to the point rather quickly with, "Well, Jack, why don't you tell the missus and me what your visit is all about."

Jack started the conversation off with the reason they were there. "We have offered Carol a position with our firm and wanted you to meet us so that you could rest easy about the people with which she will be working."

Jack went on to describe the team, their focus, and Yahveh's call on all of them. He didn't sugar coat anything but he did downplay the combat and demonic aspects so as to not scare them into thinking their daughter was seeking adventure.

Laura picked up the description by explaining the Fortress and the connection to the U.S. Military and the U.S. Government. She showed Carol's parents pictures of the inside of the Fortress and Carol's suite of rooms. She also showed them the arboretum and the swimming and fitness centers.

Jack picked up the narrative with a general description of Carol's new salary, bonuses, and benefits. Then he asked for questions or concerns.

Shirley Moffet studied the two people before her. They were young, less than thirty. They were both casually relaxed yet generated an aura of subdued firmness that came across as no-nonsense honesty. They were both incredibly fit and healthy looking and made a good couple by their listening to the conversation without resentment or irritation. She liked them and her prayer about them before they arrived was very positive.

Carl Moffet also liked what he saw but his admiration was tinged by the knowledge that he couldn't ever fit into their world. But, he sighed to himself, "this is not about me, it's about my daughter." He looked directly into Jack's eyes and asked, "I've heard about the Crossfire Team Jack, and the terrorists you contend with all the time. Will Carol be safe with you and your people?"

Jack thought, "He is direct". He answered the older man with the only assurance he could give him. "I and every member of my team will do all we can to assure her safety, but in the end it's in God's hands and it always has been."

Carol had been quiet up until that point and knew it was time to speak up. "Mom, Dad, I love you and you know I wouldn't do anything to break your hearts. You know that God calls each and everyone who loves Him to the service that He has created them for. This is that calling for me. I have seen an angel and the Father told me that this is what He wants me to do. I am not a front line soldier but an advisor for the team. The Father has anointed me with a magnificent, special calling and a unique gift so that I could help His warriors do His will. I do want your blessing, but I also want your understanding and support."

Carl smiled a wan smile and said, "Well, if God wants you to do this, then who am I to argue? Of course you've got our love and support and I'll give you my blessing tonight." He looked at the Malones, "And thanks to Jack and Laura you've got my understanding. How about you Mother?" He asked his wife.

Shirley came over and hugged Carol. "Yes, I'll let God have you this time." She smiled and asked if they could stay for dinner. They agreed but asked if Su Li could join them.

Carol said, "Mom, with my new salary we can afford to buy dinner out if you'd like not to have to do all the work in the kitchen."

Laura laughed, "This one is on us. You save your money to help your folks with their plans."

Carl liked the idea of going out, even though he had to admit his wife was one darn good cook.

They took the rental and picked up Su Li and went to one of Yuma's very good steak houses. They were able to secure a private area separated from the rest of the patrons and they all ordered their meals. Everyone talked about Su Li and her piloting and Carol's decision to join the team.

The food came and Jack was about to ask Carl to pray when Carol said, "I think I'm supposed to pray for the meal."

They bowed their heads and Carol started the prayer, "Dear Heavenly Father, I thank you for this meal and the fine company we have here asking your blessing on our food tonight. I ask you to speak to my parents and reassure them that this is your course for my life and that they will be happy for me. I would also like to ask. . ."

Carol stopped talking and everyone looked up at her. Both of her diamonds were shining with the esteem of Yahveh. The power flowing off of the diamonds carried a solid component of God's righteousness and everyone there felt conviction. Carol said, "Oh, Jack! There is danger to the team in the form of a duplicitous plan to deceive us that will bear fruit in the next four days. Be wise as serpents and pray constantly. This plan involves many of the enemy and nine humans."

The diamonds faded away and the room seemed dimmer. There was a crash at the doorway and everyone looked that way. A young female server had dropped their salad bowl as she stared at Carol. She stuttered her apology and started picking up the spilled food. Another employee came over and helped her.

Jack turned back to see a stunned look on Shirley's face and a smile on Carl's face. Carol's mom said, "You didn't tell us about the signs."

Carol was still coming back to four dimensions and simply said, "Sorry mom, I didn't know they were going to show up this quickly."

Jack decided that the news could wait until after dinner to be acted upon.

Carl said, "Okay, I will go see that we get another salad."

Dinner went well and even though he normally didn't drink, Carl decided to have a highball that evening.

Five hours later the team was reassembled in the War Room and Jack relayed the message Carol had been given. "So, are we being misled by the Hawaii effort? Is the OC going to strike somewhere else?"

The whole team started discussing their opinions and conclusions.

The next morning there was a phone call for Jack. Answering the phone he said, "Jack Malone, how can I help you?"

The voice on the other end of the phone was militarily correct and terse. "General Malone, I need to see you in regards to a message from General Miles of the utmost urgency. I will be landing at DIA in thirty minutes."

Jack said, "Certainly. Can I have your name and flight number, I'll have someone meet you at the airport."

"My name is Colonel Mason and I am coming in on a military courier jet. I'll meet your person at the private hanger exit."

Jack looked up and asked who would like to meet Colonel Mason and bring him to the Fortress. Alexis said she would do it. She got up and left quickly to make the trip to the airport in time to meet the flight.

Laura looked at Jack. "I wonder if this has anything to do with the change of administrations that everyone is anticipating."

Jack shrugged, "Don't know, but let's pray about this when we find out what it is all about."

CHAPTER NINETEEN

Alexis arrived back at the Fortress with Colonel Mason in tow. As she walked in she gave Jack a shrug which meant that the Colonel hadn't talked to her at all.

The Colonel requested to speak to the General alone so Jack took him into the office and shut the door. Jack sized up the man as a career officer with ambitions. His uniform was razor sharp and his stare steely. He was about forty years old. Mark had mentioned that he was a little long in the tooth as a Colonel but not out of the running for a one-star position as yet. Jack sat down and asked the Colonel to spell out his mission.

Colonel Mason opened a military courier bag and withdrew several papers and photos. He then eyed Jack and opened with, "Sir! General Miles is in a unique position at the present time. He needs your help but can't ask you for it due to political pressure on the White House and the President. It seems that the liberal party is going to take the November elections by everyone's prediction. The Presidential candidate of that party is of an entirely different mold than President Bolen and has publicly divorced his candidacy and the probable presidency from any black ops or even gray ops, such as your organization. In fact, he has sworn to eliminate all government sponsorship of such activities and groups. Although General Miles feels this position is short-sighted and counter-productive he has instructions from President Bollen to refrain from being involved on any level with any non-overt and sanctioned organizations. Unfortunately, with the new open records act and the incursion of the ACLU into clandestine operations he feels that he has to resort to this present method of contact. He did say that you would be less than happy but it can't be helped at the present time. Whether or not you decide to accept this commission I am simply to report back as to your decision."

Jack just nodded. "Okay, what is the job?"

The Colonel showed Jack a photo. It had obviously been taken from a Keyhole satellite in low orbit. The resolution was excellent and the details stood out in stark relief. The Colonel continued, "This is a super-secret laboratory in the middle of Iran. Its code name in English is "The Hammer of Mohammed. The General feels that the Iranians are developing a new form of suitcase nuke with Russia's aid. The new candidate wants to soften our stance with the Iranians and is not interested in any military raids. Damned foolish leadership, but a fact of life at present. The reason General Miles feels this could be up your team's alley is because the whole thing is protected on a level that smacks of the supernatural. Too many lost agents, too many foiled ploys, and worse, too many corrupted investigations by different agencies such as the CIA, NSA, and even Delta Force. They tried to do a surgical strike and were completely defeated before they even got into the place. We lost over twenty good men. The enemy knew everything we were doing even though only six people on our side, all loyal Americans, knew about the raid."

Jack thought about the situation. This was something General Miles would ask them to check out and terminate if they could. "All right Colonel, we will accept the assignment and carry it out in the next ten days. You can tell General Miles that we will find out what is going on there."

The Colonel handed Jack the rest of the Intel and left for the Airport with Alexis.

Jack went back into the War Room and laid it out for the rest of the troops. Then he asked, "Mark can you and David work up a feasible plan of insertion, investigation, destruction if necessary, and a workable exit strategy?"

Mark considered the time frame and the necessary forces. He looked at Jack, "Is this action going to supersede the Hawaii project?"

Jack nodded, "Yeah, from the Intel it looks like we need to terminate the Iranian lab before they produce these new suitcase nukes. Otherwise they could easily mess up the election by blowing up part of our country."

Mark snorted, "It would just make the new potential President want to negotiate more and more until we're all dead or imprisoned."

Jack sighed, "We need to serve the General and not carp about politics. In that case, all we can do is vote."

Mark nodded and motioned to David. They got up and went to the office to outline their initial plans.

Jack walked over to Carol. "This might be something we could use some Heavenly Intel about if you're up to praying."

Carol nodded and told Jack again how grateful she was that he and Laura had talked to her folks.

Jack smiled, "Don't think that we were instrumental in making your parents sure of your choice. I think Yahveh did that at the meal."

Carol reddened slightly, "Yes that was a sure sign for them wasn't it?"

After Carol went to her room to pray, Jack contacted the computer guru for the team. "Charlie, listen, I want you to continue with your surveillance of the Hawaii power plant problem but I also want you to dig into this Iranian laboratory and determine if what the General feels is what is going on there."

Charlie came back with, "What Iranian laboratory? You got something I haven't heard about?"

Jack laughed, "Well, I guess you aren't all knowing are you? I'll send the Intel to you in a minute or so. I've got an odd feeling about this assignment from General Miles. It just doesn't feel right somehow. I want you to see what you can find out regardless of the source, okay?"

Charlie gave him an affirmative and hung up.

Laura grabbed Jack's hand as he walked by. "I heard what you told Charlie; maybe we need to pray for guidance ourselves."

Jack thought, "Well, so much for isolated communications channels." Pulling his wife up from her seat by the offered hand he smiled at her. "Okay, let's go pray."

CHAPTER TWENTY

As Carol began praying she knelt by her bed and rested her arms on the bed. This is how she had prayed since she could remember. She felt led to sit on her bed so she got up and sat on her bed. She closed her eyes and the bed felt strangely comfortable even supporting her back. She opened her eyes and she suddenly found herself sitting in a chair in a strange but beautiful room. She noticed a pleasant looking older man sitting in another chair, watching her. He spoke in a deep and resonant bass voice that was pleasant to her ears and vibrated in her spirit. "Hello Carol, are you comfortable?"

Carol smiled, she felt completely at ease in the man's company. "I am comfortable and I have a peace within me, but could you tell me where I am and how I came to be here."

Smiling slightly the man nodded. "You are in a singular realm of Heaven. My name is Hugo. You are here at the desire of Yahveh so that you can be offered some information concerning your new gift from Him."

Carol frowned slightly, "Hugo, I have been taught to test the spirits to see if they are from Yahveh or not. How say you?"

Hugo actually grinned, which hurt a little bit because he had not grinned for decades and the muscles were not used to that. "I confess the Messiah Yahshua came to Earth, died, and was raised again through the Holy Spirit of Yahveh on the third day. I also confess that He is in me and He is in you. But, to set your mind at ease young lady." Hugo said a word that most people would not understand because it only had meaning in a different dimension than our four. Carol understood the word, which meant "Rose, come here" and the dimension it was used in by Hugo.

There was a swirl of gold and white and Rose appeared next to Hugo. She smiled at Carol, "Hello Carol, I see you've met Hugo."

Carol was happy to see Rose again. "Hi Rose! Yes, I just met him and was inquiring as to his allegiance to Yahveh as I was taught to do."

Rose drifted over next to Carol and sort of stared through her. "You are bright, aren't you? All praise to the Father for His good judgment and design. Yes, you should always test the spirits. I remember you didn't test me the first time we met, did you?"

Carol reddened slightly, "No, I assumed that the others there would know if you were on the right side or not. I was just an observer at that point. I would not have presumed to doubt their knowledge and faith."

Hugo laughed; this was another slightly less unused expression for him. "Rose, I enjoy this one. She will be a delight to teach."

Rose smiled at Carol, "You can trust Hugo. He taught me eons ago and I expect he will be doing the same thing eons from now."

Carol wrinkled her brow. "But I thought we were in the end times and that Yahshua would return soon and after that the world would end."

Rose reached out and tousled Carol's hair with her hand. "Yes, that is true, but why do you think your days as a servant of the most high will cease at that time? Do you not know of the thousand year reign and the New Jerusalem? Expand your possibilities young one, you are about to see a whole new universe." As Rose faded from sight she said, "Bye Hugo."

Carol was bemused by Hugo's humor. As the being must be thousands of years old in her time he must know some pretty interesting tales. She settled back in her chair and asked him, "What is it you are going to teach me?"

Hugo grinned again, this time it didn't hurt. "I am going to show you how to understand what you see and how many different ways the things you see can be interpreted. There are actually three to six ways of correctly interpreting what you term eight-dimensional events, but there are dozens of ways to misinterpret them. To do the Father's will correctly you will need to know the difference. To properly convert the concepts for your world is a whole different thing. First get it right, and then translate it properly."

Carol took a deep breath and listened to Hugo as he explained the universe and how it operates.

Hugo said, "First, you already know that the Father created the universe and all that is in it, including your world. He also created all of the dimensions to allow for the proper operating of the universe. You also know that humans normally only know of four of the dimensions. You are now learning about eight. It will not affect you but I need to tell you that there are an infinite number of dimensions. But for human affairs, at least on Earth, there are eleven and we will discuss the eight which are the ones that significantly affect the affairs of humans."

Carol realized she really did need to widen her expectations.

Hugo continued, "You may also be aware that time is a dimension that only affects fleshly beings. Spirit beings are not confined in a sequential flow of events but have access to events all along the time continuum."

Carol asked, "Why then doesn't Satan just go back to the birth of the Savior and stop Him from being born?"

Hugo smiled again as he thought to himself, "This one is going to a delightful handful with a mind as nimble as this." To Carol he said, "Because of the sixth dimension which has rules that have been set up by Yahveh and all spiritual beings, including Lucifer have to abide by and cannot violate. Actually, they can't be broken by anyone except Yahveh and He will not break His own rules."

Carol thought that out. "Okay, if the rules are immutable and Satan knows the future why doesn't he just give up and stop harassing the saints?"

Hugo nodded, "Good point. The reason is that there are as many possible futures as grains of sand on all the beaches on the world. Satan believes he can corrupt all people to doubt or ignore Yahveh and if he can then there will be no future punishment and he will survive to rule. Yet, if only one remains to the end with faith, he loses."

Carol took a deep breath, "Okay, then the Father must know all the possible ends for everybody and the probable conclusion."

Hugo nodded, "He does, but why do you believe that?"

The young woman smiled faintly, "Because it says so in His word, the Bible."

Hugo thought that with this intelligence it may not take as long as he first thought to train her. "There are many versions of the Bible on Earth at your time and the translations have blurred the true word. How do you know the one you read is giving you the correct information?"

Carol was ready for this one. "Because the Father will verify his word through His spirit regardless of the variations of human meddling and transliteration. I prayed over the entire text of the Bible as I learned it and He was faithful to show me the correct meanings. I trust Him and I know that I know that the word He approved is correct and honest to the original."

Hugo thought, "Yes, this would go quickly with the foundation she had already built." He told Carol, "Very good. Now let's work on event interpretation."

Carol had no idea how long she worked with Hugo because time didn't matter to her spirit and she was sure very little time was passing for her fleshly body.

As she bade Hugo farewell he faded from view and her bedroom became real again. Checking the time she saw she had been gone for only a few minutes.

Now she knew how to do what she was supposed to do and realized that her first message to Jack and Laura was incomplete and therefore inaccurate. She got off the bed and headed back to the War Room.

CHAPTER TWENTY-ONE

As Carol reentered the War Room she walked over and asked Jack and Laura if they could talk to her for a minute. They looked at each other and then excused themselves from the group and walked out into the living room.

Turning to Carol they waited. Carol was supremely confident at the moment and smiled at Laura, "Hugo said to say hello." Laura's eyebrows rose a bit and then she smiled. "Oh, you've had a session with Hugo? How did it go?"

Carol nodded her head, "Very well. I needed the training and that's why I wanted to talk to you both. I didn't do such a good job with the first interpretation I gave you both at the restaurant yesterday. If you'll remember I said, "There is danger to the team in the form of a duplicitous plan to deceive us that will bear fruit in the next four days. Be wise as serpents and pray constantly. This plan involves many of the enemy and nine humans."

I reviewed what I told you to Hugo and he showed me my mistakes. Not a great start for my using my gift. Yet, the new interpretation isn't that much different. It is a plan to deceive us and it will happen in the next two days. And, it does involve many demons and nine humans. What I didn't see was that it also will put us in great peril but Yahveh knows this and expects that we will stay faithful to Him. If we do stand in the faith in the face of insurmountable odds we will be victorious, Please understand that the rules of dimension five do not allow Yahveh to reveal all to us because then He will have violated His own rules, which He never has and never will. As things develop I will continue to pray and seek further enlightenment concerning this plan of the enemy." Carol stopped talking and let the two of them consider what she had told them.

Laura said, "This would be true if we went to Hawaii and met a superior force that we could not overcome."

Jack added, "This could also mean that we could meet that overwhelming force in Iran too."

Laura considered that. "Okay, our prayer for guidance led us to agree that we should go to Iran to combat the demonic forces that are covering the action there per Colonel Mason's directive from General Miles. We still don't have any credible information to back up the NSA information that OC is really going to attack Hawaii. OC could have generated the false information to the NSA as a setup to lure us into a trap like Mark feels it is. We don't have a leading on that yet do we Carol?"

Carol agreed that she had not had any response to her prayers about the Hawaiian geothermal facility.

Jack nodded, "You're right. It is imperative that we go to Iran and do a recon and attack if necessary and possible." He turned to Carol "Please keep us in your prayers while we are gone? We will stay in contact with you through Charlie."

Carol took a deep breath and said, "Yes I will, but, according to Hugo and the event as we saw it, I am to go with you to Iran."

Jack frowned and shook his head. "You don't have any experience or skills in combat and this could be an extremely violent mission. I would feel that I lied to your father and mother about keeping you out of the line of fire. To even get to the site we are going have to do a high altitude, low opening or HALO drop which is very dangerous for an experienced parachutist. I doubt that you've ever jumped out of an aircraft in your life, have you?"

Carol shrugged her shoulders, "I know I have not had any experience or training. I also definitely agree this is an awkward introduction for me. But as you said, when all is said and done my protection is in Yahveh's hands. I know that His will is for me to go on this mission. However, because you are the leader, I will submit to your decision. If I had my way I would never either attempt it or ask you to let me do it. It's not my choice, it's His and as scared as I am, I'll do it because I believe to not do it would be worse for all of us and especially for me. On the other hand, because you are the leader and the authority of the team, it would be wrong for me to insist on going if you believe it is Yahveh's will for me not to go."

Laura had been praying in the spirit as Carol was talking and knew the outcome of this argument. She put her hand on Jack's arm, "It will be all right, I'll look out for her."

Jack knew without a doubt that he didn't stand a chance to convince two women of his logic, especially if the Father blessed it. "Okay then, you need to be ready to go tonight due to the travel time. We will do everything we can to prepare you and defend you if necessary."

After they were back in the War Room Jack told the assembly that Yahveh had added Carol to the assault team. While Jack could sense that everyone had some reservations about the peril to the young woman they knew that Jack and Laura knew them already and accepted the change without comment.

Mark and David presented their plans for a HALO insertion by aircraft out of Kuwait City, four hours for inspection, assessment, attack as needed, and a quick ex-filtration back to Iraq by covert U.S. Navy assistance.

Jack agreed with that thought. He placed a call to Colonel Mason and explained their requirements. The Colonel agreed with the timetable and told Jack, "I will make sure the Navy will provide close-in support for your exit. Anything short of starting a shooting war with Iran that is. You know if you're caught or killed that the military and the government will have to deny any knowledge of your mission or our involvement, right?"

Jack reluctantly agreed with the officer. "I've got your word that if we need help getting out of Iran that won't implicate the U.S. that my team will get it?"

Colonel Mason said, "You've got my word and that of General Miles even if he can't say so himself. Good hunting."

After Colonel Mason hung up from talking to Jack, he set up the encryption mode and made another call. He outlined the Crossfire Team's agenda and timetable. He ended with, "Yes Sir, I think it will be a successful mission." He then disconnected his phone and sat back. Taking a bottle out of his bottom drawer of his desk he poured himself a tall double shot of whiskey. He stared out the window at the darkness of the Virginia landscape and wondered if what he was doing was good or not.

Looking deeply into the amber fluid he felt a great unseen abyss yawning wide just below his feet. He wondered if this was an omen. Downing the liquor in one gulp he let the fire burn its way down his throat. He thought to himself, "Even if the pay is good, I'm getting too old to do this anymore." He thought about another drink but instead he put the bottle away and turned off his Pentagon office lights. He locked the door and headed for his apartment in Washington, D.C.

Jack checked to see that everything was stored on the CitationX for the flight to California. They would switch to a Navy supply jet for the trip to the Kuwait City south of Iraq on the Mediterranean Sea. By tomorrow night they would be parachuting into enemy territory. He looked over and saw Laura going over the equipment and parachutes with Carol. He still had a bad feeling about taking her along on the raid. But his prayer had been confirming that she was supposed to be going along.

The next evening they were suited up and almost to their thirty thousand foot drop point. The Navy was already providing a distraction far to the east of their position that would keep all eyes on the coast rather than looking for small falling objects in the middle of the country. The site of the laboratory was ten miles north of Yatz in the absolute middle of nowhere.

Jack recalled Charlie's summary of the strike zone. "They do have a well-camouflaged facility there and it is almost an underground building. The whole thing is covered by netting and there is a pretty hefty military presence. It looks to be about two or three squads with light weapons. But, and I mean, but, I don't have any good Intel and can't get any. I think the spiritual covering is messing up my sources like it has those of the military. I did detect some of those energy fields we associate with demonic activity and there were a bunch of them in and around the place. I was also able to detect some radiation leakage so there is nuclear material there but I don't know what kind or quantity. My advice is to take it one careful step at a time. If you can recon the place and find what you think is there, then you'll have to make a command decision as to taking on the troops there. The Intel you gave me from Colonel Mason indicates that they are at their least attentive at three in the morning rather than at dawn as usual. This is apparently due to early prayers. Be careful and get out of there if anything looks out of place."

Jack didn't like it. While this was Yahveh's will it just wasn't militarily intelligent for such a small force to be grounded in the middle of a hostile nation with the intent to destroy a nuclear bomb plant, with an enemy military presence already in place. But, he had lots of experiences where he thought he was smarter than God and had come to realize that didn't work and wasn't smart. The whole team had prayed for coverage from sight by the demons so that they wouldn't warn the surrounding military or the people involved in the plant.

The red light went on and the seven people stood up and lined up for the jump as the back ramp was lowered. At five plus miles high, the air is almost non-existent and the cold is off the scale at around twenty five to thirty degrees below zero. Their suits had sufficient oxygen and heaters to keep them alive, if not comfortable, until they reached the ground. Carol was jumping connected to Sarah due to her inexperience with high altitude, low opening combat drops. Jack thought, "Hah! She'd never seen a parachute before yesterday. I bet this will be an eye-opener for her." Then he said a prayer for the safety and well-being of all of them, especially Laura and Carol. He was confident that Sarah knew how to take care of herself.

The green light came on and the line of warriors ran out the back of the plane and jumped into dark nothingness.

Carol's heart was in her throat as they left the plane and began to fall. She spread her arms and legs as she had been told to do. Sarah's breathing was in her ears and she began to explain the drop over the tiny intercom for Carol's benefit. "Well young lady, you picked probably the most dangerous and complicated parachute jump you could for your first experience. As you can see there is nothing to see but blackness. That is for our protection. Right now we are falling at one hundred and twenty five miles an hour straight down. We will continue to fall for about two minutes or until my altimeter registers twenty-five hundred feet. If you do the math you'll realize that we will only have eight seconds until impact on the ground at that time. The double chute we will deploy will slow us to about ten feet per second and we will have almost no time before we touch down. I'll tell you when and remember to bend your knees and flex as you land.

Carol breathlessly asked Sarah how she knew where she was going in the rushing dark. Sarah told her to look down and find the faint dots of light on the helmets of Mark and Jack below them. They've got the GPS coordinates mapped into their heads-up display on their goggles. They know where to go and we just follow them. That keeps us together but doesn't let any light or signal reach the ground below.

Before she knew it, and well before she was ready, Sarah pulled both chute releases and a giant hand grabbed Carol and it felt like it slammed her upwards. Sarah told her to get ready to land and Carol bent her knees even though she still couldn't see anything. Sarah said, "Now!" and they hit the ground. Carol took the landing and managed to keep her feet. What she didn't know was that Sarah, who had hundreds of jumps, used the four links between them to help her remain standing and prevented any injuries.

Sarah quickly disconnected the two parachutes and their tandem links. She gathered in the chutes and Carol helped her to bury them under the sand. Sarah adjusted her night vision goggles and saw Jack's infrared beacon fifty feet away. She took Carol by the arm and steered her over to the others as they gathered together on the sand. Laura had showed Carol how to use her night vision goggles and the combat communications equipment the night before but she was still uncertain of what to do.

Jack turned to Mark. "Ground command is yours, General Connelly." The team spread out with the most experienced in front and to the sides of the less experienced. That left Laura and Carol together in the middle. Carol was still shaking from the parachute drop and asked Laura, "Do you do this all the time?"

Laura shrugged which was lost in the dark, "Sometimes, but most of the time we have to trek into wherever we're headed. This march will be short as the objective is less than a mile away courtesy of the night drop."

Silence reigned as the raiders slogged through the cool sands in the early morning hour toward their target. Laura kept praying that the Father would cover them and keep them hidden from the demons.

CHAPTER TWENTY-TWO

The team approached to within two hundred feet of the site and were greeted by a triple set of barbed wire fences which Mark detected and warned everyone not to touch the outer fence. Using his energy detector he discovered that the outer fence was electrified and the middle one was wired with sensors to detect intruders. He quietly told the others and set to work overcoming both barriers with the help of David and Sarah.

Thanks to the nature of the terrain they didn't have too far to go to find a soft spot in the sands and were able to tunnel under all three fences. Mark carefully looked for trembler switches that would give away the tunneling but found none. After crawling on their stomachs for fifteen feet they were inside the fence line. While Jack and the others stood guard, Mark took David and slipped forward toward the building. The night was still and there were no signs of life. David did detect the smell of cooking. Probably breakfast was being prepared by some all night types.

As they reached the building, David checked the radiation detectors and found definite readings of nuclear material inside. Using their unorthodox techniques they quietly used two small MASER units to destroy the caulking around a section of the wall bricks that made up the building. The MASER did not operate in the visible spectrum and therefore did not generate a light that could give them away.

Jack checked with Charlie back in the Fortress as to the presence of any spiritual power indications. Charlie came back with, "I don't know Jack. All of the disturbances have disappeared completely. It's like they left the field all at once as you came in. That is not a good sign." Jack agreed with the crafty Oriental but was still committed to finding out what was going on here.

Mark carefully moved the bricks out of the wall and put them to one side. Then, they quickly created an opening into the building. Mark tested the structural integrity of the wall but the way they removed the bricks in a triangle had not caused any undue strain on the wall. David quietly moved two barrels that were inside their opening and the way was clear. Mark went first and scanned the inside of the building. It wasn't as big as he would have expected a manufacturing facility to be but who knew what the Iranians thought a process needed in terms of space.

Slipping along the rows of tables they found the makings of suitcase bombs and plenty of Russian markings to indicate the origin of the devices. Mark estimated that there were at least twenty five of the devices in the building. He was about to go further when David touched his shoulder. He stopped and David said, "Doesn't it seem odd to you that there are no guards or advanced detection devices like ultrasound or infrared detectors in here?"

Mark was about to agree with David when Jack told them over their combat communications system. "Make room in there guys, we've got a sizable force of soldiers coming up behind us and we can't defend ourselves out here on the sand."

Mark's heart fell at the news. "We've been set up. There's no way they could have detected us and prepared a force like that in so short of a time without a lot of activity. Those soldiers were waiting for us!"

Sarah slid through the opening in the wall quickly followed by the other four members of the team. Mark put the barrels back in place to block the entrance.

For several minutes there were noises of men and equipment moving around outside but no contact. Then the building was lit up from the outside by bright lights on all sides.

Jack shook his head, "They had to know we were coming and when."

Mark agreed, "And I would guess they know how many of us there are and what weapons we have."

Jack's silenced cell phone buzzed against his thigh. He took it out and looked at the display. "And it appears they have our cell phone number too."

He pressed TALK and said "Yes?"

The voice on the other end was obviously an English speaking Iranian, probably educated in the U.S. "General Malone? I am Colonel Giza and I just wanted to let you know that I have a reinforced battalion of seasoned troops surrounding the building you broke into. Did you enjoy our little display of obsolete Russian hardware? I hope so because it will be the last thing you see in this world."

Jack asked, "How did you know we were going to be here and what are your terms of surrender?"

Giza laughed, "General Malone, Colonel Mason gave us your headcount and time table. Don't worry about bothering your Navy to rescue you either. Colonel Mason has ordered them to ignore any calls as being too politically dangerous considering the lack of relations between our countries. And as to terms of surrender, there are none. You will die along with all of your team and be buried in the desert never to be heard of again. That was our arrangement with Colonel Mason. But we are not savages General Malone. We will give you ten minutes to say goodbye to each other." Colonel Giza broke the connection and warned the six hundred troops to keep a sharp eye for any escape attempts.

The Colonel savored the trap they had prepared and sprung on the gullible Americans. Once he had set off the explosives wired into the building there would only be the effort to dig out the bodies and bury them.

He turned to his aide and asked for cold water as he waited.

Inside the building the team realized the enormity of the situation. They gathered together and Laura told them, "This is what Carol saw as our great peril. The solution she said was to stand firm in our faith in Yahveh. I believe we need to pray for our salvation. Remember, our struggle is not against flesh and blood, but against the rulers, against the authorities, against the powers of this dark world and against the spiritual forces of evil in the Heavenly realms. Therefore, put on the full armor of God, so that when the day of evil comes, you may be able to stand your ground, and after you have done everything, to stand."

Carol added, "This is a plan of the evil spiritual forces in the Heavenly realms. It was carefully crafted to use my insight to help put us in this trap. The Father knows this and only He can save us."

Jack commented, "If it is His will that we die to serve Him then we die, willingly doing what He asks us to do. I'm okay with that. How about the rest of you?"

Each person looked inside themselves and measured their faith in the Father and realized they had said they would gladly die for His Name and it was true. They all nodded or said, "Yes, we will die for Him."

Outside the building the listening station reported to Colonel Giza that the Americans were praying to their God and standing firm in His salvation.

Colonel Giza knew that the Americans had no chance of survival. He checked his watch and saw that they only had two minutes left to live. He turned to the aide and said, "I don't care about their God. Even if He were real, He couldn't stop my execution of them and he held up the transmitter that would detonate the explosives. The men around him laughed and shouted their defiance of the American's God. Allah was triumphant over the American's God! All of the troops echoed their contempt for the American's God and spit on the ground to show that contempt.

There was the sound of a loud hiss and the Colonel stared in shock at his arm and then screamed. His hand and the transmitter were gone and the bloody stump of his arm was pulsing blood as his heart beat. His aide blanched and said, "Perhaps we should not have defamed their God." There were more hisses and the aide was knocked off the armored carrier in a spray of blood. The Colonel stared around him as small red hot stones smashed down out of the sky in increasing numbers and their tremendous velocity literally punched their way through the armor on tanks and armored personnel carriers, killed the troops as they ran or as they stood, undecided what to do. As his eyesight dimmed from the loss of blood the full body of meteorites turned from a few stones into a downpour and destroyed everything in the area, everything except the small building. Not one of the stones hit the building. The noise of the meteoric downpour was deafening outside the building but inside there was simply peace.

After less than two minutes it was over. Mark looked at his watch and said, "Apparently they've decided not to kill us. He moved the barrels and looked out the hole. Uncharacteristically, he sat back down on the floor and muttered, "Oh my God, what.. ."He ran out of words at the picture of what he saw. The others looked outside and some knelt to pray their gratitude and some like Carol were overcome with emotion and simply cried over the loss of life.

Jack crawled out the hole and looked around in the light of the false dawn to the east. Nothing was standing other than the building. The armored vehicles, the wire fences, the soldiers, all had been smashed into the ground. There was no life to be seen other than themselves in the area. An eerie silence hung over the pock-marked ground and craters which were still steaming from the heat of the meteorites. The smell was horrible.

The others came out of the building and surveyed the destruction. Mark walked over and looked at an armored personnel carrier that was broken into pieces with engine oil and blood smears on it. He noticed a small device on the ground and picked it up. He noticed a hand and wrist lying near it. He recognized it as a detonator. More than that, it was an American detonator. He motioned everyone to walk away from the site. When they were several thousand yards away Mark pushed the activate button and there was a huge explosion which utterly destroyed the building. Mark put the detonator in one of the pockets of his battle fatigues.

Jack said, "Yahveh said he would show that he was Elohim. I think He did that. Jack noticed that Alexis was taking digital pictures of what was left. Turning to Mark he asked, "Okay, combat leader, what's our exit strategy? We're still in the middle of a hostile nation and I doubt that they will be happy with these results."

Mark had been praying his awe and thanks and said, "Yahveh will make a way for us to leave. Let's go toward Iraq and see if we can raise any friendlies to give us a ride."

Charlie sat in the computer center in the Fortress and replayed the destruction of the Iranian Guard Battalion by the power of Yahveh and wept. He didn't want his friends to die, but he had watched as over six hundred people were literally smashed out of existence. It seemed such a waste. But, it wasn't over yet. He scrubbed the tears off of his face and decided how he would get the team out of Iran. He contacted the U. S. Army Command in Iraq and invoked General Connelly's authority. He backed it up with a very clear satellite recording of the destruction near Yatz. The Army had a special operations team with helicopters that committed to go in and pick up the team. Charlie then called the President of the United States and was somewhat surprised when he was patched through to him immediately.

President Bollen had spoken to Charlie once before and knew the man would not call him if it wasn't urgent and necessary. "Hello Charlie, what's the problem?"

Charlie summarized the action from Colonel Mason's visit until then and asked the President if he could get the Navy to create a second diversion to entertain the Iranians while the Special Forces extracted the Crossfire Team.

The President told him to consider it done. Hanging up he rang up the Chairman of the Joint Chiefs of Staff, General Miles. Ten minutes later a Navy battle group swung around off the coast of Iran and steamed directly for the shore. This got exactly the reaction Charlie had asked for. Not only Iran but every other major power and middle-east country focused on the Navy ships and tried to interpret their intent.

Nobody paid any attention to the helicopter incursion into Iran so far away from the coast.

CHAPTER TWENTY-THREE

Mark Connelly sat back against a bulkhead in the UH-60 Blackhawk chopper and watched the AH-64D Longbow Attack helicopter flying cover for them as the two aircraft left Iranian air space and entered into U.S. Military coverage in Iraq. The Navy must have created quite a show at the coast because they hadn't even been hailed by ground stations as they transited out of the country.

Mark dug out his cell phone and placed a priority call to General Miles, Chairman of the Joint Chiefs of Staff at the Pentagon. General Miles took the call immediately. "Hell of a show Mark. What was left?"

Mark chuckled; he knew what the old war horse was trying to do. "That won't work General. I intend to fly to Washington and personally deal with Colonel Mason regardless of the banter."

The General grunted, "Yeah, I kinda figured that. I kept the lid on your operation and the battle near Yatz. How do you want to do this?"

Mark had had time to think about what to do. He also had prayed about his burning desire to simply kill the man for his perfidy. Yahveh had taken the fire out of his revenge and given him a better idea. "General, when Jack and I get there, we will covertly come to your office. You ask Mason to come talk to you. When he gets there, he will talk, I assure you. I don't plan to lay a hand or a round on the man. Something much worse is in store for him."

The General discussed the logistics of the meeting and agreed to the arrangement. Mark told him that he would get a call when they were fifteen minutes out from his office tomorrow afternoon.

Mark used his combat comm gear to talk to Jack and explain what the Father told him to do with Colonel Mason. Jack agreed and told both Sarah and Laura about the arrangement. Then Jack called the Commander of the base in Kuwait City and made arrangements for a clandestine transfer for the team to a military jet transport inside a guarded hanger to prevent anyone from warning the Colonel that they weren't dead.

Twenty six hours later Mark made the call and he and Jack were slipped into the Pentagon by General Miles aide-de-camp Major Fenmore. They greeted the General and described the double-cross that Mason had arranged, in the General's name, for the Crossfire Team. Then Mark explained what Yahveh had in store for the traitor. General Miles shook his head in sadness for the man. He placed the call and arranged for the Colonel to be in present in the Chairman's office at three p.m. to go over some new assignments. That gave the three men twenty-five minutes to discuss the upcoming future.

General Miles frowned, "This liberal candidate doesn't like armies or warriors. He believes everything can be easily resolved by negotiations and sitting down together and working things out. Unfortunately, he has a lot of the populace in his corner because they're tired of the middle-east wars against Afghanistan, Iraq, and the one about to happen, Iran. He promises them peace and no more marching off to war. The man is demented. He obviously has never studied what history shows about appeasers and the results they achieve. But, the old man can't run for a third term and I will be cashiered as soon as the new crew moves into the White House.

Mark knew just what the General meant about the fall of America. "Is there hope that the Minute Men will still defend the country by killing all the politicians?"

All three of them laughed at that. Mark told the General, "Howard, if you need a place to operate out of, the Fortress has a lot of room and we could always use a top-notch, if slightly used, consultant."

General Miles eyebrows went up at that. "What do you mean, "slightly-used"? I prefer well-trained and well-traveled." He stuck his nose in the air like he was too good.

Mark almost fell out of his chair at that characterization. When he got his breath back he said, "Okay, part-time stand-up comic too."

Jack grinned at the inanities the two professional fighting men were engaging in at the moment. He then looked at his watch and said, "Five minutes to show time."

The General stopped smiling and motioned them both into the private bathroom off of the office. They strolled into the facility and waited. They heard Colonel Mason arrive and get seated.

General Miles asked the Colonel to describe the operations he was involved with over the next month. Colonel Mason pulled out his ledger and was looking at the paperwork intently. He didn't notice the movement behind him.

Mark silently opened the door and he and Jack walked out quietly and stood on either side the Colonel. The sudden appearance of the two men made the Colonel look up at them. The complete confusion and surprise on his face quickly turned into fear and he looked at the General, "What is going on..." In that instant he realized that General Miles was aware of his perfidy and he sagged in his chair.

Jack said, "Colonel Mason, I asked you if you had our back and you promised you did. Not so. The Navy says you told them not to help us under any circumstances." The Colonel's lips tightened as he heard the condemnation.

Mark said, "Also, the late Colonel Giza commented that you provided them with our timetable and numbers. It didn't help him."

Mason's mind spun in disbelief, "How could the seven of you defeat over six hundred trained and professional soldiers?"

Mark shrugged, "We didn't kill one of them. God destroyed all of them in less than ten minutes." Mark poked the soldier's arm. "Every last one of them died in a downpour of fiery hail traveling at meteoric speeds. They taunted God and He erased them from the face of the Earth. Too bad you weren't there with them!"

Jack sat down and held out a coin for Mason to take. Mason took the coin but was confused, "What is this?"

Mark's voice was hard as he said, "That coin represents your thirty pieces of silver you Judas. The reason Jack gave that to you is because God told him to do it."

Mason seemed as if he was going to reply when he froze in place and stared through everything for several seconds. Then he started to tremble. The whites of his eyes seemed to grow as he stared at something no one else could see. The fear in his face continued to grow until his eyes rolled up in his head and he passed out. Mark watched the man fall to the floor.

General Miles stood up and looked over his desk at the limp form. "Okay, I like it. What happened to him?"

Jack sighed, "God showed him who his real masters are. You've seen demons before General, but I'll bet he never did until now."

They took the coin out of the man's hand and sat him back up into the chair and waited. Running short of patience Mark slapped the man's face. Mason stirred and suddenly sat up straight in his chair. He looked around wildly and his breath came in big gulps. After a few seconds he settled down and with obvious terror in his eyes he looked intently at Jack, "I didn't know, honest, I didn't know, that those, those things, were involved. I was just trying to secure my retirement with a bunch of money. It wasn't personal, really!"

Mark asked Mason in a quiet tone, "If you really didn't know what you were doing and who you were serving then help us to understand what the OC and the demons are doing besides trying to kill us."

Mason took several shaky breaths and looked directly at Mark. "They're going to kill me you know. When you gave me that coin it allowed me to see them, but they could see me too. They know I've been compromised and the sooner they get rid of me the better. They told me that right then. They are coming for me. They will be here very soon, because now I am considered a liability. I don't want them to get me. Promise me you'll protect me from them! Promise me and I'll tell you everything!"

Mark shook his head. "Mason, there are consequences for everything you do in this life. This world and your existence in it is only a test. You failed miserably. Right now you are bound for hell and you will be tormented day and night for the rest of eternity." The man obviously could relate to that fate.

Mark continued, "If you want to help us and tell us what you know, that will result in good consequences. But, I can't promise something I can't deliver. You need to confess your sins before God, repent and turn away from the evil, and ask Him to protect you. He can do that if you turn to him in truth and spirit. Again, this is your choice."

The man was looking from the eternal fire of hell to the possibility of a reprieve and the peace of Heaven. The decision wasn't hard to make. "All right, I'll tell you what I know. It's not a lot but it may make up for some of the things I've done. OC has a goal of causing disasters in all forms of energy generation or production except for petrochemical sources. This will force the world to dance to the tune of the oil producing states and the refiners and speculators in oil futures. OC has infiltrated into many of the petrochemical processes in key positions to siphon off funds in the billions. They plan to eventually control the only legally acceptable power source and through that run the world the way they want to. Only now I see that they aren't in control, Satan is. My guess is that his goal is to destroy all forms of energy or force the world to depend on nuclear power which he will then use to destroy mankind. Don't you see? He will bring the world to ruin and plunge it back into chaos and anarchy."

Jack asked, "Is OC tasked with destroying the nuclear power plants in this country and others?"

Mason thought for a minute. "No, I don't think so. They never asked me for information about the military nuclear stockpiles and I never heard anything about the commercial plants either."

Mark asked the man, "Why was it so imperative that the Crossfire Team be destroyed?"

Mason shook his head over his part in that plan. "I don't know the actual reason. They told me that you were a future threat to their plans and it was critical that you be stopped. That's why I was tasked to set up the Iranian trap."

General Miles shook his head. "Mason, you realize you've admitted to committing treason against the armed forces of the United States of America? I'm hereby relieving you of your rank and privileges and will have you held for trial by a military tribunal."

Mason slightly smiled. "General, that is only a small matter compared to what I just saw. I don't care if you lock me up forever. I just want to save my soul from that foulness."

General Miles walked around his desk and removed the Colonel's rank from his uniform. He then called in two Marines and had Mason taken to a local holding cell. Sitting down again he dropped the insignia onto his desk with a sigh. Picking up his phone he called the Chaplain for the Pentagon and asked him to work with Mason and help him confess his sins, repent of them, and seek absolution for his acts." He would need all the help he could get.

After Mason was gone the General looked at Jack and Mark. "What do you think? Was he telling us the truth?"

Jack frowned, "We'll have to pray about that but my guess is that he told us everything he knew. Question is, did they tell him the truth?"

CHAPTER TWENTY-FOUR

Mark looked at the General. "Tell me Howard, what will you do if the expected dovish candidate is elected?"

Howard Miles shrugged, "Not much I can do. He's already made it clear that he doesn't want a war horse like me in this position. If I don't resign, he'll ask for my resignation or order me to resign. Any way you cut it, my time as the Chairman of the Joint Chiefs of Staff is just a few months from being over. I've given it some thought but primarily I don't want to be the military go-to guy for a President that will try appeasement before considering any type of military action. We all know where that will lead. He'll appease, they'll take. He will negotiate and they won't honor anything they sign. Finally when the wave is about to break over the country and the enemy have all the odds in their favor, he'll ask the military to save us. I don't want to be the man who sacrifices all those patriotic young men in a cause the President doomed from the start. No thanks."

The five-star General sat back in his chair. "Nope, I think I'll just take my pension and take my wife and develop a property in the western mountains that will give us shelter during the coming storm."

Mark shook his head. "I'm sorry you see that as the future of our country Howard. I've prayed about the near future and I think it's going to be far more dramatic and active than you do. I'm afraid that the lenient policies that the liberal Congress has pushed over the last few years may have paved the way for this type of President but it has also greatly emboldened our enemies abroad. Omicron is a good example. If they had completed their strike on our country there would be no elections and no new president. It is only by the protection of Yahveh that we dodged that bullet. I doubt that we will make it to the election of the appeaser because the enemy isn't going to wait for due process. I am surprised that we haven't had a major hit on the U.S. since 2001. We will have to wait and see but I'd keep your guns oiled."

Howard Miles snorted, "You've got a point there. If the new rumors coming out of the FBI and the CIA are based in any kind of fact we're swatting hand grenades as quick as we can but we're about to be hit with some artillery rounds and swatting won't stop them!"

Jack and Mark said their farewells to the General and headed back to the airport and the trip to Colorado.

As they climbed on board on the CitationX Mark had a thought. "You know, I'll bet you that those "rumors" that the General was referring to could give us some leads if Charlie can sort out the real stuff from the manure."

Jack nodded, "You might have a point there. I'll give Charlie a call and see what he can dig up."

Su Li lifted the modified corporate jet off of the active runway at Edwards Air Force Base and worked her way through the commercial traffic heading west from Washington, D.C. The flight was routine but she honed her skills as a combat pilot by watching all of her screens and instruments. That was why she caught the slight anomalies in the traffic pattern behind them.

Double checking her theory she deviated from her approved flight path to the north. She was two miles off line when ATC called her and advised her that she was out of the flight path. She corrected her line and watched the other three blips also slide back into the approved lane. They had casually turned with the CitationX and stayed on it as she veered north.

Having been attacked by Russian fighters not too long ago, Su Li was in no mood to mess around this time. She called Mark up to the cockpit and he came in quickly, rubbing the sleep out of his eyes. "What's going on?"

Su Li pointed out the multiple bogies and described her test. Mark sat down and used the aircraft radio to contact ATC for a verification of the other flights. Each one had a commercial squawk and a flight path filed that agreed with their present locations. Mark decided to make them announce their intentions. He told Su Li to return to Washington and advised ATC of the change in status.

Su Li quickly left the westbound air corridor and changed altitude and direction to move into the eastbound air corridor. Mark watched the other aircraft to see what their reaction would be. In less than three minutes, all three of the suspected aircraft had echoed the movements of the CitationX.

Mark used his "General Connelly" persona and made a call to the Air Force Air Defense Command (ADC). He explained the situation and asked what they could do to help. After six minutes the ADC came back with a feasible plan. They had two interdiction flights of mixed F-16Fs and F-22s close enough with sufficient fuel to lend assistance and both had already been vectored toward the four aircraft.

Su Li kept a sharp eye on the other aircraft and warned Mark that they were slowly closing the distance between them and the CitationX. They would be in definite missile range in about ten minutes or less.

Mark relayed the new position information to ADC. He got an assurance that the fighters would be there first.

Two minutes later ADC requested Su Li to turn to the south. The pursuing aircraft could close the range quicker but were about to meet the ADC flights. Su Li made the turn and chaos broke loose. The pursuing aircraft launched ten air-to-air missiles at the CitationX and the Air Force flights went on the attack. In less than a minute there were twelve aircraft and twenty air-to-air missiles all thrashing the air in a six mile wide sphere. Other aircraft using those corridors were doing everything they could to avoid the huge bubble of air combat going on in front of them.

Su Li accelerated way beyond the normal capabilities of a commercial bizjet and dumped flares and chaff to throw off the missiles. Two of the pursuing aircraft turned away from the ADC flights as one of them exploded in midair from a direct missile hit.

Su Li threw the CitationX into a vertical barrel roll with a twist at the top as she maxed out the engines. Most of the incoming missiles had taken the bait of the flares and chaff and the others lost the aircraft as it climbed and spun behind the chaff and flares.

Mark had endured the twisting and g-loads of the evasion and told Su Li to follow the fleeing aircraft to see what the ADC would do to them. Su Li brought the nose of the CitationX to the same heading as the fleeing attackers and held the engines in max power. They were actually overhauling the enemy when both of the planes exploded and the burning fragments started the three mile fall to the farmland below. Both Su Li and Mark heard the lead F-22 fighter call in the end of the battle. "Both remaining hostile aircraft self destructed with no action on our parts. The GPS coordinates for the downed aircraft are as follows:"

Mark shook his head and had Su Li return to their original westward direction and altitude as he contacted ADC to thank them for their timely intervention. Su Li contacted the civilian ATC and amended their flight plan for the delay.

After they settled down in the air corridor Su Li put the aircraft on autopilot and turned to Mark. "Mark, these close calls are too close. I would like to suggest we change our tactical aircraft to something with teeth and armor so that we can dish it out instead of just trying to avoid being destroyed."

Mark agreed with the irritated Oriental woman. "All right, see what you can find that will let us move the same number of people in reasonably comfortable accommodations but give us combat capabilities. I will need all possible options and costs as well as a time line to get the aircraft into operation." He thought about it for a few seconds. "You might as well get two because one could be in operation when we need another one."

CHAPTER TWENTY-FIVE

A week later the core team was summoned to hear about the results of Su Li's search. The primary core of the Crossfire Team was made up of six people. There was Jack and Laura Malone, Mark and Sarah Connelly, David Zahavy, and Alexis Hutton. At the special request from Su Li they met in the living room of the Fortress at eight a.m. the next morning. Su Li had arranged ten comfortable chairs in front of the new 100-inch DLP HDTV.

After the crew was seated Su Li and recently promoted Lt. Colonel Mike White started the presentation.

Mike had known four of these people since the beginning of the Crossfire Team during an attack on a Houston Armory and a secret high speed, transcontinental Raptor flight to Libya to chase down an international criminal. They had supported each other and fought alongside and had an easy acquaintance that allowed for direct communication without all the posturing. Mike smiled, "It's about time we had a chance to get together without it being on an aircraft or in the middle of a pitched battle." That got a chuckle out of the crowd.

Nodding to David and Alexis he continued, "I'm glad to meet the two newest additions to the team. My name is Michael White and I am a U.S. Air Force officer that has had the opportunity and the privilege of working with the team for the last couple of years. I basically function as a resource, consultant, and occasionally, pilot for the team. I helped to train Su Li in our aircraft and can say I am proud of her achievements in both fixed wing and rotary wing aircraft." He picked up a notebook and checked his notes.

"Su Li was tasked with the tough job of finding a replacement that could give the team fighter capabilities as well as corporate jet functionality. The major problem she had is that airframe development takes years to design, develop, and build and she didn't have the time. That is why she asked me to help her with this assignment."

He smiled at Su Li. "Fortunately, in early 2009 the CIA had a similar quest. Complicating the development of this particular aircraft were two rapidly changing environments. First, airframe and engine development is redefining the industry every two years. The plane would have to have the latest in both carbon-fiber frame and skin development which was just beginning to become available at that time. Second, the project would have to be a "black" project which means the whole thing was done in secret with undefined funding by the CIA, NSA, and other organizations.

The development of a completely new and unique aircraft is a hard thing to keep under wraps because of all the people in various industries needed to do it right. So it was given to Lockheed Martin's new "Skunk Works" facility at Area 51. The whole project was underway by the end of 2011 and didn't have official blessing until 2013 when the first prototype was flight tested. The world doesn't know of this aircraft and allowing you people to acquire two of them will come with some hefty restrictions and responsibility for secrecy until after it becomes public knowledge. Because you have the highest level of support in the military and the government, and because you're going to foot the bill for the aircraft, it has been agreed that you can get them."

Su Li activated the DVD player and a full-color picture of the aircraft appeared on the TV. There were appreciative comments from all the team.

Jack liked the wider and more aggressive looks of the aircraft and said so to the two pilots. "That is nice. It looks like a Citation X on steroids. I like it."

Su Li picked up the presentation. "The "Shrew" is the codename for the plane and is based not on a depiction of a harpy but the animal. The shrew is the most innocuous of rodents that looks like a small gray mouse. The true nature of the animal is defined by its need to eat its body weight every hour of its life to stay alive. It is by far the most voracious of animals on the planet, yet it looks like a little gray mouse. This aircraft combines the luxury of our present CitationX corporate jet with the performance and weapons of a modern fighter aircraft."

Mike White took up the technical description of the Shrew. "The Shrew is actually the Air Force's newest covert fighter aircraft. Don't let the corporate business jet look fool you. The combination of stealth, supercruise, maneuverability, and integrated avionics, coupled with hidden weaponry and improved maintenance support, represents a new dimension in hidden warfare capability. The Shrew shares a great deal of its critical components with the most modern air dominance fighters. The development time and cost of the Shrew was cut by seventy-five percent due to the parallel developments of the F-22 Raptor and the F-35 Lightning II. The Shrew uses the Raptor's combination of sensor capability, integrated avionics, situational awareness, and some of its weapons and can provide a first-kill opportunity against threats. The CF-88 Shrew also uses a variation on the Raptor's sophisticated sensor suite allowing the pilot to track, identify, shoot and kill air-to-air threats before being detected. Significant advances in cockpit design and sensor fusion improve the pilot's situational awareness especially in the use of helmet mounted display from the F-35 rather than a HUD or heads-up-display as in the F-22."

Mike smiled at the assembled team. "In the normal configuration the Shrew carries four AIM-120 AMRAAMs and two AIM-9 Sidewinders. Due to its clandestine nature, the Shrew does not share the capability to attack surface targets. Advances in low-observable technologies are somewhat limited by the commercial appearance but still provide significantly improved survivability and lethality against air-to-air threats. The CF-88 engines produce more thrust than many current fighter engines. The combination of sleek aerodynamic design and increased thrust allows the CF-88 to cruise at supersonic airspeeds of greater than 1.5 Mach. This characteristic is known as supercruise. Supercruise greatly expands the CF-88's operating envelope in both speed and range over most known current fighters, which must use fuel-consuming afterburner to operate at supersonic speeds. The sophisticated CF-88 aerodesign, advanced flight controls, thrust vectoring, and high thrust-to-weight ratio provides the capability to outmaneuver almost anything currently flying except for fighters of the F-22 Raptor's level."

Mike stopped to take a sip from his drink, and then he continued. "The CF-88's characteristics provide a synergistic effect ensuring lethality against most advanced air threats. The combination of integrated stealth and integrated avionics, coupled with supercruise drastically shrinks surface-to-air missile engagement envelopes and minimizes enemy capabilities to track and engage the CF-88.

The general characteristics of the CF-88 whose primary function is covert air dominance are as follows: The prime contractor: Lockheed-Martin, Boeing through the Skunk Works facility located at Area 51. The power plant for the aircraft is two Pratt & Whitney F119-PW-100 turbofan engines with concealed two-dimensional thrust vectoring nozzles. The afterburner capability was deleted to provide for less detection by unfriendly forces. It really isn't needed unless you plan to engage top echelon enemy fighter jets and that isn't the CF-88's mission. Each of the engines produces a thrust in the 35,000-pound class. "

Mike put a three view drawing of the aircraft on the screen. "Note that the wingspan is only ten feet wider than the standard Citation X at 74 feet, 6 inches which is due to the increased body width. The length has been stretched to 75 feet and 1 inch, and the height is now 19 feet, 8 inches. The Shrew still looks lower because the under cabin space is larger to accommodate the more massive internal engines and the weapons bays."

Su Li pointed out the other specifications. "The empty weight is 25,700 pounds and the maximum takeoff weight is 93,500 pounds and that number has to include the passengers, crew, fuel, weapons, and everything else. Let's try to not have to use explosives to give us boost when flying off of deserted islands, okay Mark?"

Mark thought back to the sabotage that had forced them to use a makeshift JATO made out of Sematex. "That's simple; just don't land on any deserted islands in the future."

Su Li rolled her eyes at that. "The fuel capacity is 24,000 pounds on the internal tanks and we can have 44,000 pounds if we use two external fuel tanks. Our speed is way up with the fighter engines. Using the supercruise feature at altitude we can travel at 1,100 miles per hour and we'd darn well better not do it around civilians or cities because we will leave a sonic boom behind us. Still our range will be more than 2,550 nautical miles on internal tanks and over 3,200 nautical miles with external wing fuel tanks. The operating ceiling is three thousand feet higher than the standard Citation X at somewhere above 55,000 feet, or roughly ten miles high."

"The armament is carried in internal central weapon bays and consists of two AIM-9 infrared air-to-air missiles and four AIM-120 radar-guided air-to-air missiles. The standard crew is two and the maximum for the rear seat party goers is eight, ten in a pinch."

Mike summed up the presentation with, "You can have all this fun at the low, low unit cost of $220 million dollars U.S. and be thankful that they built three extra aircraft and that the CIA's funds were cut and they can't afford them. That is probably the only reason you even heard about these babies."

Mark raised his eyebrows and looked at Jack. "I know we can afford four hundred million dollars but that's going to drain the budget right to the bottom."

Jack smiled, "You don't have to worry about your bonuses. I've already talked to Victor Chamberlain and he's going to put up the funds for the aircraft on the stipulation that he gets to ride in one now and then."

Mark shook his head, "I guess for four hundred million we can let him do that."

CHAPTER TWENTY-SIX

Su Li had done some extensive photo cataloging of the new jet and ran the photos by one at a time for the team to see what it looked like.

True it had the same look and feel of their present ten million dollar plane but there were more than subtle signs that this was a warplane rather than just a fancy business jet.

On the right hand side of the front curve of the body below the co-pilot's seat was a one-foot square outline. If desired, and the right buttons were pushed, the panel snapped up into the body and an electronic M-134 minigun with electronic computerized targeting could give the pilot an alternative to missiles.

The rear seats swiveled to the rear and a panel slid out of the way to give both seats access to another two fully functional M-134 miniguns with computerized targeting capabilities. There was a counter-warfare panel that allowed the rear gunners to eject chaff and flares to mislead radar and infrared guided missiles. The panel also included the controls for radar jamming and laser blinding projectors which were behind panels at the tail of the plane. The rear defensive positions were in full contact with the cockpit and could also be run by the pilot/copilot as needed.

The tables between the third row and fourth row of seats converted to AWACs control systems even though the look-down and side scan radar was only a tenth of the AWACs dish. It was still brutally functional in determining the air domain around the Shrew in that it gave other war craft the information they needed to coordinate an attack or a series of maneuvers.

The flight deck looked innocent enough until the right series of switches was thrown and then the combat displays and coordinated attack instrumentation was revealed. One physical clue was the reticule-equipped flight helmets for the pilot and copilot. Anybody who had been in the modern Air Force, Army, Navy, or Marine aircraft of today would recognize them as being from a modern military fighter.

One of the very noticeable redesign clues that differentiated the Shrew from a normal CitationX was the lack of engines on the body and a huge intake under the pilot's position. The expanded body and even wider section below the waistline changed the cross section of the aircraft significantly. If you looked at it correctly it looked a lot like the F22 in the front end with a door and windows in the sides of the body that any real fighter wouldn't have.

Su Li related that the Shrew was capable of vertical climb directly from liftoff which only the most powerful fighter jets could accomplish. The operational parameters of the Shrew were exceptional and even though the majority of the team couldn't appreciate it like Mike White or Su Li they understood the fantastic new capabilities of this pocket-battleship of fighter planes.

Colonel White continued with the description of the Shrew. "The CF-88 features a cockpit speech-recognition system (Direct Voice Input), which improves the pilot's ability to operate the aircraft over even the current-generation of F-22s. The CF-88 will be the second U.S. operational fixed-wing aircraft to use this system after the F-35, although similar systems have been used in the AV-8B. The system is integrated by Adacel Systems Inc with the speech recognition module supplied by SRI International. Although helmet-mounted displays have already been integrated into some fourth-generation fighters such as the Swedish JAS 39 Gripen, the CF-88 will be one of the first, along with the system developer and prototype of the F-35, in which helmet-mounted displays replace a head-up display (HUD) altogether."

"Another feature of the CF-88 that is borrowed from the F-35 is a phased array sensor suite that allows the Shrew to travel at supersonic speeds on the deck, below one hundred feet. The integration of the side-scan radar and the body sensors give the pilot unprecedented feel for the proximity of the terrain and upcoming obstacles. The CF-88 can also integrate satellite and AWACs information to plan a course that will use or avoid all blocks to its supersonic flight at ground level. Let me show you a gun-camera film of such a flight."

Su Li ran a video that was essentially a pilot's eye view of the aircraft as it flew just thirty feet off the ground at 1250 miles per hour. The film was slowed down so that the human mind could adjust to the changes in altitude, attitude, and direction that the computer was accomplishing. It was an awesome demonstration that included a sudden change to flight with one wing up and the other down as the aircraft flew between several buildings with less than one hundred feet of space. Then Mike ran the same video on a split screen and showed what the supersonic shock front did to the things behind the aircraft covering a mile in slightly more than three seconds. Water exploded, buildings exploded and imploded from the seceding shock waves, people died from the shock.

Su Li turned off the video and shook her head. "Of course, we won't do that in populated places unless it is absolutely necessary. This aircraft is as much a military weapon as any fighter. I got a lot more than I asked for when I wanted to be able to defend our aircraft. I'm just grateful that we have this plane and the enemy doesn't."

Laura tilted her head to the right and studied Su Li. "Su Li, are you having second thoughts about piloting this aircraft? You have to know that a lot of its capabilities will be called on and there could be a loss of life involved in that action. Are you all right with that?"

Su Li thought for a few seconds. "I guess I'm alright with the killing of the enemy and those that seek to harm us or the country, but my hesitation is with the effects on non-combatants, innocents if you will, that could be killed simply by the passage of my aircraft"

Sarah spoke up, "Su Li, I agree with you completely. It there is any way we can prevent collateral deaths of non-combatants we should do it. But, sometimes there comes a hard choice between survival of the team and the possible death of innocents. That isn't really a choice. We try to avoid it at all costs but if there is no chance to avoid it. Then you have to choose the team's survival over the others."

Su Li slowly nodded her head. "I see. Well, I will do everything I can to keep from having to make such a choice. If I can't then I will do what I have to and give my emotions to Yahveh."

Mike White brought the discussion back to the subject at hand, the Shrew. "Guys, I also want you to know that there is a complete medical station built into this plane. The fourth row of seats can be converted to an operating table and there are lights and oxygen built in to support a full surgical procedure. But, you need to have a surgeon available to make that important."

Jack shook his head. "I think you can see why this aircraft costs as much as it does. I think it's a heck of a bargain and can't wait to get my hands on one."

CHAPTER TWENTY-SEVEN

Colonel White concluded his presentation with a warning. "Guys, you will have to sign several documents that will make it a federal felony if you allow the existence of this aircraft to be known outside of your group. They will prosecute you if you do. I know you won't reveal the aircraft or the type of plane it really is to anyone, even accidently. But once you land at a general aviation field or even a commercial airfield, people will be asking "What is that airplane?" This could lead to complications that won't be easy to answer without potential disclosure. I like your security compound at DIA but with the Shrew being there rent-a-cops won't meet the security requirements. I suggest that you upgrade the security both there and here at the Fortress by using the Air Force Special Forces. Besides providing better airport security at DIA they could improve security and maintenance at your helicopter operations. The 720th Special Tactics Forces work out of several bases in Colorado and California but this could become a premier training assignment due to the actual combat requirements such as the attack against the Marines on the mountain top recently."

Mark nodded his head, "Not only the helicopter operations but we need better military security for the supply of the troops of all branches that train here. We discussed upgrading the facilities and the operational defensive force for the training troops and administrators after the attack and that will include an increase in the number of troops here. By adding the troops from the 720th we could resolve a lot of makeshift portions of the operation. Let's also suggest that the 720th provide troops to train in defensive investigation of possible attacks with the assistance of our ComSec group. It could not only help us but give them a real-time, real-world situation on which to train."

Mike thought that the Commander of the 720th would be interested in that operation. "Could Charlie work up a curriculum for such training that would meet all the different needs?"

Charlie's voice appeared conversational in mid-air next to the Colonel. "Consider it done Colonel Mike. That works into our scheme very well."

Mike was familiar with Charlie's disembodied voice. "Thanks Charlie. Could you have a good rough draft in three weeks?"

Charlie snorted, "How about day after tomorrow?" Mike laughed, "Okay."

Mike then added, "I will ask Su Li to accompany me for the next two weeks to train on the avionics and weapons systems as well as the supercruise capability. The aircraft handles a great deal more like a fighter than your current model and requires a fighter pilot mentality. We will be putting civilian tail numbers on both planes and will have them FAA approved as a variant of the CitationX which will be called the CitationXS. Don't let anyone not authorized into the cockpit and only have Skunk Works mechanics service the aircraft to prevent the loss of secrecy. You will have to keep the performance toned down when you are near airports or military units to make this seem like just another version of a good old civilian biz jet."

The team agreed to the restrictions. The Colonel then asked, "Why did you decide to get two super expensive aircraft instead of only one?

Jack smiled, "Because our operations are quickly coming too fast for a single pilot and single plane to get everybody where they have to be in time. Su Li is working ten to sixteen hour days, sometimes seven days a week flying us everywhere and sometimes having to fight with us and then fly us home. Our projections indicate this trend is not about to slacken off as we travel farther into the last days. So, we need additional air support which means another aircraft and another pilot."

Mike thought for a few minutes. "I really don't know where you can get another pilot as talented and knowledgeable as Su Li. Also, I don't know if I will have the time to train them."

Laura asked, "How about you? You're already trained and obviously you're as talented as Su Li."

The Colonel stared at Laura for a minute. "Have you been praying about this?"

Laura nodded.

Colonel White stood there for a few minutes as he summed up his present life in his mind. His wife had passed away from cancer three years ago and he knew that since he was never able to spend enough time with her due to his career he felt guilty about that. His three children were grown and had lives of their own now and really didn't need a father very much. His career was peaked out and he should have been a full bird Colonel by now but he was focused on the flying and the equipment more than officer politics. He could hang on in the Air Force for eight more years until he had his twenty in but that would leave him too old to do much starting over. These people were his friends and, from what he'd heard, paid really well. He would be flying into danger every time. "WOW, sounds like a win-win situation".

Looking up he smiled, "I'm pretty expensive."

Jack looked at Mark, "Oh, I think we can cover your salary and expenses."

The Colonel took a deep breath and in his mind he said, "God, if this isn't what you want me to do, block it. If it is, make it work." Verbally he said, "You've just hired yourself a pilot. I will need the rest of the month to finish Su Li's training and process out of the service. Will that be soon enough?"

Jack stood up and shook Mike's hand. "It was quicker than we thought it would be. Tell you what, let's do the paperwork today and start your employment with the Crossfire Team on Monday. That way you won't have to skimp on things while you get started."

Su Li grinned. She really liked Mike White and his piloting. She gave him a hug and said, "Your salary will be more than twenty-five million Yuan a year!"

Mike did the computation between Chinese Yuan and U.S. Dollars and came up with a number above two million. He thought to himself "That would be more than two hundred thousand a month! I can't even spend that much if I had my own aircraft." Looking up at Jack he said, "Sounds reasonable."

Everyone laughed at the dry comment.

CHAPTER TWENTY-EIGHT

That afternoon Su Li accompanied Colonel White on a flight to California and to the Skunk Work's new secret base at "Area 51". Colonel White gave Su Li the basic information. "Area 51 is a remote tract of land in the southwestern portion of Lincoln County in southern Nevada in the western United States. Situated at its center, on the southern shore of the dry lakebed of the Great Salt Lake, is a large military airfield which is one of the most secretive places in the world. The base's primary purpose is to support development and testing of new military aircraft and to analyze foreign aircraft and weapons systems."

"The base lies within the United States Air Force's vast Nevada Test and Training Range. Although the facilities at the range are managed by the 99th Air Base Wing at Nellis Air Force Base, the Groom Lake facility appears to be run as an adjunct of the Air Force Flight Test Center (AFFTC) at Edwards Air Force Base in the Mojave Desert, around 160 miles from Groom Lake, and as such the base is known as the Air Force Flight Test Center Detachment."

"Names used for the facility include Dreamland, Paradise Ranch, Home Base, WatertownStrip, Groom Lake and Homey Airport. The area is part of the Nellis Military Operations Area, and military pilots refer to the forbidden airspace around it as "The Box"."

"Groom Lake is not a conventional airbase, as frontline units are not normally deployed there. It is used during the development, testing, and training phases for new aircraft. Once these aircraft have been approved by the United States Air Force or other agencies such as the CIA, they are allowed to operate the aircraft from Air Force bases as long as security can be maintained. Operation from a civilian airport or landing field is normally not permitted until years after the aircraft has been released."

"Though no ICAO identifier for the base appears on any official document, in December 2007, airline pilots noticed that the base had appeared in their aircraft navigation systems' latest Jeppesen database revision."

"Groom Lake was abandoned After World War II until 1955, when it was selected by Lockheed's Skunk Works team as the ideal location to test the U-2 spy plane. The lakebed made an ideal strip from which they could operate the troublesome test aircraft, and the Emigrant Valley's mountain ranges and the NTS perimeter protected the test site from prying eyes and outside interference."

"Even before U-2 development was complete, Lockheed began work on its successor, the CIA's Mach-3 high-altitude reconnaissance aircraft, a later variant of which became the famed USAF SR-71 Blackbird. The Blackbird's flight characteristics and maintenance requirements forced a massive expansion of facilities and the area surrounding the valley was made an exclusive military preserve."

"The first prototype stealth fighter, a smaller cousin of the F-117 Nighthawk first flew at Groom in December 1977."

"The airbase has the IATA airport identifier code of KXTA and listed as "Homey Airport" in aviation GPS databases, has seven runways including one that is now closed. The other runways are two asphalt runways, the 14L/32R with a length of 12,000 feet and 12/30 with a length of 5,420 feet. There are four other runways located on the salt lake. These four runways are 09L/27R and 09R/27L, which are approximately 11,440 feet, and 03L/21R and 03R/21L, which are both approximately 10,030 feet."

Mike then switched the conversation to the new aircraft.

"The CF-88's cockpit is a variant of the F-22's cockpit which is an "all-glass" cockpit. There are no traditional round dial, standby or dedicated gauges. "

"Like the F-22's cockpit, the CF-88 represents a revolution over current "pilot offices", as it is designed to let the pilot operate as a tactician, not a sensor operator. Humans are good differentiators, but they are poor integrators. The CF-88 cockpit lets the pilot do what humans do best, and it fully utilizes the power of the computer to do what it does best. "

"Using the power of the onboard computers, coupled with the extensive maintenance diagnostics built into the

CF-88 by the maintainers, that workload has been significantly reduced. The idea is to relieve pilots of the bulk of system manipulations associated with flying and allow them to do what a human does best, be a tactician."

"Aircraft startup and taxi are excellent examples of harnessing the power of the computer to eliminate workload. There are only three steps to take the CF-88 from cold to an airplane ready for takeoff: The pilot places the battery switch 'on,' places the auxiliary power unit switch momentarily to 'start' and then places both throttles in 'idle.' The engines start sequentially right to left and the auxiliary power unit then shuts down. All subsystems and avionics are brought on line and built-in testing checks are made. Then the necessary navigation information is loaded and even the pilot's personal preferences for avionics configuration are read and the systems are tailored to those preferences. All of this happens automatically with no pilot actions other than the three steps. The airplane can be ready to taxi in less than 30 seconds after engine start. The concealed engines in the CF-88 are the same engines as in the F-22 with the exception of no afterburners."

"You are familiar with the heads-up-display or HUD that is used on the F-22 but this new system is even better. The helmet displays replace the HUD and give you a better integration of information and symbols and allow for quicker reactions."

"The Stand-by Flight Group is always in operation and, although it is presented on an LCD display, it shows the basic information (such as an artificial horizon) the pilot needs to fly the aircraft. The SFG is tied to the last source of power in the aircraft, so if everything else fails, the pilot will still be able to fly the aircraft."

"The Primary Multi-Function Display (PMFD) is an 8"x8" color display that is located in the middle of the instrument panel, under the ICP. It is the pilot's principal display for aircraft navigation including showing waypoints and route of flight and Situation Assessment or a "God's-eye view" of the entire environment around the aircraft."

"Like the F-22, the CF-88 features a side-stick controller and two throttles that are the aircraft's primary flight controls. For the CF-88 the controls are duplicated for the co-pilot's seat."

"The cockpit panels in the CF-88 feature extended life, self-balancing, and electroluminescent edge-lit panels with an integral life-limiting circuit that runs the lights at the correct power setting throughout their life. It starts at one-half power and gradually increases the power output to insure consistent panel light intensity over time. As a result, the cockpit always presents a well-balanced lighting system to the pilot. The panels produce low amounts of heat and power and are very reliable. The aircraft also has integral position and anti-collision lights (including strobes) on the wings. The low voltage electroluminescent formation lights are located at critical positions for night flight operations on the aircraft. There are similar air refueling lights on the butterfly doors that cover the air refueling receptacle."

After landing at Groom Lake and processing through the paperwork they walked into the hanger with the CF-88s. Su Li was impressed by everything but she especially was awed by the aircraft.

Mike White looked at the smile of satisfaction on the young woman's face. "Well, Su Li, we'd bettered get started with the hands on before the simulator. I only have so much time left in the Air Force and most of that will be training you on these beauties."

CHAPTER TWENTY-NINE

The hands-on tour was completed and they were granted eight hours of simulator time because there weren't many pilots for this particular aircraft. The simulator was so close to reality that it was hard to find clues that it was a simulator. Except of course, when you were killed, you got to try again.

Su Li had read the manuals and already knew most of the controls and displays from her time learning and flying the F-22 and its simulator. There were differences in the operating envelope but for a "supposed-to-be" civilian aircraft it flew and even fought like an F-22. After a full week of simulator there was only one area that eluded Su Li and Mike couldn't tell her how to improve on it.

He was upset that he didn't have the knowledge needed to perform the needed maneuvers. He called one of the Air Force pilots that had done the first experiment flights and then the qualification flights for the Shrew. Mike explained that he couldn't get the nose of the aircraft up and around quickly enough during air combat. The simulated enemy had out turned them every time.

Tom Caldwell laughed at his friend's discomfort. "Don't feel bad Mike, I had the same problem until I talked to one of the designers. Len Malton showed me a fact I didn't know and you don't know either. I'll come over in a few minutes and meet you at the aircraft in the hanger."

Twenty minutes later the pilot showed up and was surprised to meet Su Li. He was intuitive enough not to try to act like a VIP to impress her like he tended to do with women. Something about her warned him that would be a big mistake. So he stuck to business, but he had hopes. He had the electrical and air power connections made to the plane and then went up into the cockpit while the other two stood to one side. Suddenly a seven foot, forward pointing canard wing snapped out of the fuselage above the engine intake and below the pilot's cockpit. Then it snapped back into the fuselage leaving only a two inch thick edge flush with the body.

Tom reappeared and had the services shut down. Walking back over to the two surprised pilots he grinned. "See? I told you that there were facts that even you didn't know. They built the canards into a scissors extension that snaps out when you push the right button. It gives you twenty percent better maneuvering during combat. The reason for them being hidden is because this craft isn't supposed to be a combat fighter and the canards are a big indicator of its real capabilities so they forgot to put their operation into the early manual that you have. Now, as far as I know this is the only "secret-secret" that I've been told about. Come on inside and I'll show you the magic button." As they entered the pilot's cockpit he admired Su Li's form until he caught Mike's disapproving frown and warning shake of his head.

After learning the "secret" of the canard wings Su Li's score went up very quickly. She "graduated" after only ten days with six solo flights of the first Citation XS. Mike told her to take it to Denver and he would bring the other one early the next month which was only fifteen days away anyway.

Su Li said her good-byes to Mike and to Tom who had lingered to help with the training. Su Li recognized his interest in her as healthy social activity and was grateful for the attention. But she was about her business and stuck to the training program. When she told Tom goodbye she hugged him and gave him a card with a number he could reach her later. After talking to Mike about Su Li and her occupation, Tom thought he'd have to think a great deal before getting involved.

Su Li walked up to the beautiful aircraft and did her walk around before boarding. She sat in the cockpit and savored the beautiful mixture of fighter jet and luxury personal jet for several minutes while she became one with the aircraft. That completed, she donned her helmet with the integral weapons aiming equipment and she flipped the switches and set the throttles at idle.

After warm-up she taxied out of the hanger and waited for the tower to give her access to the runway. She lined up on the runway and accelerated like she was a normal commercial jet. She lifted off and worked out of the small pattern at Groom Lake as she came up to flying altitude.

The plane was a fighter jockey's dream to fly and she realized that Mike had been right. It was more of a full-time fighter pilot job than a commercial jet pilot job. She had to monitor the displays, plan flight requirements, and keep a watch for unfriendly aircraft. All at the same time she had to maintain her image as a normal Citation X. Still, it was fun and it kept her edge up as far as flying a fighter jet.

On the flight to Denver, Su Li realized that all her training of Mark and Sarah was essentially wasted by the enormous changes to the new plane. "Oh well," she thought, "I'll just have to train them a lot more."

Following standard procedures she got permission to land at DIA after a 757 heavy and set the plane down with no hops. Taxiing to the Crossfire Hangers she was surprised by the addition of the Air Force Special Forces troops manning the perimeter and handling the security duties.

She taxied into the hanger next to the normal Citation X and shut the engines down. Completing her post flight checks she grabbed her gear and exited the plane. She conferred with the men there and told them to refuel the aircraft by truck inside the hanger to keep it out of sight.

Taking the Cadillac XTS-V she had driven down to the airport, she headed back to the Fortress.

Eventually she walked into the War Room and greeted the team members there. Alexis got up and gave her a hug and asked her if she had seen any aliens at Area 51.

Su Li grinned, "Maybe. I think one wants to date me."

CHAPTER THIRTY

Mark ran into the War Room with a worried look on his face. Jack looked up at the commotion and asked him "What's the problem?"

Mark frowned and shook his head. "I just got a call from the British Secret Service with information they received about an OCsponsored, resurgent ASF terrorist group that has smuggled a nuclear weapon into a major city. Their tacticians believe the terrorists are going to detonate it tonight."

Laura asked, "Can't MI-5 find and stop the terrorists and why call us rather than the FBI?"

Mark shook his head, "In answer to your first question, MI-5 can't stop them because it's an American city that is under attack. Their informant says it is Houston, Texas. The second answer is because there is some kind of demonic protection that is killing their agents and actively preventing communications to American security forces. Apparently, we fall below the demonic radar as to the communications blockage."

Sarah quipped, "Or it's another trap for us."

Jack cleared the war plan boards and told Mark to give them whatever he had from MI-5. As Mark was bringing up the information Jack called the FBI and explained the situation. Gary Rhodes got the call because as Director of the Denver Office of the FBI, all potential nuclear incidents went through the Director's desk.

Gary was in an upbeat mood at the moment and was glad to hear from the Crossfire Team. "Jack, it's good to hear from you again. What's the flap about a nuclear weapon in Houston?"

It was Jack's turn to frown. "I take it your office hasn't heard anything about this?"

"No, our nuclear detection and defense board is clear and we haven't been informed of anything like that. The Houston area would normally be handled out of the Dallas office at any rate, but at least I would have been given a heads up."

Jack studied the MI-5 information and had Mark send it to Gary. "I'm sending you what we just got from our British friends. They say that they have been demonically blocked from sending to any of our alphabet agencies, including yours and Homeland Security. It looks like it could be good Intel and we need to be concerned about the timeline. Tonight is only six hours away."

Gary said, "Let me check this out. I'll get back to you." Hanging up the agency man thought that the Limeys had bought into a bad Intel feed and were probably confused. The nuclear detection equipment and teams the U.S. had deployed around cities like Houston was top notch and nothing had caused them any concern. They were very careful to check inbound shipping around cities like Houston. Plus, the CIA's threat board was silent at the moment concerning ASF activities.

Jack hung up and prayed for guidance. Looking up at his team mates he said, "Yahveh says to keep working on it as a real threat. Alexis, will you call Sarah, David, and Carol? They're in the chapel praying right now. I hate to disrupt them but their skills may be needed."

Less than two minutes later the three walked into the War Room and took their seats. The information was on their screens and it didn't take any of them long to understand the situation. Carol started to pray again and suddenly the diamonds on her head and throat glowed white hot.

The others began contacting their sources to see what they could find out about the threat. They were getting conflicting information in some cases. It was Al Qaeda or a different splinter group of Arab terrorists other than the ASF. Each source thought that they had the right information. Mark commented, "This does look like demonic masking because everyone is so sure but they all have different information."

Carol spoke up suddenly. There was a sob in her voice and she was crying. "It's too late! It's too late! Yahveh wants us all to pray for his children." She put her head down on her arms and continued to sob.

The phone rang and Jack answered it. It was Gary Rhodes and he sounded thoroughly shaken. The FBI man said, "The British Intel was right, a nuclear weapon was just detonated at the waterfront in Houston. Major widespread death and destruction. I'm just getting the first flash but it looks to be a bigger bomb than a suitcase nuke, probably a ten megaton ship-borne bomb that has a Pakistani nuclear signature. How they slipped it in past the NRC detectors is a mystery. Stay in touch, I'll get back to you when I know more."

There was a stunned silence in the War Room. Laura told everyone, "You heard Carol, let's pray for the Father's children."

The news coverage began five minutes later. The newscasters were terribly shaken but tried to convey the horrific details as best as they could. Some of them had relatives and friends in the blast area. CNN's coverage was the most detailed. "The nuclear bomb, set off in Galveston Bay next to Seabrook, Texas has devastated the area and the city of Houston. According to government sources, NASA's facilities are completely gone and half of the tall buildings in Houston proper were knocked down by the blast. The damage and the death toll is total within a five mile distance of ground zero and the heat and blast effects have taken a tremendous toll farther out. The destruction is catastrophic west as far as Sugar Land and north as far as Humble. Completely obliterated besides the NASA facility are the following: Seabrook, League City, Baycliff, Friendswood, La Porte, and Texas City and its oil refineries. Heavily damaged are Galveston, Port Bolivar, and everything east to the Louisiana border. All shipping in the area has been sunk or damaged beyond use by the explosion or the tsunami created by the blast. The death toll will be in the hundreds of thousands, if not millions. As far as radiation contamination, it is unknown at this time."

For the team, first came the horror, and then the anguish. After that came the righteous anger at the people that would do such a thing. The death was already done but the justice needed attention.

Two hours later Sarah did an all-call on the communications link. "Folks, one of the African operations of the Mossad have just identified a fifteen hundred member group in Zyngola as the core group of people behind the bombing of Houston. They also identify the newly rebuilt AFS as the leading organization. And again, the Mossad lost agents to mysterious and probably supernatural attacks, which prevented them from relaying the information out of Zyngola. Like the British, they had the information two days ago but were prevented by this same force from even warning Israel about the impending attack. No form of communications, even satellite phones were working and any agent that tried to leave to personally warn the outside world was killed."

Jack commented, "Reminds me of Jacob's prayer and the answering angel being held up by the Prince of Persia, preventing the answer to his prayer, for a time."

CHAPTER THIRTY-ONE

Carol was still very somber after the emotional message she had received from the Father. She quietly called everyone's attention to the news channel on the television.

The Presidential Seal was displayed and the announcer was saying that the President was about to speak. President Bollen looked haggard and pale, but determined. He sat at his desk in the Oval Office and looked into the camera. "Ladies and Gentlemen of the United States. A second day of infamy has overtaken us and we have lost loved ones and friends to an enemy that doesn't care about our feelings or our lives. I have declared the entire area of southeastern Texas, surrounding the city of Houston a nuclear disaster area and have mobilized National Guard and U.S. Army troops to lend any and all help to the survivors of this attack on our country."

"More important than that, we need to return to our roots which area firm belief in God. This country was formed on Christian morals and principles and the ungodly have worked tirelessly to remove God from our lives. Houston is proof of the removal of Godly protection from our country. The day of lawyers and courts dismissing Christianity and God from our schools, our government, and our lives is over. Every form of "religion" is tolerated except to one that made us what we are. God has been pushed aside in the name of tolerance. Well, unless you want more attacks like the one on Houston, God is going to make a comeback in America!"

"After I conclude my comments we are going to have a prayer session for the dead, dying, and injured plus the families of those injured or lost in the attack on Houston. We are going to get down on our knees like we did during the poisoning two years ago and plead with Christ to give his love to those so evilly destroyed. If your attitude is that you prefer Allah, or Buddha, or some other God that is fine. In this country you are free to pray as you wish. But, in God's name, so am I and the rest of us. Christianity will not take a back seat to any other religion or group in this country again."

He got up and walked around his desk and sat on it. "Let me make one thing perfectly clear. We DID NOT bring this attack on ourselves regardless what some people will try to make you believe. We were attacked by an enemy that is implacable and non-negotiable concerning our freedom and our lives. This enemy will make treaties and contracts with you, knowing that you will honor the pact but they do not have to honor them because their form of government by "religion", says they don't have to honor an agreement with a person not of their religion. Don't misunderstand me. I am not declaring war on Islam. But I am declaring war on Islamic radicals that would do such as was done to Houston and the Islamic population that either promotes or allows people to do these things in the name of their religion."

The President was coldly furious. "Not more than ten months ago, I gave the Zultarian religion an ultimatum. I told them, "After the attempted mass bombings of the United States of America and England, the need to find a resolution to these types of attacks has become critical. The ultimatum the United States of America is issuing today is the same for the Islamic religion as it was for the Zultarian religion then. Since the last century the U.S. has always held to the concept of religious freedom. We have never pointed fingers at one religion or another. Until then and now. The group identified as plotting and executing the Houston bombing are Islamic extremists who make up a resurgent terror organization called the Arab Strike Force."

The President took a sip of water. "These people are denounced and rejected by the mass of Muslims. But, the fact remains that they espouse a twisted expectation of world domination through violence in the name of their religion. For the last fifty years these misguided and violent men, women, and yes, even children; have dealt death and injury in the name of Allah. They strike, and if they don't kill themselves, they melt into the general Muslim population and disappear."

The President took on a very serious look. "Enough is enough! It is time for the Islamic people to take a stand. Your population is not only the breeding ground for these terrorists, but it is also their fortress. I would say that the average Muslim is a peace-seeking, honest contributor to society. But many of you know who the terrorists are and protect them by not saying anything and even contribute to their cause and in some cases work with them. We, the free world, cannot attempt to root these violent people out of your population without a great deal of collateral damage to uninvolved Muslims. But, you can show the world where you stand by how you react to this request. Cleanse your faith of the unfaithful that are killing others in the name of Allah. Because, if you don't, we will. There are hundreds of thousands of Americans dead today because of these rabid terrorists. There is no excuse, regardless of previous wrongs or perceived wrongs for this attack. Today the world is changed by these vermin and no sane person will stand for any more "safe havens" for them."

The President pounded his fist on the desk. "I say that any American that declares that these vermin were right to attack us is not an American but a subversive that requires being added to the ranks of those who seek our deaths. Our first amendment to our Constitution grants freedom of speech to everyone. I am not declaring that null or void. What I am saying is that this country needs to wake up and see the truth. Each of us needs to support this country, not other countries, or relocate to your preferred country. If you want to run down the United States of America, you had better do it from a foreign soil. You're either for this great country or you're not. Make up your mind right now.""

President Bollen looked directly at the camera. "Homeland Security, the FBI, the CIA, the NSA, and others have been warning us about this eventuality for years, now it has happened. The administration has done everything within our power to prevent it. We have stopped over thirty-eight attempted nuclear attacks against our cities and civilians since 2001. Unfortunately, one facet in our country and in our government is determined to remove our protections and prevent our safety, in the name of fairness and equality to all, especially these terrorists."

The President looked like he had eaten something that didn't agree with his system. "The enemy has used that "waffling" on a strong and determined stance by America.

The destruction of Houston is the direct result of the actions of those who declare our country socially bankrupt but praise the enemy. No more! As a free society we have vulnerabilities that other, more closed countries do not. The vermin that just drove a dagger into America used that acceptance by some politicians and our vulnerability. Now they will celebrate. This is what I say to the appeasement group of liberal subversives in Congress and to the enemy. Because of their actions and this unthinkable horror perpetrated on America, I will also repeat a statement I made three years ago after the poisoning of millions of our people and the people in Israel. We, the United States of America will find out which group or groups did this horrendous act of cowardliness and we will arrest them, try them and, if found guilty, execute them. Any group, state, or nation that wants to protect or promote them, will be at a full state of war with this country. We will win and we will revenge our fallen countrymen. I swear this as my oath to America in front of God Almighty!" We will also determine which subversive actions within this country aided the enemy and we will prosecute those responsible!"

The camera shifted to the President's left side and he turned to address the country from that angle. "From this moment on, I am declaring America First, for those of us who live here and love this country. Those that don't support this effort should be seen as aiding and abetting the enemy and will be handled as such. This applies to all of us that govern this country, administrative, congressional, and judicial. I will appoint a commission today that will be made up of patriots from all three branches of government and both major parties, to root out the leaders and followers that have deliberately aided and abetted the enemy through their actions. This will not be a cabal or a witch-hunt. The investigations will be public and open and all dealings, including mine, will be investigated."

The President looked soberly into the camera. "If you are in public office, or were in public office, you can count on all your statements and arrangements being held up to the light and the public. No longer will we bow our knees to non-American people or policies. Oh, we will retain our honesty and our original view of fairness, but God save the people that enjoy our freedoms yet seek to destroy our country.

The President shook his head. "Don't be fooled by nay-Sayers in the Congress or other bodies. Their view will no longer be tolerated and the horror of the attack on Houston will never happen again. I am authorizing all branches of the military to ratchet our border protection up to RED Immediately! All foreign shipping is being turned back by the Coast Guard until they can be thoroughly inspected. If we had done this a week ago, everybody in Houston would be alive today. But as long as we have appeasers in the courts and in the electorate that label our country's good intentions as "Foul!" and "Not Fair", giving the enemy leeway to overcome us, we cannot stand. I personally hope that they are happy today. They demanded our rights be second to others and resisted the reasonable use of force to prevent this type of attack. No More!"

"The mushroom cloud over Texas leaves us no option but to become what we should have ten years ago. A country of people that respect God, loves our country, respects each other and one that takes defense of American from terrorism seriously. Cry dictatorship or foul all you want, we will not use our reasonable defense as a political football any longer. I expect everyone in the government and those running for office to join together to right this wrong and to make our country strong again."

"Good day."

Mark looked at Jack. "I think he just threw down the gauntlet for all parties and they will have to make a stand. Personally I don't think I would want to stand up anywhere in public right now and advocate restraint or appeasement."

Jack nodded."This is just the beginning. Remember, these are the end times and the lines are going to be drawn exactly as prophesied in the Bible."

CHAPTER THIRTY-TWO

Mark sat there in thought. "Sarah, what was the information you gave us before the President's speech?"

Sarah thought for a second. "There is a fifteen hundred member group in Zyngola who are the core group of people behind the bombing of Houston. The newly rebuilt AFS is the leading organization. There is also a demonic element in the killing of agents and the delaying of information."

Mark turned to Carol. "Carol, I know you're still upset by the last message you heard but we need you to seek Yahveh and the plans of this group as well as our direction. We will pray with you and support you."

Carol felt exhausted by the emotional drain of the last hour but she nodded her head. The rest of the team bowed their heads as Laura led the prayers. "Dear Heavenly Father, we give our grief and sorrow over the death of your children in Houston into your loving hands. We seek your peace and to do your will. We ask in humble servitude that you direct our path and lead us in your will so that we can walk before you in honor and love."

Jack glanced at Carol and the diamonds at her forehead and throat were glowing white. As they continued to pray and sing homage to the Creator of the Universe, Jack felt the familiar heaviness that he associated with the presence of the Father's Spirit among them. He felt, more than saw, the brightening of the room they were in. Opening his eyes he beheld Caleb floating above the War Room console. Jack said, "Hello Caleb."

The angel was in his warrior white and a fearsome sword was in his hand. The angel looked at Jack and did not smile. "Jack, the Most High has need of you and your team. He has assigned a cadre of angels to accompany your team to Zyngola to destroy this new ASF threat at its roots."

Mark asked, "Why didn't the Father send us there before they could kill so many?"

Caleb looked at Mark. "There are things that have happened and will happen soon that will seem wrong and that Yahveh could have stopped. These things must be allowed to happen because of the end of the era is here. Many, many more of His children will perish in the next short period as is foretold in His Word. If they are His they will not know the end. They will be with Yahshua and Yahveh in an instant of time. If not, they will die and face judgment. The time is upon us to make our stand!"

Laura asked Caleb, "If this is the end, why do we need to destroy the people in Zyngola?"

Caleb smiled for the first time. "This is one of the things you will need Carol to answer, as the answer is too large for you at present. Be of good cheer in Yahveh, Laura. He is true and faithful and will not send you into danger for no reason. It is imperative that we stop this group because it has violated the Lord's decrees. The leaders are directly controlled by Satan's demons and even though it seems inexplicable to you at this point, their actions will delay and interfere with the coming of the man of perdition. I don't have the words to explain why this is or why it has to be stopped to fulfill the prophets and history. But it does and Yahveh has chosen your group to find a way to stop them."

Caleb rotated and looked at each of them except Carol who was still in continual prayer with the diamonds glowing. "This will be an extreme test of both your spiritual capabilities and your fleshly combat skills because the enemy has invested heavily in the demonic protection of this group. Again, I can't tell you what to do and prayer will lead you on but not direct you this time. Yahveh cannot interfere with the earthly action and must depend on your faiths and abilities to achieve a victory over this group. And it must be a total victory. There are women involved and perhaps some children. It is still not clear, depending on how you arrange the assault and battle. Be assured that Rose and I and many more of the Heavenly host will be there with you but cannot interfere in your dimension. This time your training is over and we will follow your lead because the spiritual pressure against us is so great we cannot see what is to occur. Yahveh can but is bound by His own word and rules not to disclose what is to be, even to us.

Be strong and courageous and stand for the Lord and the Son. Be in prayer and seek the Lord's grace and protection."

Caleb turned to look at Carol who had stopped praying and was staring at him. "Carol, you have limited disclosure to the future. Be very careful not to interpret the multidimensional plans wrongly. It is designed to mislead one who is not diligent in studying and understanding the patterns. You do have answers but be very careful how you reveal them so as not to mislead the team."

Caleb held his sword up and said, "Until the battle." and faded from sight.

The room seemed darker without his glow. Laura sighed and looked to her husband and Mark. "The added obligation to lead the angels and the attack is serious and important. Let me know what I can do to help you guys."

Mark wanted to sigh a big sigh but Laura had just done that. "He asked Carol, "What do you see that you can tell us?"

Carol shook her head, "Everything and nothing. I need to pray about this and concentrate on it. Give me a couple of hours and I'll give you what I can be sure of by then."

Mark nodded and Carol got up and went to her room. Mark said, "Troops, let us get to work with what we have and what Intel we can get. Sarah, you and Alexis see what you can get from the CIA and NSA. David, see what your old firm can give you. They are the ones that identified the group involved at some expense in the lives of their agents. They should be willing to work with us to revenge their losses and to end this threat. Jack and I will work on the tactical end of things. We have to set our own timeline this time."

CHAPTER THIRTY-THREE

The team had been working for over an hour when Laura announced, "There is an Ultra Secure, Hi-Priority Flash Message coming in from General Miles."

Jack coded in his response code and the message was delivered. After decryption by Charlie's computers the message read: *"Crossfire Team, the President of the United States has tasked me to determine the originating group that was responsible for the nuclear weapon detonated today in Houston, Texas. All agencies reporting: We have isolated the origination of the weapon and the team that delivered the weapon to Zyngola, Africa. The President and the Congress concur that this base must be eliminated."*

In coordination with the British Secret Service (MI-5) and the Israeli Mossad we have concluded that only a small radical segment of the Tymerian based government and council were complaisant in the arrangements and the Mossad will attend to them. The problematic conclusion is that the base for the resurgent ASF operation that authored the plan and the team along with the bomb is tactically defended by a supernatural force that is undefeatable by current military strategy. Based on your team's history of combat within this realm, would you consider combating the supernatural force and neutralizing the base? The multinational security team estimates that they have at least five more weapons they plan to use on the U.S., Israeli, and our other allies. We cannot allow this to happen and will respond with a nuclear weapon ourselves if they are not neutralized within sixty hours. Since the base in question is only three miles from Tymeria, the entire city would be destroyed. Respond with your intentions ASAP. - Chmn, JCS.

Jack opened up an all-team conference on the communications net. "Ideas, problems, tactics, suggestions?"

Many of the team made suggestions and recommendations but in the end it was up to Jack to decide if they were to go or not. "All right. We each need to seek the Lord on this matter because there is a good chance we will not come out of Zyngola unscathed this time."

Each person went to where they could best pray and listen to Yahveh. Jack and Laura went to their room and settled into two lounge chairs next to each other and began to pray for wisdom and direction. After a while Jack got up and paced for a few minutes. Laura asked him what he was concerned about.

Jack smiled, "Actually, I am not concerned, as I am trying to understand the leading I got. It is odd. I feel Yahveh wants us to tackle the assault and "neutralization" of the base. But he isn't giving me any direction as to how or assurance that we will be successful. That is exactly what Caleb indicated we would face. How about you?"

Laura equivocated for a few minutes as she tried to determine what to tell her husband. She loved him more than anything except Yahveh and Yahshua and it pained her to realize that one or both of them most likely would not be coming home after this mission. She made her decision and said, "There is a good chance that my abilities will not be sufficient to combat the demonic forces at Zulnoth", which is the demonic name for the base in Zyngola. In that case I could be overwhelmed and destroyed by the demons there."

Jack shook his head. "Then you are not going, period!"

Laura laughed a small laugh that came out flat even to her. "Jack, Jack, we don't determine our fate. You know that. If I am to go then I will go and your love for me won't protect me by leaving me here. I will still be destroyed if that is what Yahveh has in store for me. No, I will go and I will fight the good fight and if I fail…" There was a short silence while Jack waited to hear what the one woman he loved in the world finished her statement. Laura looked up at him, "Then I get to pick out the curtains in our Heavenly home and you'll just have to like them!"

The sudden shift from super serious to humor caught Jack flat footed. Then he realized she had always been the one to realize the truth first. He just pulled her off the couch and encircled her in his arms as if he could keep her there forever.

She loved his closeness and realized what she could lose, but again, this wasn't her choice. It was Yahveh's choice and she would be a warrior for Him. She quietly said, "Remember, I am going to have babies who will be warriors for Yahshua?"

Jack held on to her, "Yes, but Rose never said "we" or indicated that it would be me that is the father of those children."

Laura thought about that. "You will be. They may be spiritual children, too."

The alert tone on their communicators rang and they headed back to the War Room.

Carol was sitting in the War Room when the team reconvened. After everyone got settled, Jack asked her what she had learned.

Carol sat there for a few seconds putting her comments in order. Then, looking at Jack she said, "There are many possible assumptions to each of the multidimensional concepts. I'm sorry, I know these are poor words to describe the activities of Heaven but they are the best that we have."

She took a sip of water and continued. "There are conceptual plans upon plans that are designed for effects with time added in later. Time is only a concept that was added to the human dimension for our benefit. See, we can only understand things in a linear manner although our minds do make intuitive leaps which are a shadow of the multidimensional thinking. Pertaining to our present quandary concerning the terrorists in Zyngola, there are three overlapping plans in motion as of this morning. First, the enemy has been given permission to hide the terrorist's operations from the entire world as long as they remain in that particular location in Zyngola."

Carol looked at Mark, "Second, the enemy is aware of our capabilities and has obtained permission to spy on us, probably including right now. They have been denied the right to attack us from the spiritual dimension unless we are attacking them first.

Carol then looked at David, "The third plan that I can be certain about is that they have requested permission to attack Israel next, like Houston. I believe they are going to do a similar attack in the next five days."

Carol glanced up and looked somewhat sheepish. "I'm sorry that I don't have any more to tell you right now.

Some things are too murky to my sight and others could be false plans that are there to mislead us."

Mark nodded, "That is helpful Carol, thank you for having the guts to go back into prayer so soon after your Houston revelation." He waved his hand around the table. "We all know that was hard for you."

Carol just smiled her thanks. Mark continued, "We don't have sufficient information about the base or the force of terrorists and we also don't have enough insight into the spiritual side. Still we have to move on this right now, any suggestions?"

Laura asked Carol, "Do we have the ability to counter this permission to spy on us?"

Carol nodded her head in response. "Yes, that is one of the variables allowed in the permission. But, I was restricted from telling you that unless you asked me first."

Laura said, "Let's pray for concealing of our plans and us from the enemy's sight."

CHAPTER THIRTY-FOUR

After the prayer for concealment, Mark said, "Alright, we have actually gotten a pretty good idea of the base and the number of terrorists. I wanted to wait until we wouldn't give away everything we know."

Carol spoke up. "Actually, I can now tell you about the spiritual side too. Please understand that I am bound by my knowledge to obey the rules and conditions of Heavenly conduct. When the enemy is aware of my new abilities, they include requests that I not reveal information I become aware of until the people involved, which is you, make certain choices and do certain things."

She looked around and saw understanding and love in the eyes of the team and she felt special and accepted.

Carol began to detail the spiritual forces involved. There are six major demons or strong men protecting the base. They each have been tasked with one aspect of coverage. One handles communications and observation. This is the one that kept Israeli agents from communicating the Houston attack. He works through deception, primarily. The agents thought that they had communicated the event two days before it happened. Problem was that they were communicating with this particular demon, named Proloth, a servant of Pyro, the demon of falsehoods and lies. This demon is aptly suited to deceiving agents."

She prayed quietly inside her mind for the Father to cleanse her spirit and not give any of these entities an open door into her life by talking about them.

Carol continued, "Secondly, there is Xloner, an agent of Vetis, the demon of corruption. His job is to interdict any opposing forces. He is the one that has killed the British and Israeli agents. This one you have to be ready for because he likes the "kill" part of his assignment.

Those are the two you will have to contend with in any attack. The other four are tasked with keeping the ASF forces in line and moving on the attacks against the west and the moderate Arab states. Two of them are involved in transportation of the weapons to keep them hidden from all sensors and detectors.

They are aware that the team has been assigned the attack on their base and they are prepared for it. Since they can no longer spy on us they can only guess what we are doing by our activities. I suggest a major misdirection to mislead them. You will get an advantage that way but will still have to contend with Xloner and Proloth when you get there."

Mark thought about the rouse concept. It reminded him of a mission he had when he was in the SEALs. The memory was important to the present mission and he attempted to remember all the details of a SEAL mission that occurred over four years earlier.

-----------------------******-----------------------

The sky had been blue and cloudless above the trees covering the government camp in the mountains of Argentina. Three ranking U.S. government officials had been kidnapped by terrorists and were demanding release of many other terrorists being held in U.S. jails. Because the governments were working together to recover the officials, Mark's SEAL team as well as three other SEAL teams were coordinating with the government troops at this camp.

One of the government troops caught Mark as he left the latrine and asked for a light for his cigarette. As Mark lit his cigarette the man softly spoke to the Navy SEAL leader. "Be careful, we lost many troops yesterday because someone on the command team is a terrorist plant and lets the terrorist know our plans. We don't know who it is but they have burned us twice. Please be warned."

The two men walked away in different directions and Mark realized that they needed to accomplish several different plans with the enemy watching their every move. He also noted that the man had not been able to identify the traitor in the group.

Mark called the leaders of the other three SEAL teams into a private conference and explained what he wanted to do. The other leaders agreed with his plan and would play along until the time to strike.

Mark walked into the office where the government officers were gathered and called them all to a map on the central table. Looking at all the interested faces he explained his plan. "Gentlemen, we know that the terrorists are watching us and will have time to warn their comrades before we attack. So, we are going to fool them. We will move two squads of your troops and two SEAL teams up to the obvious attack point, but they won't really attack. The other two SEAL teams and the rest of your troops will move around to the east side of the compound. While the terrorists are focused on the troops at the front side and organize themselves to defend the camp, the real attack will come from the east and catch them unaware."

The officers thought that it would work and it had the added benefit of leaving the troops at the front to reinforce the east troops as the terrorist turned to the attack on the east.

They set the feint up for 0200 hours with the troops told that they weren't going to actually charge the camp but be ready to reinforce the actual attack group. The actual attack group had the heavy weapons and the two tanks backing them up. They would give the feint twenty minutes to draw all the terrorists to the front of the camp to defend it and then they would smash their way in, catching the terrorists off balance and unprepared for the hidden force.

At 0145 hours local time, the South American jungle was only mildly noisy with the sounds of nocturnal animals hunting and being hunted. There was a slight breeze from the south that carried the fetid smells of the dead vegetation and rotting wood. The area of the camp was fairly quiet and dark.

Mark passed the word to the "feint" team to lock and load. They moved up toward the front of the camp and immediately ran into defensive fire from at least eight points. The SEAL team snipers went to work and the defensive fire fell off rapidly. Then Mark gave the signal and the entire force charged the camp as the prepared charges blew sections out of the fencing. The government forces raced forward with the SEALs and infiltrated the camp quickly. The terrorists had been prepared to repel the "supposed" main attack from the east and couldn't bring themselves into a good defensive alignment in time to repel the frontal attack that was quickly enfilading their positions. Just as they turned to fight back, the second front attacked from the east and caught the terrorists in a pincher movement, which quickly eliminated the terrorist's troops.

Mark took one of the SEAL teams and split off from the assault and headed toward the cabin holding the hostages. They arrived before the terrorists knew that the camp had been overrun. In a one-sided firefight the terrorists to a man, died quickly.

Two of the SEALs with medical training found the three Americans hidden in a closet and released them from their bindings. Checking them over and finding no serious injuries they rapidly dressed them in bullet-proof vests, helmets, and fatigues.

The camp was quickly reduced to a hunt for any remaining terrorists and any Intel the troops could find. Three of the injured but surviving terrorists were being interrogated by the government troops. Their technique was crude and probably less than legal, but got results. They had the name of the traitor back at camp and they had the proof which was a message from him on the cell phone they got from the body of the leader of the terrorists. He had warned them of the feint and the real attack which was exactly what Mark had wanted him to report.

There were three serious injuries to the SEALs who were quickly airlifted offshore to an American carrier and medical aid. There was a handful of fatalities for the government troops whose body armor was not as effective as that of the SEALs.

-------------------------*****-------------------------

Mark turned that event over in his mind as he considered how to attack the ASF camp. To the positive, they didn't have any hostages to worry about. On the negative side, the demons wouldn't be so easy to fool with a reverse fake attack. He decided to pray about the ideas that he was entertaining.

CHAPTER THIRTY-FIVE

Mark called a meeting of the core members of the Crossfire Team. He had a whiteboard set up in his offices and sat the others around the board and started illustrating his ideas.

Using a black marker he outlined the base and the probable locations of the troops and the remaining nuclear weapons. Then he took a red marker and started detailing the attack. "This is the dual heart of our attack, right here and here." He indicated both, a large building toward the back of the base from the front gate, and the bunker with the weapons.

"This building doesn't house troops but is crucial to our attack because the enemy will be completely surprised when we launch our attack from it and the weapons bunker."

He took a blue marker and indicated arrows leading out from the building and the weapons bunker, toward the other three main buildings. "These will be the attack lanes and we will be on them before they have a chance to regroup! The officers and leaders of the AFS are based in these three buildings and we want to try to find any Intel we can get."

David cocked his head and asked, "How about the rapid reaction groups they have on the base to respond to any attack not from the outside? They have 1500 members on that base and we are only six."

Mark shook his head, "Not important."

Sarah looked at her husband as if he had lost his mind. "Okay, how do we get into the building and the bunker in the first place? And, how do we stop them from detonating one or more of the weapons? And, what about the remainder of those 1500 personnel?" She was obviously agitated. "These things are important!" Her anger and irritation were quite evident.

Mark showed his wife the grin he saved for his triumphant occasions. "Okay, let me spell this out. First, we are going to drop into the building and the bunker in a new version of the HALO drop I call the HANO drop. I'll explain that in a minute. In answer to your second question of weapon detonation, they won't have time to prep and detonate any of their weapons before you and I eliminate the entire force of the enemy in the bunker. And, number three; we will kill all the rest of the personnel simultaneously with our arrival."

Laura asked, "What about the satanic Strong Men?"

Mark shrugged. "Okay, we have some fine points to work out there but we should be ready to go by tomorrow."

Jack laughed. "Okay buddy. Great words, now explain it in terms we can all understand."

Alexis put in her concern. "If it is only the six of us, how do we handle the Zyngolan Army who is probably somewhat complaisant in this endeavor?"

Mark sat back with that same grin. "True, there will only be the six of us going in and coming out. All of these concerns were good questions that were obviously considered by the powers behind the ASF. And I mean the "powers" behind them, both human and otherwise. I looked at this situation every way I could and could not come up with a solution that had a chance of victory. Then I realized the flaw in their reasoning. They only considered all the possibilities of current technology and planning."

A light lit up in Jack's eyes, "The Generators?"

Mark nodded, "Partially."

Alexis and David asked at the same time, "What Generators?"

Jack waved his hand to Mark so that he could handle that one. Mark stood up and said, "I'll be right back." He walked out of his offices and headed for the vault that the crucifixion nail was kept in. Alexis and David looked at each other and wondered. David sat back and checked the sharp creases in his trousers. Mark walked back into the office carrying one of the Force Generators. He asked everyone to come with him to the firing range located on the next level down.

After the six of them were there, Mark lifted the hinged surface and walked out into the firing range about twenty feet and strapped the Generator on and activated it. Checking the green light he nodded to Jack who had stopped to get an M8 from the armory.

Jack indicated that the others needed to put on their ear and eye protection. After they were set he put his on and turned to his friend on the range and emptied the full sixty rounds of SOCOR 6.8 MM. rounds directly into Mark. The muzzle flare and the hammering of the full auto discharge were disconcerting even to the seasoned warriors. There was little smoke from the new rounds and Mark was still standing there smiling at them.

He walked back to the range counter and opened the counter again. He walked out and took off the Generator. Seeing the looks of incredulity on the faces before him he explained. "Last year Jack commissioned a scientist named Clashire to develop this device. Jack had gotten the plans from Yahveh but couldn't understand the science involved. Clashire could and was able to make these items which we call "shield Generators". Jack and I watched as explosions, bullets, knives and other weapons were used on a girl wearing a Generator and then tried them along with Dr. Clashire with no damage. I'm talking about five "pounds" of C4 being detonated within inches of us! Later, Jack and I used them in a trap that the OC set up for us. Again, with no damage to us."

Alexis said, "That would change the entire world of warfare. There would be no one that wouldn't want one and would kill all of us to get them."

Mark shook his head, "No, they won't. Only a very small segment of humanity can use the Generators. Why don't each of you try it on and activate it, one at a time?"

Each person did and was rewarded with a green light. Mark called up to Charlie to bring one of his programmer wizards to the firing range. When they arrived Mark had the programmer try on the belt and Generator and switch it on. The light came on red and didn't change. Charlie asked to try it. He did and the light changed to green. Mark retrieved the Generator and thanked them so they could go back to the ComSec floor wondering what that was all about.

Mark pointed at the Generator. "Unless you are a servant of Yahshua and have Yahveh's Spirit living in you, the Generator is useless. The green light means that you are protected by the shield generated by what we now call a "Force Generator". Now, let's go back upstairs and I'll explain my plan.

On the way back to the War Room David commented to Alexis, "If you live your life for the Savior you could only use these Generators for defense because Yahveh's will is love, not violence for personal gain."

Reseated, they watched as Mark detailed his attack plan. "First we time out our fall time in a HANO drop. That means, High Altitude, No Opening. We are going to drop at full terminal velocity directly into the large building and the bunker. You four will hit the four-story, main operations building and Sarah and I will hit the nuke bunker. As we fall we will have eighteen, three hundred pound, solid steel needles that have been dropped from near space, pacing us. The combined energy of those needles will be somewhere in the equivalent of two tons of C4 when they hit all the buildings except the two buildings we will hit and the three that we want to comb for Intel. The USAF has been developing these passive energy weapons for the last nine years and I have seen the effects on ground targets when they hit. No explosives, just sheer kinetic energy that is off the scale. There won't be any troops to bother us as the needles will produce enough shock waves to also kill anyone in the open within a hundred yards of a strike."

David shook his head. "Amazing, just like those Generators. How does the Air Force direct the needles for precise hits? They've got to make midcourse corrections for wind, don't they?"

Jack shook his head, "No. The computers that release the needles in near orbit altitudes take everything into consideration including any significant winds at every altitude. Once they reach their terminal velocity the winds have only a very slight affect on them. I saw the tests of the latest versions used in Iraq. The news said that they were bombs. I saw a six story Insurgent-infested building reduced to granular rubble, spread out over three blocks in less time than you could say, "Boom"!

Sarah looked at the small Generator. "Okay, Mark. Are you sure the Generators will keep us from harm on the way down or when we hit the buildings? And, if these things can prevent any damage to us, how do we fight from them?"

Mark pointed to a small switch on the side of the Generator. "Push that and you can fire out without interfering with the shield. It is then synched to your rifle and stops for enough time to let the round leave its sphere of influence. Of course, I wouldn't attempt to do that during an explosion or when you're taking a high volume of incoming fire."

Alexis' quick mind was racing with the possibilities of the Generators. "Aren't we going to be similar to the needles as energy weapons on the buildings we hit?"

Mark nodded, "Yes, but with a significant difference. Our dimensional mass will be dissipated over more of everything we hit. It shouldn't be as bad as the needles. Of course it's never been done and I really don't know what will happen. The concern is the bunker and possibly detonating one of the nuclear weapons. I called Dr. Clashire and his take on the subject is that the shield spheres will dissipate the effects enough that we should be halted by the time we breach the first three floors of the big building and due to the heavier construction of the bunker, only its outer layers. It is a chance we need to take if we are to stop them before they head for Israel."

Laura looked at her husband with a concerned face. "Honey, will those Generators stop attacks by the demons? How do I fight out of one?"

Jack looked at Mark. Mark said, "Honestly, I don't know. I think we need to ask Yahveh those questions.

Laura nodded. She bowed her head and started praying her heart to the Creator of the Universe.

CHAPTER THIRTY-SIX

The rest of the team realized the burden for spiritual battle that their technologically-advanced attack would leave on Laura and joined her in her prayer. This became an extremely earnest prayer by honest people that loved Laura and would die with her before they would leave her to face the enemy alone.

Jack and Laura felt the heaviness of the Spirit of the Father as they worshipped and prayed their hearts. With the suddenness of a thunderclap they felt displaced and looked up. The glare from the brightness of the energy released by the being in front of them and the pureness of His Esteem, which made them feel like ugly rags drove them both to their knees with their faces to the ground. The feeling of complete power went so far off the scale they couldn't even compare it to anything they had ever known in their lives. Both of them felt the words being spoke more than they heard them with their ears.

"Do not be afraid or discouraged because of this strong army. For the battle is not yours, but ours! Tomorrow, march against the strong men in Zyngola. You will have to fight to win this battle. Take up your positions; and stand firm and see the deliverance I will give you. O My children do not be afraid; do not be discouraged. Go out and face them tomorrow, and I will be with you. Laura, My child, I love you and your anointing will overcome the demonic Strong Men arrayed against you. Battle like the consuming fire I have made you. Leave none of the enemy standing, none! My messengers will be there to aid you, but you will be My message to the enemy. No more will they assume they are all powerful but they will know I AM Elohim! Go in my love and mercy as an all-consuming fire of Heaven!"

Suddenly they were back with the rest of the team. David started and frowned somewhat. Jack tried to reorder his senses to the normal world as he looked at David. "What?"

David looked intently at the two of them. "Your faces are shining like the sun. There is great power radiating from you both. You look as if you had seen Yahveh himself."

Laura quietly said, "We did."

Jack took a huge breath and said, "We're ready."

Sarah had big eyes and rapidly shook her head, "Not good enough. We need more words, tell us all that happened?"

After Jack and Laura told what happened the entire team was filled with boldness and confidence that they could defeat the enemy. Laura thanked everyone for praying for her and supporting her.

Mark started detailing the steps each person would take after they "dropped in" on the ASF base. On the second repeat of the arrangements there was a knock on the door and Carol walked into the office. She looked happier than she had since the knowledge about Houston had been laid out for her. To see with no uncertainty, in the Heavens the death and disaster that was unstoppable had been like a searing flame to her spirit. Still, her grit and determination would not let her stop praying and worshiping a Father she knew was loving and compassionate.

Her time in prayer with Yahshua had led her to understand the necessity of the event regardless of the pain and suffering. She realized that she could have been in Houston when the bomb had gone off and she would have been with Yahveh now. Her heart echoed the Father's at the loss of those who would not turn to Him through His Son. But time in prayer had given her the perspective that Yahveh wanted her to have. She still felt horrified by the bombing and the effects but now saw that it was a part of the end time's history that was being played out across the world.

She started to apologize for interrupting their deliberations but Laura just smiled at her and waved her into the room. "What do you have, Carol?"

Carol looked around at these wonderful, deadly people that she had begun to think of as her family. She was moved by their humanity and their constant ability and obedience as Yahveh's warriors. "I just wanted to tell you that the plans in the Heavens have changed somewhat. The original reason you brought me up here, the Geopower facility in Hawaii, has disappeared from the enemy's plans. The defense of the base in Zyngola is now the major effort. Strangely, there is a feeling of defeat in the picture. It isn't frantic, just a slight resignation to a possible defeat. I don't think the enemy knows what you're going to do but your flame is starting to burn more brightly than that of the enemy in that area. I think that is what the resignation is about."

Laura had been praying while Carol had been talking and she confirmed the younger woman's feelings. "Yahveh has spoken and they know it. They don't know what He has said, but they know it's probably not good for them." She got up from her seat and walked over and put her arm around Carol's shoulders. "Would you go up and talk to Charlie on the fifth floor? Just use your key in the elevator and select "COMSEC". I think you two could collaborate on the planning and monitoring during this attack and our exit from Zyngola. Trust Charlie and his wife, Linda. They are crucial to the team's operations and well-being. I think you'll find you three have a lot in common."

Carol hadn't been told about anything on the fifth floor and was intrigued by the reference of her compatibility with the Oriental couple that she had only met once so far. She hugged each and every one of the assault team. She smiled at them and told them, "I know that I know that I will see all of you when you get back."

Mark got a message and left the room for a few minutes to return with four additional shield Generators. "Let's all go to the firing range and try these out so that your faith in Clashire's technology is increased before you step out of an aircraft at forty-plus thousand feet without a parachute."

That got everyone's attention.

As they walked to the range, Sarah asked Mark, "If you've only tried these in one battle, how do you know they will work to shield us as we fall into buildings? And how far will we go through the building?"

Mark shook his head, "I really don't know how it will work. I was just given the idea and ran with it. As far as my not being worried about it, I prayed and asked Yahveh to block it if it wasn't a good idea and tell me if it was. I got a definite leading to continue with the idea." He looked at his wife, "Think about it. The function of the Generator is to prevent a sudden increase in energy from damaging the wearer. Hitting a building traveling 183.3 feet per second will release a great deal of energy which the shield will absorb and redirect, or whatever it is that it does with the energy. I doubt that we will feel anything from the impact."

Sarah nodded and said, "True, but what about the rest of the fall, like the sub-zero temperatures, wind blast, and lack of vision?"

Mark smiled, "We'll dress for the wind and cold like always and use our oxygen and night vision goggles. My gut says it will work."

Sarah sighed, "If it doesn't then all of our guts will be all over the place." She implicitly knew that Mark was always careful and accurate and she was confident that the Generators would protect them. It was just the unknowns that pestered her mind. Everything about this assault seemed to be fairly unknown.

CHAPTER THIRTY-SEVEN

Fourteen hours later the six warriors stood at the exit ramp to a U.S. Air Force C5A Starlifter flying at 43,000 feet above Zyngola. Each one had their full jump gear on including their oxygen for the altitude. Everybody checked the other people's gear, checked their ForceGenerators, and mentally prayed for Yahveh's protection.

Laura thought back about their discussions on how to combat the Strong Men the enemy had in place and knew that Yahveh would guide her into the battle as He wanted it to play out. She just had to have the nerve to do His will. She took a deep breath and steeled herself to the upcoming battle.

The red ready light came on and they mentally prepared to step out into the black void without parachutes. The green light flashed on and all six members jumped out of the aircraft at the same time.

To Jack the jump was almost exactly the same as the last several HALO jumps he had made. His mind knew he was falling at 125 miles per hour straight down but it seemed that he was simply floating in blackness as he breathed oxygen and watched his altimeter on his left wrist. The wind raced by his body and he worked to stay level with the small lights he saw on Mark's suit. He couldn't see the others and they maintained tight radio communications silence so that they didn't warn the enemy on the ground of their arrival. Jack knew that the deadly space needles were close around them and he made an extra effort to keep himself tightly arranged with the formation of warriors so that his entry would be far enough away from the needle's impact points.

Watching for the dispersal signal from Mark, Jack prepared himself for where he would take over as the leader of the four story building group while Mark and Sarah moved away to align themselves with the bomb bunker. The flash of blue light indicated the shift and Jack pushed the switch on his left wrist that turned on his "flight lights" so that the other three in his group could close in on his position. He checked the GPS positioning and tipped his body to the left to line up on the top of the four story building they were aiming at in the compound below.

They had been falling for almost four minutes and only had ninety seconds left before impact. Jack reached back and switched on the Force Generator and was rewarded by a green light. He didn't notice much difference in the fall but knew that the wind wasn't enough energy to cause the Generator to modify his protection.

With just forty seconds left before impact, details started to become visible on the ground. There were lights and glows that quickly organized themselves into a pattern. Jack's mind did the interpretation and the pattern of lights resolved itself into small buildings and vehicles that were rushing up at him at a frightening speed. Jack's prayer for the protection of the others as well as himself was not only urgent but heartfelt.

With nothing to slow them down they were about to slam into the target building at a little over 183 feet per second which equaled 125 miles per hour. The building seemed to suddenly grow large as the last seconds ticked off. They each had a target "impact" zone in one quadrant of the building roof. Jack's was the northern quadrant and he side slipped to line up the point of impact and rotated his body so that he would hit feet first. He checked the others and noticed that David was too far to the left. Before he could say anything the clock clicked to zero.

The actual impact happened so fast it was over before he realized it was started. As the Generator field touched the building the energy from the impact powered the unit in increasing strength and all Jack saw was a blur as the roof exploded downward and away and the next three floors disassembled away from his path. He saw people, both men and women being blasted away from his descent and slammed back by one of the other impacts.

Jack found himself standing on a pile of rubble on the ground floor and looking out at the falling debris around him as the building disintegrated completely. There was nothing left of the structure or the crew that was manning the operations building. Jack saw, more than felt, the impacts of the others and the space needles by the redirection of debris in waves from each of the other impacts.

When the last particles had stopped hitting the ForceGenerator field, the field essentially released Jack to walk on his own. Jack climbed down off of the smashed debris below him and joined up with the others. David came running around from the far side of the rubble. David called Jack to tell him that he missed the building altogether. It didn't matter because the building was totaled by three of them, anyway. The only problem was that David had to climb out of the twenty-foot deep hole his fall had created without a building to cushion it.

The Crossfire warriors headed toward the three buildings not targeted by falling bodies. The three buildings were damaged but still standing. There were no lights showing and the warriors quickly activated their night vision goggles.

Laura was still in prayer and seeking Yahveh as to the position of the Strong Men. They would not have been bothered by the physical assault and would be seeking the cause of it.

As the warriors aligned themselves into a squad formation and headed toward the closest target building David glanced behind him at the remains of the building the other three had hit. It still didn't seem real to his older mind. He hadn't grown up playing the realistic video games that the others had. His eyes saw what was left of the building and his ears told him about the destruction that was still continuing with remaining walls falling and water being blown away from broken pipes. It seemed like a dream rather than reality. Suddenly, a large propane tank exploded and the flame front rushed at them in the blink of an eye.

David watched as everything around the four of them was incinerated by the flames, but the four warriors kept moving around debris and broken objects secure in their Generator fields. The flame quickly ran out of fuel and faded away leaving every combustible thing on fire.

As the four warriors approached the first building they could see movement inside. Four or five weapons, rifles and handguns started firing at them and the Generators stopped the bullets and sucked the energy out of them so that they fell to the ground.

Jack and Alexis returned the fire and the Generators worked flawlessly in allowing them to fire out by flickering off and back on. The people shooting at them fell back and stopped shooting.

Laura was praying and noticed that her prayer was deepening and being echoed in her spirit. A large demon came around the corner of the building with anger burning in his eyes and a large black sword held high.

David fired at the demon with no effect because it had permission to exist in the human dimension in this place.

Laura felt her body tremble at the sight of the large and powerful demonic spirit that exuded evil and destructive powers. But her spirit was not going to give into the fear. She made her choice to do what Yahveh had told her to do, regardless of the seeming odds against her. She felt the power the Father was pouring into her growing at an exponential rate that shook her mind as to the energy involved.

CHAPTER THIRTY-EIGHT

Xloner stared with hatred at the four humans facing him. They did not tremble with fear. He realized that the base and its large staff of humans were no longer usable and no doubt these "humans" here were involved in, if not responsible for, the destruction of his project. He would make them pay for their insolence in attacking him.

It also quickly became obvious, to him that the one closest to him was challenging him. It made him laugh when he discerned that it was a female! Even so, he felt the waves of spiritual power emanating from her. She was strong in power and she knew that it would be a battle to the death. "Good!" He thought, "I will take her first".

He raised his sword to high guard and rushed at the woman, shaking the ground with all the power and weight he normally exhibited. A warning came to him as he neared her. Usually, the humans quailed at this point. He noticed that the woman not only didn't seem afraid but actually was moving toward him. That was troubling in a basic way. He wasn't stupid and he stopped suddenly while he was still two lengths away from her. He expected a trap and was sampling the spiritual arena around him. He recognized the angel warriors of their God but they were holding back and therefore were not the danger.

The other three humans were not advancing on him but watching the action. Logically, that only left the woman as the problem. He felt her power but it wasn't really that much compared to his power. So, he decided that he would end her existence quickly. NOW!

As he closed with her he saw the transformation from normal human to armored and armed warrior of the Most High as Laura's armor and the sword of faith exploded into visibility. The power rolling off the sword was enough to make Xloner weak. But it paled compared to the power radiated by the woman herself. He recognized Yahveh's hand in this trap and knew he was facing a directed agent of Yahveh. He could sense his fellow demons fleeing and knew his time on this earth was over. He tried to swing his sword but it seemed to be mired in mud it moved so slowly. He brought it forward only to see it cut cleanly in two by the pure power of the woman's blade.

Before he could move back, the flaming sword flashed in a reverse cut and Xloner felt fear for the first time as it ripped through his chest and cleaved his spine. All the humans, demons, and angels he had destroyed seemed to be standing around him applauding his death. He wanted to scream but it only came out as a whimper. The great demon of death that had ruled and destroyed as he wished, died and found himself bound to the walls of the pit awaiting judgment. It had happened so quickly it was over before he knew it. He hung his head in defeat knowing his master would laugh at his failure.

As Xloner's body turned to an ugly red-black smoke that was lost in the darkness of the ruined camp, Laura felt the power with which Yahveh had foretold He would anoint her. It was pure righteous anger at the enemies of the true Elohim. It didn't give Laura a personal feeling of power but it gave her courage to destroy those that stood against the Most High.

Laura raised her sword and called out the other Strong Man. Her voice seemed to fill the silence of the shattered base and echoed throughout the spiritual world in that place. "PROLOTH! SHOW YOURSELF! Yahveh CALLS YOU TO ACCOUNT IN THIS PLACE!"

Laura felt the power of Yahveh and slammed her sword into the ground with such force that it shook the earth. The other three Crossfire warriors staggered to maintain their feet. The front wall of the middle building couldn't take this additional abuse and fell in ruin, taking the rest of the floors with it.

Yahveh gave voice through Laura and had her call on His warriors to find the enemy and bring them forth to do battle! He did this using two words which have no meaning on the human plane. The words seemed to gather strength and radiated out from Laura's position like ripples on a pond, except that they got stronger the farther they moved.

In the aftermath of the pronouncement of the two words, silence fell. As Laura waited alert for attack, there was a fluttering of gold and white that resolved itself into the angel Rose.

Rose's eyes grew large and she moved back in awe of the Lord's power flowing out of Laura. She grinned at her human friend and resisted an urge to bow to her. "They have all fled from you Laura. Your challenge was as strong as a sun in their dark universe. You have literally put the fear of Elohim into the rank and file of the demons here. Proloth was the first one to go with his tail between his legs. This stampeded the rest of the demons. I daresay that your destruction of Xloner and the rout of the other demons will resound throughout their dark world. I give you a word of caution. This elevation of yours will undoubtedly bring you to the attention of Satan himself. Stay alert and on-guard in the spirit at all times. I will be there to assist you. I am so blessed by your bravery and courage and am pleased you stood the test. I must go, farewell for now."

Rose whirled into a swirl of fierce white and gold and faded from view.

Laura, kneeling next to the sword, prayed her thankfulness to the true Power of the Universe. Jack would always recall the image of the golden warrior that had just destroyed a major demon kneeling in supplication. "Father, I humbly thank You from the bottom of my heart for this service You have granted me and Your power you invested in my hands even as my human soul shook in dread. Please protect us from attacks of the enemy and cover us with Your eternal love. I love You and pray all things in the Name of Your Son, Yahshua."

As Laura finished her prayer her armor and the sword faded from sight and she felt the power ebb away until she felt normal. She stood to her feet smelling the death and destruction of the base. She checked her Force Generator for a green light and put on her night vision goggles. Unslinging her M8 she turned to join her husband and friends in seeking the leaders of the attack against America.

Jack put out his arm to stop her progress and stared at her face with a mixture of love and deep respect. "You were so awesome in battle. I can't even begin to tell you how glad I am that you are on our side." He lifted her goggles and looked closely at her. He saw the gold flecks in his wife's eyes again. This time he was comfortable with it. He leaned in and kissed her on the lips. Laura hugged him to her as best she could with all the equipment they had strapped onto themselves.

She looked up and smiled. "I liked that." She pulled away from him, "But, I think we need to get back to the matter at hand before David tells us to get a room."

Jack laughed and they both put their goggles back on. Together they turned to approach the looming building ahead.

David and Alexis went to the back of the building and they synchronized their entry to put the most pressure on the inhabitants. Laura was surprised by how little the total destruction of the rest of the base had affected the interior of the building. There were things knocked over and some glass breakage but it was minimal.

The building was obviously a living quarters and had heavy drapes over the windows. These must have caught most of the shattered glass and prevented it from trashing the rooms.

As she and Jack combed the front rooms she talked on a hush microphone to Alexis and David who were doing the same thing from the back. None of them had seen any sign of life. But there had been people shooting at them from the building so they had to be here somewhere.

Jack followed a trail of papers down a flight of stairs and to a wall. The trail ended there but there was a piece of paper stuck under the wall. He used his Streamlight NightFighter flashlight to examine the wall for a way to open it. Failing that, he spoke into his combat microphone. "Fire in the hole!" and used the 40mm grenade launcher.

The grenade struck the door in the middle and blew it apart. That blast was followed by a flurry of rifle fire and a sudden detonation. The blast tore through the tunnel and body parts and debris were blown out through the hole where the door had been. Jack advanced on the tunnel and checked through it. None of the officers or directors and their aides had survived their own blast. They probably didn't understand the weapons and managed to blow themselves up trying to set a booby-trap for the attackers.

Jack keyed his comm channel to the one for group call. "Mark, Sarah, we have found a tunnel that runs toward the bunker. There were some ASF personnel trying to flee through it. They were killed in an explosion but I don't know if any are still in the tunnel headed your way. We will sweep it toward your end. We should be there in a few minutes."

CHAPTER THIRTY-NINE

As the Crossfire Team had fallen from the aircraft, Sarah had been praying that the Father would protect all of them as they fell from the heights toward their targets. She remembered that Mark had side slipped away from the others to align himself on the weapon's bunker. Sarah had matched his moves and was about ten feet from him as they reached the roof of the bunker, traveling feet first at almost two hundred feet per second. She recalled that the roof had seemed to jump up at her for the last hundred feet. She reveled in the functioning of the Force Generator as the reinforced roof of the bunker had collapsed downward and away from her.

She came to a halt about three feet into the concrete flooring of the weapons bunker in a large assembly area. The lighting failed and she flipped her night vision goggles down over her eyes. The interior of the lab was a shambles from her entrance but she looked in vain for Mark. She keyed her combat microphone as she slung her M8 around and went looking for targets. Sarah's combat training in the Israeli Defense Force and the advanced training in the Mossad took over and let her move quickly throughout the bunker looking for the enemy.

Mark responded to her call and said he'd be there in two minutes. She continued to search the property and came to a heavy door that was marked with a radiation symbol and secured by a wheel-activated lug system. She spun the wheel and pulled the door open to find Mark standing there. He smiled and pointed upward. She looked up and saw the sky and the huge hole he'd made as his entrance.

Mark moved over to the four assemblies lying on work benches and examined them. "These are the nuclear weapons, but we're missing one."

Sarah looked around, "That's right, there were six bombs sold to the ASF according to the Mossad's Intel. One went to Houston and four are here. That means the other one is probably on its way to Israel right now."

Sarah watched as Mark snap aimed his M8 over her head and triggered a three round burst that avoided her shield's field and she heard a scream that choked off. She rotated and saw a man with a rifle falling to the floor with his chest riddled. There were more of them behind him and she added her weapon's firepower to that of Mark's.

The incoming fire was stopped by the Force Generator shields and the outgoing fire was devastating fatal to anyone who showed their face. The one-sided battle lasted only a minute and the enemy was either dead or had retreated.

Sarah looked at Mark and quickly moved to the vault-like door and scanned for other attackers. While she was there the door started to swing shut as one or two of the ASF troops tried to trap them in the vault.

Thinking quickly Sarah stepped into the way of the closing door and the frame. The door tried to crush her but the Force Generator used the pressure against itself and held it open. Sarah held out her M8 in both hands, aimed around the door and fired off three, three-round blasts. The door swung open to reveal three bodies on the floor. There was more movement in the dark behind some cabinets and Sarah ducked as Mark threw a fragmentation grenade into the area. The blast ended the movements.

Sarah grabbed one of the corpses and jammed it into the frame so that the door couldn't be closed without exposing the enemy to their gunfire.

At that point they got a call from Jack warning about possible people in a tunnel heading their way. Dousing their lights they waited until light became visible as a door opened in one wall.

Mark slid out of the darkened vault and to one side. Sarah went the other way and hid behind a large machine. Jack and the others came into the bunker and Mark said, "Welcome to the bomb factory".

After they swept the entire bomb bunker for remaining enemies they met by the four remaining nuclear weapons. Jack sighed, "I know the Father said to destroy everyone, but I wish we'd had one to question about the missing bomb.

David held out a sheath of papers, "We don't have to question anyone. They laid it all out in some of the documents we found in the first building. The timetable for the bomb delivery by submarine of the second bomb and their target, Israel."

Sarah shook her head, "Don't these vile characters ever learn that Israel isn't just sitting there expecting the normal types of attacks?"

David shrugged, "I hope they never learn. It makes the job easier for the IDF and the Mossad. I suggest we call them and let them handle this attack. With the demons gone it should be fairly easy for the IDF to locate and eliminate the submarine before it gets close to Israel."

Mark looked at Jack and Laura with a question on his face. Both of them nodded their assent and Mark told David, "Do it."

David used the encrypted ciphers to alert the Israeli forces of the impending nuclear attack and the information they had gleaned from the paperwork. David got a clear air message back that it would be handled and that operation "Drive-in" was underway with an ETA of eight minutes.

CHAPTER FORTY

Mark ran back into the vault and climbed onto several workbenches and attached shaped charges to the roof in a predetermined pattern that Charlie had worked out as soon as he got the pictures of the vault and the damage done by Mark's entrance. Mark set all the charges to a single remote control button and left the vault. Meanwhile, the others had moved back to the other side of the assembly room.

Mark joined them and without discussion triggered the remote. There was a massive explosion that blew debris and dust out of the vault. Mark ran back and waved in the others.

When they entered the vault it was obvious that Charlie knew his explosives. There was no roof over the vault anymore and surprisingly little debris. The shaped charges had blown the roof structure up and away from the vault. Everyone else got busy attaching the lightweight lift cables David had packed in, on the remaining four inert bombs.

David got a call and he took three of the Streamlights and set them shining up out of the hole where the roof had been. There was a disturbance and then the sky was blotted out by a black Osprey in hover mode.

A heavy cable snaked down into the room and Mark hooked it to the loops on all four bombs. At a word from David the entire set of bombs were cleanly lifted up and out of the hole. A minute later the VTOL moved away from the hole and another one took its place. A cargo net fell into the room. David gathered in the Streamlights and stowed them in his pack.

The six members of the team then grabbed onto the outside of the net and gave the word to the aircraft which lifted them out of the building into the air. While they were being winched into the open back hatch of the aircraft they started taking rifle fire from the ground. David pointed a laser pointer at the major source of the fire, which was the third building that hadn't been knocked down, and called for air support. Out of the night two F-35 fighter bombers flashed behind them and the explosions of the four 1,000-pound GBU-32 Joint Direct Attack Munitions flattened the area including the two remaining buildings that were standing. The gun fire ceased and the V-22 continued to move out of the area as the team was helped into the aircraft by the support crew for the trip to the Red Sea and the waiting U.S. aircraft carrier. The USS Ronald Regan had two flights of F-35 fighters covering the two Israeli VTOLs as they exited across the Sudan.

The U.S. Government had preemptively notified all the nations around Zyngola and reminded them of the terms of supporting any ASF forces which would amount to an act of war against the U.S. and its allies. There was no effort to interdict the flights or even any complaints about the strike on the base. Zyngola was given seven days to prove they weren't aware of the activities by the ASF on their soil or face war with the free world.

Everyone was fairly sure that at least part of the Zyngola government was complicit in the existence of the base, if not the bombing of Houston, but politically it would not be in the best interest of the free world to simply go on suspicion. There would be significant leverage available for the free world if Zyngola wanted to continue to exist.

Meanwhile the IDF was implementing pre-existing plans to find and destroy the submarine that was being used by the ASF to bring the last nuclear weapon close to Tel Aviv/Jaffa, Israel by the sea. This was not a new concept and had been carefully thought out by the best naval and aviation minds in the Israeli Military and the Mossad.

Hundreds of sonar listening buoys and seabed listening posts were being scanned and monitored for any undersea activity and the Israeli Air Force was using dozens of airborne detection systems in the effort.

In the midst of the activity the IDF added six of the so called, "Death Sharks" or what the IDF branded as the "Protector". The Rafael Industries weapon is equipped with four cameras, as well as a sonar or radar system and electro-optics capable of providing three-dimensional images. The cameras operate with the same distance and high definition as satellite cameras, being able to capture a

that is the only one anywhere near Israel. Two, with only ten submarines Iran wouldn't risk a second one as a gambit. I say it's the real thing and Crayton agrees with me to 99.999%."

Mark relayed that information to David who called it in to the IDF. The U.S. military concurred from their own information and then the final nail in the coffin of the submarine was a flash message to the Mossad from the U.S. NSA. Since there was no longer any demonic coverage the NSA could clearly detect nuclear fissionable material on the submarine. Since the submarine was not a nuclear boat, it had to be a bomb.

The ASROC was launched while the submarine was still over 100 miles from the coastline. Four minutes later there was a major nuclear explosion in the depths that caused a small tidal wave on the coasts and upset the earthquake monitors around the world. The water depth contained the majority of the radiation and only a superheated mushroom cloud erupted from the surface of the Red Sea.

Israel deflected the public storm by preempting the Iranians with a news conference condemning the ASF and the Iranian complicity in attempting to attack the Jewish state. They provided pictures of the mushroom cloud as proof that the submarine had a nuclear bomb on board. They demanded the UN also condemn the action. Iran countered saying that the Israelis had used a nuclear torpedo on an innocent ship.

That came to a sudden halt a week later when a captured ASF spy confessed to the plot and named names in Iran who had conspired with the ASF to bomb Israel.

The fallout from the bomb was mostly dissipated by local rainstorms and was minimal in strength when it came ashore on the Egyptian and Israeli coasts.

After delivering the remaining nuclear weapons to the IDF and a special contingent of the U.S. FBI, the Crossfire Team met Su Li at the Ben Grunion Airport and headed home in the Shrew.

CHAPTER FORTY-ONE

As the covert military/commercial, armed and armored jet winged its way across the Atlantic in Supercruise, the team slept, talked, and tried to help Su Li.

Laura and Jack were praying hours later as the jet flew into the next morning and neared the North American continent. Besides their love and thanks to a loving and present Elohim they were expressing their thanks for the successful mission in Zyngola.

Jack was deep in prayer when Caleb appeared in his mind. Jack was pleased to see the angel and smiled in the vision. Caleb stared at Jack for a few seconds and then spoke. "Jack, you and your fellow warriors were faithful and humble in your victory in Zyngola. There are new dangers now facing the team by the recent actions in response to the bombing of Houston. The Lord is proud of you because you walk as He tells you to."

Caleb hesitated for a little and then spoke softly. "The Most High wants you to know that the Force Generators cannot be used very often. He knows it would be easy to use them all the time but it violates a Heavenly balance of power or fairness. Ask Carol about this when you see her. They are a gift only for use when the odds have been shifted by the enemy without permission, like they did in Zyngola and on the ship that destroyed Houston, Texas. They had not asked for nor received permission to shield the weapon from human knowledge or sight outside of their base in Zyngola. To restore the balance Yahveh allowed your team to use the shields against them."

Caleb smiled, "Yahveh will let you know when they're to be used next. Until then be on your guard as your team has now gotten the full attention of the enemy and they will test you as hard as they can. In these last days the enemy of mankind is willing to risk anything to eliminate any challenge to his domain. You have just become a serious challenge worth his time and effort to destroy you. Rose and I will be watching and will support you as you do

Yahveh's will but it will require the faith in Him for each member of the team to stand against the enemy.

Caleb faded out of view and Jack continued to worship and for the first time he felt a desire to give up this mortal world and join Yahveh in Heaven. Sighing, he knew that his battles were not over, yet.

He opened his eyes and looked around the darkened aircraft at the sleeping people and listened to the soft sound of the conditioned air as it flowed through the compartment. He had a thought and reached out with his spirit to see if he could feel anything in the quiet morning hour. He was startled to realize he could sense a spiritual "aura" from each of the people around him in the plane. He couldn't sense any troubled or deceptive spirits coming from the people resting or flying the plane. He focused his senses on his wife and for the first time in his life understood a major reason he loved her so much. Her resting spirit was joyful and confident and buoyed up by a greater love. Jack realized he was sensing Yahveh's Holy Spirit in his wife. He also felt Laura's love for the Father and, wonderfully, for him. It was a pure love without regret or disappointment. The tears fell silently as he looked at her with love and realized she was a perfect match for him and that meant that Yahveh had desired them to be together forever. He also knew that even though she was asleep she was aware of his attention and his love. She smiled in her sleep.

Jack praised Yahveh and asked Yahshua to keep his wife safe from the enemy and from the troubles of this world. He then realized he was asking for something that had already been granted.

As he contemplated this new dimension of his life, he realized that it was because of the Holy Spirit in each of them that he could sense them. He smiled to himself in a flash of understanding that they all were right where Yahveh wanted them to be.

CHAPTER FORTY-TWO

The team returned to Denver and the Fortress with the victory of a successful mission diminished by the outpouring of grief and sadness for those lost in Houston.

The nation had staggered financially from the attack but had rallied to help those still living after the attack. The dead, those that had been far enough away to still be identifiable as a human corpse, had been located and buried. The entire area was cordoned off because of radiation and damage. There was no looting because it was too dangerous to approach the devastated area. One Sheriff had mentioned on the evening news that they would be able to locate looters easily since they would glow in the dark with a sickly green-blue color. The nation was in various stages of mourning, anger, and just an overwhelming sadness that so many could be exterminated so casually by a small group of people, who hated all life that didn't do things their way.

The President's rallying cry had been heard and most Americans agreed with him. But, since he was a lame-duck President there were those that dared to counter his arguments and blame the people of America for "making" the ASF attack Houston with a nuclear weapon, After all, that was their only means of making a statement that would be heard. Unfortunately, the people of the rest of the world heard the Muslim view of things and that was not favorable to America. Eventually the hue and cry of the "injured" Muslims that had so been "so cruelly" depicted by the President started demanding that America stop catering to the false Christian god and embrace Allah as the true god of the world. Some in the country agreed with the foreign attitude and started campaigning for removal of the entire federal government, especially the present President and his cabinet.

When the question was raised about the death and destruction caused by the bombing and who did it, it was brushed off as unimportant compared to the "disregard" Americans showed to the rest of the world and especially to

Muslims. The tide was turning against the Christians as foretold in the Word of God.

Meanwhile the sun was setting on the ruins of downtown Houston and the rescue workers dressed in anti-radiation suits turned on their floodlights to continue searching for any remaining survivors of the horrific destruction.

George Hallis and Lorene Turner were using a sonic detector to listen to the sunken areas below buildings for anything like cries for help, moans, or shouts. They had been doing this for four days, twelve hours on, twelve off as they and another crew spelled each other. There had been several people detected and rescued. Maybe half of them would live out the next month due to radiation exposure.

As the night darkened they were working their remote sensor robot as it probed the twisted steel and debris covering a collapsed building that had been on the west side of I-610 near Bellaire Blvd. The majority of the building had been blasted to the west but the three lower floors were shielded from the direct force of the bomb by the interstate structure had fallen in on themselves.

Lorene thought that she had been at this too long when she heard singing. She reached over and tapped George on the arm. Keying her microphone in her suit helmet she said, "Turn to channel two."

After George had changed his listening channel she could see his face frown behind the glass of his helmet. He looked up at her with a questioning glance. She smiled back and keyed her microphone to the inter-agency channel and requested diggers and cranes to move the debris.

Five hours later, just after midnight local time, one of the diggers signaled that he had made contact with more than one person. The rest of the teams converged on his position near the east end of the buildings remains and worked to make a passage into the depths.

Thirty minutes passed and the first survivor was helped to the surface and immediately decontaminated and provided shelter in a radiation-proof trailer designed specifically for these types of operations.

All in all there were forty-two people rescued and processed by the teams on the scene. Debriefing personnel worked with the rescued people to determine what they had been doing at the time of the attack. It turned out that they had been attending a Christian convention and were viewing a modern diorama of Jerusalem at the time of Christ. The blast had trapped them all in the dark but they had encouraged each other and rationed what food and water they'd had until they had been rescued.

The chief medical doctor on the scene walked into the command trailer still shaking the decontamination rinse off of his suit. He held up a sheaf of papers and smiled. "Not one of these people has any radiation poisoning! I've never seen anything like it. The combination of the sheltering by the Interstate to the east and the amount of debris that covered the site must have prevented them from getting radiated."

The military Chaplin assigned to the team looked up and asked the doctor, "You know, it could be their faith and God that prevented them from getting poisoned."

The doctor was an atheist and just laughed, "Then why did the other three hundred of their equally faithful followers die in the initial blast in the convention hall?"

The Chaplin smiled back at the man, "Ask God why. Only he knows the purpose for saving these and not those."

The doctor knowingly shook his head. "Face it Reverend, it was just chance and circumstance that made the difference."

The Chaplin nodded, "Exactly! Now ask yourself who arranged the circumstances so that these survived, all of them, without injury or radiation poisoning."

Outside in the dank, deadly open air, George Hallis and Lorene Turner were moving on to other possible sites looking for more survivors. Lorene was buoyed up by the huge find they'd made and was determined to find anyone else they could in the remaining hours to the end of their shift.

CHAPTER FORTY-THREE

The core team was meeting in the War Room to determine what their next mission might be when the Washington Hot Line annunciator chimed. Laura pushed the right button and answered. "Crossfire Team, how can we help you?"

President Bollen's voice was decrypted and presented by the premier electronics so well that you would have thought he was in the room. "Hi, Laura. Is everyone there?"

Laura smiled, "Jack, Mark, Sarah, David, Alexis, and I are present."

The President seemed satisfied. "Okay, I've got some breaking news for you that will change the election picture in November for all of us. The Liberal candidate who was picked by his party to run for President, Senator Bill Curtis, was assassinated by Muslim terrorists this afternoon."

There was a complete silence in the War Room while everyone contemplated the fallout from this new development. Jack frowned, "I'm sorry he was killed. Wasn't he the great Muslim fan that was campaigning for the U.S. to show favor to them even though they nuked Houston?"

"Yes, he was." stated the President. "But, unfortunately for Senator Curtis, he decided to switch sides when it became apparent that the majority of Americans did not like his stance and the fact that his popularity was plummeting like a rock. This morning I learned, according to the FBI, Curtis had several secret meetings with a group called "People for a United World" which is supposedly a "one-world" group but also serves as a front for Arab terrorist organizations. They provide funds and recruit local personnel to the Muslim terrorist groups in America. Curtis supposedly pledged to promote Allah over Christ so that the Muslims would get sympathy and, they, in turn, would back him for President."

Mark spoke up, "And just how do we know this?"

The President was solemn. "The FBI had an agent on the inside who recorded the talks. Apparently, Curtis realized he had a tiger by the tail last week and made the decision to make a complete break with the terrorists. The terrorists apparently, also had a man on the inside of Curtis' campaign organization. When Curtis went to get in his car this morning, one well-placed, 208-caliber round ended his career and his life."

Sarah shook her head, "Doesn't the killing of Senator Curtis sort of implicate the other party, your party?"

The President laughed a dry laugh, "True but again, terrorists being what they are they just had to take credit for the hit and denounced Curtis as a traitor to the true cause of Allah. Plus, a bystander accidentally got a good video of the shooter. Turns out to be the not-so-late and never lamented Sam Sturgis."

Mark came up out of his chair. "Sturgis! That piece of filth was supposedly killed in the Congo two years ago. They even had a DNA match for him. How certain is this identification?"

The President spoke quietly. "Oh, it is him. The CIA made a definite match with four different identifications, including prints on the abandoned rifle, DNA on a shell, a bio-mass analysis, and the video. He must have faked his death in Africa and is hiring his talents out to terrorists of the world again. How would your team like to hunt this human demon down and end his career of murder and evil?"

Mark was nodding his head as were the others, so Jack said, "Yes Sir, and we'll do this one free for you Mister President."

Mark asked, "Can you get us all the Intel available on Sturgis?"

President sighed, "I'll see what I can do. Even though there is four months until the election, the pollsters are telling me and everyone else that I'm in the twilight of my tour and not everyone is giving me one-hundred percent, anymore. Some politicians smell the odor of a new administration and are changing their colors as fast as they can. That means I don't have all the access and support I used to enjoy. But, I will get you what I can and I'll also see if I can get the JCS to give you a hand before the liberals bring down the curtain on my Presidency and his term, too."

Laura spoke up. "Thank you, Mr. President. A couple of thoughts first. If the only real Liberal candidate was just killed why do you think that party will win the election? And, if things do look shaky for you and your family after leaving the presidency because of a shift in politics or loyalties, you and your whole family are welcome to live here at the Fortress. We'll do what we can to keep you safe and comfortable and you don't have to work, either."

David quipped, "And we can do a lot to keep you safe."

The President was quiet and when he spoke next you could hear the emotion in his voice. "I just might take you up on that offer. You realize you could be hurting your cause and team if you do that?"

Laura laughed, "We'll take our chances just like you did for us during your terms."

The President said his good-byes and hung up.

Sarah had been thinking about Laura's offer to the President. "He's got two grandchildren as well as a daughter and a son and a son-in-law. We'd better get that Army designer back in here to set up an effective and comfortable living quarters for them before we lose our pull with the military."

Jack considered that and agreed with the thought. "Okay, you two see what you can get Major Gary Danning to do in the next five or six months, before the change of administrations. In the meantime, we just took on a mission. Mark, what do you know about Sturgis and his associates?"

Mark sat down and collected his thoughts. "This assassin is a real pro on all levels. He is an expert marksman with a wide variety of weapons, knows Brazilian Karate. I think he has a fourth degree black belt in it. He also is a meticulous planner and very careful about setting and avoiding traps. He's always been well funded and is probably a multimillionaire in his own right. He does not allow sentiment or emotion to get in his way. He'll kill a whole city block of people to get the one he wants and laugh about his efficiency. He operates out of a state of anger which is sated when he can hurt people. He apparently has the ability to channel his anger so that he functions, not in a rage, but icy cold and calculating. If he has to interrogate someone it is usually fatal and it is rumored that he is fascinated and enjoys watching the evil done to the victim. Sturgis is a seriously bad person who can be a real threat to all of us if we go after him and we miss. He'll come after us with a redoubled vengeance."

Sarah looked at her old boss. "David, didn't you once have some insight into this vermin?"

David frowned. "Yes, but it is not fit conversation for decent people. Samuel Sturgis is an ex-patriot Irish citizen and if a human being can act like a demon, then this man is a walking example of the worst case. He is such a stone cold killer that his reputation is enough to frighten seasoned law enforcement personnel into leaving him alone. The stories that are told of his evil tactics would cause everyone to blanch and feel sick."

David looked around at what had become his best, and only, friends in the world. "I don't know that we did the right thing in accepting this mission. The man is highly resourceful and intelligent in the worse way. He is ruthless and relentless once he has a target and we will become that target as soon as we strike at him or his organization."

Jack smiled. "Since he sounds like the devil himself he is a natural target for us and eventually our two forces would come to blows whether we initiated it or not. If this is the man Carol is talking about then we are already his target. I suggest we pray and ask Yahveh if we are doing His will by accepting this assignment, which I feel is His will, and for a game plan to eliminate him on first contact so that he doesn't have another chance to strike us."

Mark grinned and slapped his hand on the desk in front of him. "I like the way you think!"

CHAPTER FORTY-FOUR

Sam Sturgis stared at the body on the table before him without compassion or even concern. The man had resisted to the bloody end. Never even got the slightest admission out of him as to what group or entity for which he was working. The man's greatest fear had been of mutilation and the loss of his manhood. So those were the last areas the doctor had worked on. The amount of pain the man had taken would have broken anyone so Sam decided that the man might of been telling the truth when he said he didn't have a clue about what Sam wanted in the way of information.

Sam walked away from the pile of burnt and torn flesh that had recently been a good looking young man. Sam was irritated that they had wasted so much time on a dead end. That thought made Sam smile. It was a real dead end for that guy even if he wasn't an enemy after all.

Looking back at the two Arab henchmen he had been given he said, "Take the Israeli and bury him in his blessed desert where he won't ever be found. Then clean this place up so that even a forensics team couldn't tell he was here." Sam then exited the soundproof room, walked up the stairs, and out to his luxury car. He got in and started the car.

Sitting there he planned out his next three moves and considered any chances that he could be compromised by this operation. Doubtful. Putting the car into gear he drove carefully away from the abattoir, dismissing the whole operation from his mind. Sam had trained himself carefully to compartmentalize all of his knowledge and operations in his mind. When he was done with a thing, a hit, a deal, a woman, he flushed the memories and the concerns out of his mind entirely. Since nothing useful had been gained and no future harm to him could result from it, he would not consider or remember this operation again.

As he started the drive to Damascus, the capital city of Syria, he discovered yet again that his mental control still hadn't let him forget about his earlier life. He remembered his hard scrabble youth in Ireland where he had to fight to get anything or to keep what he had. He'd run away at sixteen and joined the British military, faking British heritage and his age. He'd managed to rise through the ranks to the level of Staff Sergeant due to his attention to detail, his tenancies, and his quick wits.

It had been noted that he was more than cool under fire; in fact some comments indicated a borderline suicidal coldness. At that time in the British Army with many being deployed to Iraq his "fearlessness" was a needed quality and he became a highly experienced troop leader and strategist. His reported stand-offishness, which was a result of not trusting anyone, did not make him popular with the troops but he seemed to live a charmed life and walked out of every firefight unscathed and sometimes, the only one to survive.

His penchant for inflicting pain didn't come to light until he'd been in Iraq for almost a year. When the Army discovered he'd tortured three insurgent fighters for information to point of their death he was quietly cashiered out of the service. He chose to stay in the Middle East rather than go back to England and eventually met up with others as cruel as himself. Again, his exceptional talent at dispensing death and pain was noted and he rose in the ranks of the illegal drug trade as an enforcer. Since the penalties in Muslim countries for dealing drugs were terminally severe his survival showed a talent as an exceptionally effective assassin. He charged high fees and quickly became independently wealthy.

What no one knew, not even Sam was the carefully molding of his anger, violence, and hatred by the demons assigned to him at birth. This was to be one of Satan's chosen weapons to be used against the forces of good in the world. Many times bullets had been deflected and bombs muffled so that Sam didn't get hurt. His egotistical pride increased every time he escaped harm when those around him were maimed or killed.

Over the next ten years he went to Brazil and learned martial arts and supplemented his income by smuggling weapons to both sides of any conflict and odd jobs as an assassin. He'd refined his skills to the point of professionalism when he became involved in world politics.

He was the point man in reorganizing governments by assassination which also made him one of the most wanted of Interpol fugitives. The major countries of the world continued to turn up the heat until they had apparently killed him in Africa.

His staged death gave him a breathing spell and he went to ground as another person, whose identity he had borrowed after killing the man. But the enemy of mankind knew exactly where he was and when it was time for Sam's repayment of all the loving care he'd been given by the devil he was contacted by an underground facet of the Arab Strike Force.

His tenth assignment for the ASF had been Senator Curtis, the liberal front runner for President of the United States. The assignment was actually quite simple for a good sniper. The law enforcement forces of the United States normally aren't that efficient concerning personal protection. Other countries such as Russia and China were more in tune to the necessities of protection. The U.S. hasn't really faced the challenges of daily assassinations or attempts that would bring out their best. That will change, maybe after this event.

Thinking about his strategy he mentally patted himself on the back. Simply good Intel, good timing, and an excellent shot from a moving vehicle. Per his instructions he had made sure that there was at least one video camera that would catch him firing the fatal shot. The media in this country could be led easily. The young man that took the video worked for an associate of Sam's and would be paid very well by the hungry media as well as by Sam's organization.

Now that he had successfully completed that job, his identification as "the" world assassin was assured. He was also forewarned about an unspecific threat against his existence from America.

As he drove into Damascus Sam knew that he had no limitations, which meant, in his mind that he was supreme above any "god". He not only didn't believe in God, he felt faith in God was just a crutch for weak people to lean on because they couldn't handle life by themselves like he could.

After he settled into the safe house he had been given he played host to several of the ASF's surviving bigwigs. They had word from sympathizers in the U.S. about the President's assignment to the Crossfire Team to eliminate him. The message the ASF wanted Sam to send to the west was that the ASF was unstoppable. This would be amply proven by the violent termination of this American team. So they gave the job to him.

Sam got all the information available on the American team and carefully planned how to eliminate them in a spectacular way. He needed six more capable men half as good as himself and a workforce of twenty enforcers.

The ASF promised him the personnel in the next thirty days. Sam then gave them a list of weapons, supplies, and travel arrangements he would need. They didn't even blink at the requests. They had access to large sums of money which was supplied by the west in the form of oil income. Ironically it was the west that would supply the means for him to destroy one of the west's antiterrorist teams. Sam found that satisfying on several levels.

Sam considered the Crossfire Team's accomplishments and the supposed involvement by powers beyond the earthly ones the team could provide. He was fairly certain that "godly" support was actually being provided by the administration in Washington instead of by fairy-tale deities such as a god. He would plan for that and make sure they didn't have a chance to escape his plans for their destruction. They would be dead long before the rigged elections in November and the hold on America would shift to people whose alliance was with groups considered as antithetical to the present American policies and freedoms.

CHAPTER FORTY-FIVE

Carol Moffet woke from a sound sleep in her suite at the Fortress with a start. She felt an urgent need to pray. As she prayed the dim light in the room was overcome by bright white light from the diamonds at her forehead and throat. Carol didn't see the light as she had her eyes closed and was concentrating on understanding what she was seeing. All of the dimensions of Heaven opened up to her and her comprehension of events took in all of the facets of thousands of events, time lines, requests, approvals, denials, and strategies. One event that had been started decades ago drew her attention and she sailed in her mind along the timeline and studied the ramifications of the operation.

Praying for true guidance and understanding she spent what seemed like days avoiding the subtle misdirection and gross fakeries that were part of a satanic plan until she saw the entirety of the enemy's desire. Realizing that a time like this was why she had been given this gift in the first place she focused on the next movements as related to time in the human world.

After coming to all the conclusions she could make she prayed that the information she was about to give to the team would be complete and true and not a deliberate misleading by the enemy.

Feeling Yahveh's conviction about the message she prayed her thanks to the Father and spoke of her worship of Him and His love.

The light died down as she left the Heavenlies and she picked up the micro recorder she had next to her bed. After dictating everything she knew about the plan she laid back in bed and tried to look at the thing from all angles. Finally, as sure as she could be of her facts, she got up and went to freshen up. Dressing quickly she noted the time was five in the morning. She picked up her communicator and asked the computer to connect her to Laura Malone.

Laura's voice didn't betray any sleepiness when she answered. "Hello Carol, what's up at this hour of the morning?"

Carol apologized for the early hour and asked Laura to meet her in the kitchen to discuss an urgent matter.

Five minutes later both Jack and Laura walked into the kitchen dressed in cammo fatigues and boots and ready to go in any direction. Laura walked over and picked up the pot of coffee Carol had started. She poured some into two cups and brought them to the table for her and Jack. She smiled at Carol and tipped her head to one side to indicate that they were there and she could divulge whatever she had that needed them up at this predawn hour.

Carol nodded and looked directly at Laura. "I was brought awake an hour ago by Yahveh to pray and seek the Heavenlies for something very urgent, very important. Only a few minutes passed but it was like a whole day there. One event line was brought to my attention and I spent the majority of my time analyzing the events and the implications it has for us."

Carol took a drink of her coffee to steady her voice for this next part. "What I was shown is the possible end of the Crossfire Team and all of us."

The solid, no-nonsense way she said it and the heaviness of her spirit added emphasis to the news. "There is a man with a team of his own who has been tasked with destroying us. I know others have had the same mandate so that this is nothing new. But, this person is probably one of the best assassins in the world and he is at the top of his form right now. He is being guided and aimed directly at us by a fourth-level demon named Stabolethe, a destruction demon. Stabolethe is giving this assassin the information on where we are at any time and everything the enemy knows about us."

Carol searched the eyes of the two people across from her looking for any signs of fear or distress. She was heartened not to find anything but intelligence and interest in her disclosure. "The reason the Heavens are concerned that this one will succeed where earlier attempts have failed is because this man and his team are being funded and supported at the highest level. There will be an attack soon on this base; while it will fail it will set in motion a series of events that could lead our Team out of the security of the Fortress and into direct combat with this assassin and his team. He will be aware of our decisions and will be prepared to eliminate the team completely. His probability of succeeding if we act according to Stabolethe's plan is in the upper eighties right now."

Jack prayed quietly and contemplated the news Carol had given them. He was asking Yahveh for direction and understanding on how Yahveh's Will could be best served in this matter. There wasn't a hint of concern from Jack about any of the team's lives or deaths. He simply wanted to do Yahveh's will regardless of the outcome.

Laura had been praying the entire time that Carol was speaking and had already heard from the Father. Now she waited until her husband got the same message.

Jack looked up at the two women and smiled. "I believe we are to prepare for the attack against this place but we also need to preempt the assassin's schedule and be on the attack against him and his team even before he attacks here. He looked at Carol, "Did you see anything that would give us an idea who this assassin is or where he is?"

Carol nodded her head, "Yes, he is Samuel Sturgis, the man the President told you to find and eliminate."

Jack nodded, "I'm not surprised. His demon probably told him about the assignment tasking the Crossfire Team to eliminate him and it would be expected that he would try to preempt us. He was easily identified during his killing of the Liberal nominee for President and I believe that was on purpose to allow identification of him and to get the President to point us at him."

Laura looked at Jack, "Why do you think it was on purpose?"

Jack smiled, "Well, I think it had to be on purpose because Sam is supposed to be the best assassin in the world yet he allowed himself to be videotaped, left a rifle with his fingerprints on it, and a shell casing with his DNA on it all on one mission. Pretty clumsy for a top assassin unless he wanted to be identified."

Carol laughed, "Very good Jack, Yes, he wanted to be identified for that reason and also so that he would be identified as the best assassin in the world after that mission. There was a lot of personal ego in deliberately allowing himself to be noted and identified. The enemy knew that about him and allowed him to do it so that the President would use us against him."

Laura sighed, "I've got a bad feeling about this."

CHAPTER FORTY-SIX

Charlie Wu considered the elusiveness of Sam Sturgis and his well-documented professionalism as a hit man or better yet, as an international assassin. The man was very careful about keeping his whereabouts a secret from his employers and his employees. No one but Sam himself would know where he was, or where he would be.

This was proving to be the toughest case Charlie had ever tackled and he felt fairly sure he couldn't solve it by himself. He also considered his wife's inputs and realized their limitations even as a formidable couple. They were very good at the spy/counterspy game but they were only human. This assassin was being aided by demonic forces and therefore this needed a spiritual solution rather than just a human one.

Charlie pressed the buttons that caused the liquid crystal composition of the glass around his office to darken and completely obscure the glass. He locked the door, and sent an electronic "DND" or "Do Not Disturb" notice to all his employees and the rest of the team. He dimmed the lights in the office and knelt down on a pillow he kept there for just these occasions. He started to worship Yahveh and quietly sing songs of praise to him. Charlie didn't rush his worship nor did he let the urgency of his needs pollute his worship. Once started he gave himself over to the praise and love he felt for the creator of the universe. A creator that he hadn't even known existed several years ago in China. He relaxed and let his heart take over the singing. He felt the heaviness he associated with the presence of the Father's spirit and also felt the happiness spring from his spirit at the nearness of Yahveh's spirit.

Charlie had studied hard to understand his Christianity and his relationship to the Father Yahveh and with Yahshua, the Son. He knew the Father knew his requests before he could bring them up, so he didn't bring them up. He waited on his Elohim to speak to him so that he could find the answers in the response.

Charlie felt a presence and opened his eyes. In the dimness of the office the bright whiteness of Caleb's garb stood out clearly. Caleb looked at the smaller Oriental man and smiled. "Yahveh has heard your praise and it pleases him to guide you in your quest. Your answer is not to seek Sam Sturgis' location but to determine it for him. Then you will be able to pinpoint his whereabouts for the rest of the team. He wants to destroy the team and he takes personal satisfaction in being in on the kill. He is more interested in finding and executing the team members than anything right now. He will attack you individually rather than as a team. He feels each success will make it easier to take out the rest of the team because he will be seen as unstoppable and their death inevitable. Your answer was in your question." Caleb faded from sight and Charlie continued to thank the Father in praise for a while.

Climbing to his feet he shut off the DND signals and cleared the windows in his office. The bright light of the Colorado sky flooded his world through the visionports in the computer center which ran from the floor to the top of the ceiling.

Charlie had the computer contact Jack and Mark for him. "Guys, I have a suggestion for you. I'll be down in a second."

After Charlie had explained his revelation to the two men he mentioned that he could "accidentally" leak information as to one or more team member's future locations so that Sam could use it to set his trap. Only they would be there first to set their trap around his trap.

Mark smiled at Charlie. "That was pretty much what we had concluded too. I have an idea that could bring the slime ball out into the open. A target of opportunity he could not refuse." Mark grinned a big grin. "That would be me."

Jack looked at the cool professional soldier who had become his best friend in the world after Laura. "That could be dangerous. This character has a real string of extremely hard to hit targets with confirmed kills on each one. Why do you think you'll be able to avoid becoming dead?"

Mark smiled a canny smile. "I'll just use his weaknesses against him just as he plans to use ours against us. Remember, I've been a professional sniper just as he thinks he is. Sturgis likes to do splashy executions with a lot of publicity and the harder to reach the target, the better he finds it because it feeds his ego to go the target one better. I think we'll give him the hardest target he's ever tried to take out and make him really work for the kill. In the process we will profile his efforts against what we already know about him so that we can take him out of the picture for once and all."

Jack had gone through this with Mark before. "Okay, that's great, but, how will you stay alive to make him go through multiple attempts?"

Mark sat forward in his chair. "All good assassins study their targets carefully before they plan the kill. Sturgis is known for doing that. We don't have any real routines and it will have to be a suck job for him to use what little he knows about us to set a trap. In other words, he'll have to use some kind of lure to get us out of the Fortress and into his sights. We're going to tailor-make his lure for him and set the situation up for him before he can."

David had walked in and stood quietly to one side. "You mean you'll give him a verifiable lure that we are already aware of like a person to abduct or a target to threaten?"

Mark nodded, "Yes, and it will have to be very, very soon."

CHAPTER FORTY-SEVEN

Sam Sturgis was just finishing up his planning and design for his first strike against the Crossfire Team when he got the phone call he had been waiting for all week. His contact in the Justice Department let him know that his number two target was going to testify in front of a Congressional committee on Wednesday, three days away. He got the time of the subpoenaed directive for Mark Connelly to appear. Assuring his contact that the reward for his information would be in the usual place Sam disconnected the call.

Now came the guessing game part of the program. How would Mr. Connelly travel to the Congressional hearing from which airport? He dug into the computerized records and had a lock on the airport and the method of travel in less than four minutes. Connelly and his partner Jack Malone always landed at Ronald Reagan and took an armored SUV from the airport to the Senate hearings. Four trips, four repetitions, no variance. "Dumb", Sturgis thought. "Mark Connelly thinks his armored car will keep him safe."

Sturgis checked his planning and contacted two of his shooters and gave them precise directions as to time and place to be on Wednesday. He would refine the operation as the target moved out of the airport and onto interstate 395.

He checked several times over the next three days to ensure that there were no special flying squads or SWAT teams activated at the time of Mark Connelly's arrival. Nothing at all indicated that there was anything directed at the Crossfire Team's leading counterterrorist arrival or trip. There were teams being fielded but they were nowhere near Interstate 395 or the airport.

Wednesday had dawned with a light rain but it cleared up toward noon, the expected arrival time for the target at Ronald Reagan airport. Sturgis looked out of the window of the H2 Hummer he was sitting in as a small private jet prepared to touch down. It had no special markings and was a normal Citation X in its usual white color. He watched the plane land smoothly and taxi into a private hanger. Using his powerful binoculars Sam watched Mark Connelly walk down the stairs of the jet and climb into the black SUV. The doors on the hanger were being closed and temporarily interfered with Sam's view but the SUV quickly moved into the middle of the hanger and slid out before the doors could be fully closed. Sam watched as the big SUV headed for the exits.

Sam started his engine and quickly pulled over where he could watch the exits in his rear view mirror. If anything looked suspicious he would call off the strike and try again later. He watched the black half-truck, half-car move through the express lanes that allowed for a quick exit by radio tagged vehicles. He let several other vehicles get in between the SUV and himself.

Calling his accomplices on the disposable cell phone he made sure they were in position and ready. The SUV stuck to the speed limit and wound around on the I-395 as it prepared to cross the Potomac River. He closed up slightly and told the others to start moving.

He used his binoculars but could only see a vague silhouette of Mark Connelly in the back seat due to the heavily darkened windows. Sam switched to the IR mode and was gratified to get a body heat signature from the silhouette proving it wasn't a ploy using a dummy.

As the SUV approached the river crossing there were two semitrailer trucks each with two, twenty-foot trailers hooked on behind each truck. The trucks were in the center and right lanes. Just as the SUV driver was about to swing to the left lane the truck in the center lane moved to the left lane leaving only the center lane free. The SUV driver saw his chance and accelerated between the trucks.

Sam picked up the remote control and as the SUV was passing between the very back trailers of both trucks Sam pushed the little red button and stepped on his brakes at the same time.

Two massive explosions erupted out of the rear trailers on both trucks at the same time. The huge shaped charges channeled all of their energy at the SUV. The armored vehicle was designed to stop an IED or deflect an RPG round as well as defy gunfire. But its designers never thought to plan against simultaneous massive explosions from both sides. The sides of the SUV were literally smashed together and the whole vehicle width was reduced in a second to less than three feet. The concussive energy alone would have killed anyone in the vehicle. The additional overkill on energy just made sure by mashing everything inside of the vehicle into paste. So much for Mark Connelly.

As the explosions occurred, the rear trailers separated from the front trailers and the trucks sped off away from the violence occurring behind them. $$$$$

Sam had come to a halt fifty feet behind the wreckage and noted the red stain leaking out of what had once been a stylish SUV. He swung to his right and drove around the mess. Smiling as he took the next off ramp he headed back to his hotel to pack up and plan for the next member of the Team to die.

Purely accidently, Sam's design had not even injured any of the other people on the highway. It was a surgical strike and a very professional one.

As he pulled into his hotel parking lot he noticed another car swinging out of its lane to pull into the parking lot. That raised the hairs on Sam's head. Somehow there was someone interested in him and that wasn't in the plan.

Pulling quickly into a parking place, Sam exited the Hummer and walked quickly into the hotel only to immediately exit the building at the rear through a predetermined escape route he'd arranged two days before.

Sam duck walked beside two other vehicles and got into a non-descript rental Ford Focus. He quickly put on a loud Hawaiian shirt over his $300 silk shirt and added a floppy hat. He drove carefully out the other driveway and into the evening traffic. He didn't spot any police cars or even any activity near the Hummer as he drove away. Probably just paranoid he thought. But it was better to be safe than sorry. Now that he'd done in the tactical leader of the Crossfire Team he'd have to be ever so much more cautious on his next hit. Sam smiled; maybe he'd take out more than one target at Connelly's funeral.

CHAPTER FORTY-EIGHT

The news that night highlighted the action on the I-395 as a gangland execution style killing. No names were released and the story about what happened was vague enough that it could have been anyone that had been killed. Sam didn't care what the public thought. He'd gotten his confirmation that he'd eliminated Mark Connelly through his Justice Department snitch.

Connelly didn't make his appointment and significantly there was no hue and cry from the panel. In fact there was no warrant issued for Connelly as defying the Congress. Little things meant a lot. The only sour note for Sam was that no one knew he did it except himself and a couple of hired hands. He did have a very clear video recording of the hit. Maybe he'd play that for his employers someday.

"Oh well", the price of fame could have been a little too high this time Sam thought. He pulled out his files on the remaining members of the team and tried to pick his next target.

1,500 miles to the west of where Sam sat in Washington, D.C. those potential targets sat quietly in the War Room and listened to Jack as he detailed Mark's funeral.

"I think that we'll keep it to a minimum as far as the number of people invited. Mark would have preferred it that way. Per his wishes we'll use the same cemetery where our first pastor was interned. Obviously we won't advertise the event, any comments?"

Sarah shook her head. As the widow she could have demanded anything she wanted but this would do. She got up and walked out of the War Room and went to her suite upstairs. She thought she'd like a little private time right about now.

Laura watched her leave and looked at Jack. "You think she'll be all right?"

Jack nodded, "Yeah, she's a lot tougher than we give her credit for."

Laura frowned, "She's an ex-Mossad agent who's probably the deadliest member of the team and can do almost anything except walk through walls. How much tougher can she be?"

Jack smiled, "I meant emotionally she's tough."

Laura nodded, "Okay, Mr. Guy. I happen to know that you have emotions too. Just because you're male doesn't mean you can't be sensitive. Women are naturally more emotional because of our makeup, that's all."

David laughed, "Don't you two ever listen to yourselves? You're both saying the same things in different ways. Sarah is probably one of the toughest people I know but at the same time she has a delicate spirit and that would be the place of tenderness that could be hurt."

Alexis just grinned and shook her head.

Upstairs in her suite Sarah sat on the bed and sighed. Looking over she said, "Do you think my husband would be all right with us being alone in a bedroom?"

Mark thought for a few seconds and said, "He'd bettered. I'd be a lousy husband if I said it didn't matter."

Sarah lay back on the bed with her feet still on the floor. "Do you think Sturgis fell for it?"

Mark nodded. "Oh yeah he fell for it. That last little bit at his hotel was the clincher. He doesn't know if there was anything to the sudden movement to follow his Hummer and that would be just enough of an anomaly to make the whole thing realistic. Otherwise it would have been too perfect, too good."

Sarah reached over and took Mark's big hand into her hand. "Okay, now he thinks you're dead so he'll be gunning for the rest of us. I hate to admit it but that shaped charge idea was very good and innovative. If you hadn't suspected he'd go for you on the highway I hate to think I'd be planning a real funeral for you."

Mark sat up and smiled. "Right, and that's where he's going to try for more of us. The advantage we have is that he thinks I'm dead and the spiritual covering we've been praying for should keep his demons from telling him differently. See? He's no longer expecting me. That's going to be his undoing."

Sarah grinned. "Okay, how do we keep the rest of us alive at the funeral while you bag him?"

Mark pondered for a few seconds, "A little more sleight of hand."

Sarah shook her head. "That switch of vehicles to the remotely piloted one in the hanger got by him completely. He wouldn't have gone through with it if he'd thought it was decoy. Even the bagged faked blood and the two small heaters to give the driver and the "victim" a realistic heat was neat. You have to give it to Charlie for piloting the SUV from the Fortress. It looked like a real driver was doing the steering."

Mark absentmindedly nodded. "I think we're going to stress Mr. Sturgis if he makes a play for you at the funeral. It's going to require his personal touch, up close and personal. Then we're going to bag him!"

CHAPTER FORTY-NINE

Finding out which cemetery was going to be used for Mark Connelly's funeral wasn't hard for Sam Sturgis. Operating as the Obit editor for he contacted every cemetery within a fifty-mile radius of the team's hideout and found that there were only going to be six funerals on Saturday and nine on Sunday. He eliminated all but two and picked the one where the team had buried their first pastor over a year ago.

The small cemetery near Idlewild, Colorado was picturesque and beautiful. But it was challenging to Sam due to the terrain. The cemetery was located in a small valley right up against a small mountain on its west side. As a trained sniper he could have used the high ground but then these people weren't stupid. They would have that angle covered. So, he'd have to improvise like he always did.

Two days before the funeral, Charlie Wu called Mark and Jack to the ComSec center and showed them the video recordings from the previous night. It seems the night maintenance man was very busy planting things. It wasn't customers but explosive devices. Charlie showed where each and every device was located and then showed their crew disarming all of them and removing them from the site. He looked up at his friends, "I had them leave the sensors so that Sturgis will believe that they're still there and when he activates them they'll respond, but no boom-boom. Did you know he used nothing but mega-Claymores? He's planning to kill everybody in the cemetery just to get a few of us. One very sick human being that's what he is."

Mark just nodded. "Make sure you've got firepower for the team handy and that you inspect them to see if the protective gear they will be wearing doesn't show."

Charlie nodded, "Don't worry, it'll be cool and windy up there at five p.m. and everyone can wear long black coats that will cover their armor easily."

Mark thought for a moment, "Remember that the armor makes one a little awkward when exiting a vehicle and Sturgis could be watching them to see who he thinks he'll bag."

Charlie smiled, "Not to worry. This is a capable crew and he's the one that's going to get bagged."

The next two days flew by while everyone was making preparations for the big event. Charlie and his crew worked especially hard on their part of the big event.

On Saturday Charlie climbed into the limo next to Jack and Laura and his wife, Linda. "I've got the damping field set up in triplicate just in case. Sturgis will have to come within fifty yards to set off his explosives and then he is ours."

The short procession only included the hearse and four limousines. They wound up the simple road to the site. There was no room for the vehicles in the small cemetery so everyone piled out on the road adjacent to the cemetery. A light mist was falling which allowed everyone to use large black umbrellas further confusing anyone watching.

Jack, David, Charlie, and three of the SOG soldiers took the casket out of the hearse and carried it to the gravesite and set it on the straps holding it above the open grave.

As a very brave but highly nervous pastor Tim Carson began to read the prayers, Charlie watched a small video screen which was a direct satellite feed from the ComSec center in the fortress. Quietly whispering to Jack he said, "Sturgis has tried to detonate his bombs without success. He'll become aware of the RF damping field very soon and move in to activate the explosives."

Jack said, "There is a cemetery maintenance man slowly approaching us from the building side. He keeps looking at his hands. I think it is Sturgis."

Charlie was about to answer when a bullet struck him in the chest and he flew backward to land on the ground. Everyone got down quickly as more rounds flew through the space they had occupied.

Jack said, "What is going on?"

Charlie rolled over onto his side and coughed. "Dang that hurts" he said as he rubbed his chest. He looked at the display and coughed. "There are about twenty men approaching from the street side firing rifles, at us, now!"

Jack thought, "Great, tell me something I don't know." He reached up and pulled the coffin off of the webbing and onto its side on the ground. Yanking the top open he started handing out M-8s to everyone. Taking one he sighted on the rapidly approaching men and started squeezing off rounds. Two men went down quickly as the volume of fire increased from both sides. Suddenly there was the sound of rolling thunder as Mark got into the game from the mountainside. His Barrett M50 .50 caliber Bullpup-design sniper rifle was knocking the enemy soldiers off their feet in rapid order. The M500 is designated as an "anti-material" weapon used to knock out enemy vehicles, helicopters, and fixed facilities at ranges up to two miles. Mark felt it worked very well against body-armored troops too.

A hundred feet away from the team members in the cemetery Sam Sturgis knelt behind a gravestone as bullets smashed against it. He pulled out a miniature set of high-powered binoculars and trained them on the mountainside. It came as no surprise when he picked out Mark Connelly firing a sniper rifle with great efficiency. He turned back to the on-coming people shooting at the team and wondered who they were. He realized his plan had been thwarted and he was in as much danger as the team of being overwhelmed and killed by this unknown force that was trying to accomplish what he wanted to do in the first place. "Oh well," he thought, might as well get one of them myself. He pulled out his .40 automatic and tried to get a shot at one of the team. As he was taking aim an unimaginably giant force slammed into his left shoulder and chest. The gun flew out of his hand as he was slammed backwards.

Sam lay there dazed for a few seconds trying to get his wits about him before he realized that Mark Connelly had shot him from the hillside. His left arm wasn't working and he felt the blood running freely down his left side. He slid behind a large headstone that kept him out of Mark's view and checked his shoulder. The body armor he was wearing had taken most of the punch out of the 1500-grain round but hadn't stopped it completely. He had an entry wound just below his left shoulder but he couldn't find an exit wound. "Not good!" he said. He took out a handkerchief and stuffed it into the leaking hole. Looking around he found what he wanted in a small wall that ran back to the building behind him. Gritting his teeth against the pain and dragging his left arm he crawled to the building and then, leaning on the building he levered his numb body upright. He stumbled around the building.

Charlie was still rubbing his chest with his left hand while firing his M-8 with his right. The attackers had gone to ground and were sniping at the team. Laura, Sarah, and David had taken cover in the new grave and were firing at any target of opportunity while Alexis, Charlie, and Jack were behind headstones doing the same.

Occasionally the boom from Mark's sniper rifle would sound and another of the enemy stopped firing but it was still a touch-and-go situation with the attackers outnumbering the team members three to one.

Jack got a cell-phone call and heard Su Li's voice. "Get as low as you can, I'll try to miss you."

Jack smiled, "Bring the rain". He yelled, "Duck and cover, the air force is here!"

Suddenly there were four rapid explosions and the sound of two chain guns ripping the ground, tombstones, and people to pieces. The whole thing couldn't have taken ten seconds but it was extremely thorough. The Air Cobra hovered menacingly with the gun smoke wafting off of the barrels of the two miniguns sticking out from below the cockpit. Su Li still had a few thousand rounds she wanted to expend. But, nothing was moving on the bad side of the line.

Jack and Alexis moved quickly up to the attackers and verified the ones that were still in one piece were quite dead.

Mark called Su Li and told her to look for Sturgis. "I know that I hit him and I saw a blood spray so he's hurt."

Su Li quartered the area but found no sign of the assassin. "Sorry Mark, he's gone."

As the team searched the area of the cemetery Alexis found the blood track that Sturgis left. She followed it to the side of the building but it ended there and there was no sign of the man's passage after that. It was starting to get dark and the police were arriving in droves. The team put down their weapons and explained what happened. Charlie showed the police the aerial view from a keyhole satellite that confirmed the initial attack by the unknown force.

Sarah caught Jack's eye and tipped her head to one side. Jack excused himself and walked casually over to the dark-haired beauty. "What do you have?" he asked in a soft voice.

Sarah showed him a wallet from one of the attackers. No driver's license, no identification, only money and a slip of paper showing the location of the cemetery and the time to attack. "I think we've run into some more mercenaries from OC. I mean, they're not Arabic but Caucasian, typical weapons like before, and they are definitely mercenaries."

Jack nodded, "But, were they in cahoots with Sturgis?"

Sarah shook her head. "From what I saw they were trying to shoot him too. I think the OC just saw a chance to take us out and took it. Unfortunately it gave Sturgis the opportunity to get away."

Jack nodded, "Yeah, but Mark says he hit him and it's not an easy thing to overcome a hit from a BMG .50 caliber round, even with body armor."

The wind picked up blowing the smell of cordite and the coppery smell of fresh blood and other battle odors away from the two team members. Sarah frowned, "Yeah, he's probably seriously hurt but he's still running. But, I think we're going to see more of him before this thing is over and done with."

Jack sensed that Sarah was right about Sturgis. She had the most experience with combat second only to Mark. "What do you think he'll do next?"

Sarah laughed, "He has to not die first. Then he'll either be too maimed to continue his war with us which will mean his sponsors will probably eliminate him, or he will have learned a painful lesson about the Crossfire Team."

Jack nodded and watched her walk back to the rest of the team. He turned and felt the first cold breeze of fall caress his face. It was late September in the Rockies and it promised to be a cold winter this year." He saw Mark walking in from the mountain carrying the M500 over his shoulders. Jack walked over to meet him. Jack thought, "This should be an interesting post-combat review."

The Crossfire Team will return in ***"Russian Crossfire"***.

If this story has awakened your spirit or moved you to seek the love of Christ and His power for your life, whether you've never accepted Jesus as your savior or you've fallen away, repeat the following prayer and begin a most wonderful journey into eternal life with Him today.

Father God in Heaven, As You said in Your Holy Word, (Romans 10:9) that if we confess the Lord our God and believe in our hearts that God raised Jesus from the dead, we shall be saved.

(The prayer on the next page is a sample prayer when asking Jesus into your heart as your Savior. You can also pray this in your own words.)

Salvation Prayer

Dear God in Heaven, I come to you in the name of Jesus. I confess to You that I am a sinner, and I am sorry for my sins and the life that I have lived; I need your forgiveness. I believe that your only begotten Son Jesus Christ shed His precious blood on the cross at Calvary and died for my sins, and I am now willing to turn from my sin.

Right now I confess Jesus as the Lord of my life and my soul. With all my heart, I truly believe that your Holy Spirit raised Jesus from the dead. Today I accept Jesus Christ as my personal Savior and according to Your Word, right now I am saved.

I thank you Jesus, for your unlimited grace which has saved me from my sins. I thank you Jesus that your grace that never leads to license, but rather it always leads to repentance. Therefore Lord Jesus, transform my life so that I may bring glory and honor to you alone and not to myself.

I thank you Lord Jesus, for dying for me at Calvary and giving me eternal life.

Amen.

If you just said this prayer and you meant it with all your heart, believe that you are now saved and have been born again.

You may ask, "Now that I am saved, what do I do next?" First of all you need to get into a spirit-filled, bible-based church that teaches the Scriptures, and you need to study God's Word.

Once you have found a church home, you will want to become water-baptized. By accepting Christ you are baptized in the spirit, but it is through water-baptism that you publically announce your obedience to the Lord Jesus. Water baptism is a symbol of your salvation from the dead. You were dead but now you live, for Jesus Christ has redeemed you for a price! The price was His atoning death on the cross. May God Bless You!

www.ingramcontent.com/pod-product-compliance
Lightning Source LLC
Chambersburg PA
CBHW071329250626
47159CB00004B/1533